Mr Knightley's
Diary

Mr Knightley's
Diary

AMANDA GRANGE

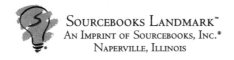
SOURCEBOOKS LANDMARK™
AN IMPRINT OF SOURCEBOOKS, INC.®
NAPERVILLE, ILLINOIS

Published by Sourcebooks Landmark, an imprint of Sourcebooks, Inc.
P.O. Box 4410, Naperville, Illinois 60567-4410 USA
(630) 961-3900
FAX: (630) 961-2168
www.sourcebooks.com

Printed in the UK by CPI William Clowes Beccles NR34 7TL

10 9 8 7 6 5 4 3 2 1

SEPTEMBER

Tuesday 22 September

I was very sorry to have to tell Weston that I will miss his wedding, as business calls me to town, but I am looking forward to seeing John and Isabella again. I can hardly believe it is seven years since they married. It seems like only yesterday they were courting, and John was neglecting everything in favour of walking over to Hartfield to see her. It was fortunate for him that he found a wife so near. She could hardly have been nearer! And now they have five children. It is, perhaps, time that I, too, thought of taking a wife.

Wednesday 23 September

I rose early and spent the day looking over my accounts, making sure everything was ready for my trip to London. I gave William Larkins his instructions, and having satisfied myself that he knew what to do in my absence, I walked over to Hartfield to take my leave.

When I was shown into the drawing-room, I found Emma and her father sitting with Miss Taylor. It was an attractive group. Miss Taylor was looking well, as befitted a governess who was about to be married. Mr Woodhouse was talking to Emma, and she was sitting on a low stool beside him. As soon as she perceived me, she stood up and came forward to greet me.

'Mr Knightley, I am so pleased to see you. We were just saying, were we not, Papa, that we hoped Mr Knightley would look in?'

'Yes, my dear, though I hope he has not taken a chill. You did not walk, Mr Knightley?' he asked me.

'Of course I walked!' I said.

'You would have done better to use your carriage,' said Mr Woodhouse anxiously.

'What! use the carriage on a fine night like this, a mild evening in September? What could be more pleasant than a walk of a mile to see old friends?'

'I cannot believe it was so very fine. It was misty this morning, was it not, Emma?' he asked querulously.

Emma and I exchanged glances, for he always says this when I arrive at Hartfield.

'Yes, it was, Papa, but the mist soon lifted. You must not concern yourself about Mr Knightley. He is used to the walk, and it never does him any harm.'

'Perry is not in favour of autumn walks. He has known them lead to very bad colds,' said Mr Woodhouse.

I was about to remark that Perry's opinion did not interest me when I thought better of it on account of Mr Woodhouse's advanced age, and besides, I did not want to distress Emma.

'But Mr Knightley does not have so much as a cough,' said Emma.

'Well, my dear, I am sure I am very thankful of it, but you must not think of coming out to see us again, Mr Knightley, when the weather is so inclement.'

'I was just about to ring for supper,' said Emma, distracting his attention. His face lost its anxious look and settled into more harmonious lines. 'You will take some with us?' she asked me.

'Yes, thank you,' I said, as I sat down next to Miss Taylor.

I cannot help thinking it a pity that Emma has only an old man for company, especially as his habits have always made him appear even older than his years. When Miss Taylor leaves, Emma will be alone with him. Fortunately, she has a cheerful disposition and does not mind. Quite the contrary, she is only too pleased to see to his comfort, and to make sure he is happy.

'Is everything ready for the wedding?' I asked Miss Taylor.

'Yes, thank you,' she said.

I hoped that talk of the wedding would cheer Mr Woodhouse, but it only made him more anxious.

'Poor Miss Taylor,' he said with a heavy sigh, as though she was about to be carried off by pneumonia, instead of by a respectable gentleman. 'You will miss us all terribly. What a dreadful thing marriage is, to be sure.'

'Come, now, you will hardly know she is gone!' I said rousingly. 'She will be living no more than half a mile away, and you will see each other every day, either in the morning, or in the evening.'

'But it is not the same as having Miss Taylor in the house. She will have to leave her house to visit us, or we will have to leave ours to visit her. It will be a dreadful thing for the horses,' he said sorrowfully.

'They will like the exercise,' I said. Then, thinking there had been enough sighing, I went on: 'I am going to London tomorrow. Do you have any commissions for me? Isabella is always eager to hear from her father and her sister.'

'Will you take these letters to her?' said Emma, giving them to me. 'And pray give her this cap. I made it for the baby.'

'This is prettily done. Would you like me to take that one, too?' I asked, seeing another on her work-table.

'No, it is not finished, but no matter. I am making it in the next size. Little Emma will need it by the time Isabella visits us, I dare say.'

'All, poor Isabella!' sighed Mr Woodhouse. 'It is a long time since we saw her and her children. I wish she would visit us more often. London is such an unhealthy place.'

'But not Brunswick Square, Papa. Brunswick Square is a very healthy area. You know that Perry said so.'

'Ay, he did, but it cannot be as healthy as Hartfield, my dear. I do not like to think of the children playing in all that smoke.'

'There is no smoke in Brunswick Square, Papa. Is there, Mr Knightley?' she asked, appealing to me.

'Very little,' I said. Then, seeing his worried face, I remarked: 'When the children play, you know, they go to the park, where there is no smoke at all.'

'You see, Papa, there is no need to worry about the children. What message would you like Mr Knightley to give Isabella?' she asked. 'You know she will want to hear from you.'

'Tell her that Perry says she must not think of taking the children sea-bathing again,' he said. 'He says that she must wrap them up warmly. It is very chilly now that autumn is here. And she must not go out in the rain. Perry has known many people take ill and die from going out in the rain.'

As he talked, I watched Emma and wondered what is to become of her. She is of an age to be married, but she spends her time with people who are so much older than she, that she is never likely to meet a husband. And if she does, I do not know if she will wish to marry. She is too comfortable where she is. Her father is easy to please and she can do as she likes with the household. A husband will have his own views, and Emma is not likely to take to that way of living.

But if she does not marry, what then?

Thursday 24 September

I set out for London this afternoon. The autumn day was drawing in and I did not arrive at Brunswick Square until after dark.

The house was as neat as always, a credit to Isabella. John could not have found a better wife if he had searched the length and breadth of England. With her domestic character and her gentle, quiet manners, she must be one of the few women in the country whose amiable and affectionate disposition would allow her to tolerate his short temper.

As I was shown into the drawing-room I was greeted by a perfect domestic scene. Isabella and John were sitting there, surrounded by their five children. The baby was sitting on Isabella's knee, whilst Bella and George were playing on the hearthrug. Henry and John were more active, as befit their advanced years, and as soon as they saw me they ran up to me with squeals of 'Uncle George!' and then they clamoured to be thrown into the air. I obliged, sending them both up to the ceiling, before setting them back on their feet.

'Again! Again!' said Henry.

'You are too heavy! You must be five years old by now—' I teased him.

'Six!' he cried in delight.

'Then it is no wonder you are so big.'

He tugged at the tails of my coat and I relented. 'Very well, one more time then,' I said.

Nothing would do but that I should treat little John in the same way, before I could sit down.

'Enough,' said my brother John, as they clamoured for more. 'Give Uncle George some peace. He has ridden all the way from Surrey.'

'Here,' said Isabella, giving them some wooden blocks to play with.

The boys sat down on the hearthrug and occupied themselves by building a tower.

'How was your journey?' Isabella asked, as she moved the baby to her other knee.

'Better than usual,' I told her. 'At least, this time, the weather was dry.'

'I wish you would not ride,' she said. 'It is too far. You should use your carriage.'

'Too far?' said John. 'It is only sixteen miles. No more than a three-hour journey.'

'I should not like to ride so far on horseback,' said Isabella.

'Then it is a good thing I was the one who undertook the journey, and not you,' I remarked.

She gave the baby to John and took Bella on her knee, for Bella had started to cough.

'How is Bella's throat?' I asked.

'Better than it was. I am using an embrocation of Mr Wingfield's devising, and it seems to be strengthening her. But tell me, how is my sister? She is not too lonely, I hope?' asked Isabella.

'No, not yet. Miss Taylor is still at Hartfield. She is not Mrs Weston yet.'

'Poor Emma,' said Isabella. 'And poor Papa. They will be very lonely without her. She has been with them for such a long time. It is sixteen years since she arrived. A sad business.'

'A sad business!' cried John. 'Not for Miss Taylor! To go from being a governess companion, to being a wife? It is an excellent business, and a very good match for her. As a companion she was a dependent, no matter how much she was loved, but as Mrs Weston, she will be a woman with a home of her own. I am very glad to have her marry. A more sensible and respectable match I have yet to see.'

'But it is a sad business for Emma,' said Isabella.

'It will do her good to have some time to herself,' said John.

'It will give her a chance to finish all the things she has been meaning to finish for the last five years,' I said.

'For shame!' cried Isabella.

'You have always been hard on Emma,' said John.

'And if I am not, who else is there?' I said. Little George came and stood by my knee, his face a picture of concentration as he sucked his thumb. 'Her father thinks she can do no wrong. Miss Taylor is hardly any less doting. There is no one in the village who cares to question her, as she is the most important woman in the neighbourhood. Someone has to tell her when she goes wrong.'

'And when does Emma ever go wrong?' asked Isabella.

'On many occasions, particularly when she thinks she has nothing to learn. It is not entirely her fault. She has been taught to think well of herself by everyone around her—'

'Would you have her think badly of herself?' asked John,

'I would have her think less of herself altogether. For that is the evil. Emma is the centre of Emma's world.'

'She will think differently when she marries,' said Isabella.

'But will she marry? What is there to tempt her?' I asked, as George climbed on to my knee. 'She is already the mistress of her father's house. She has her nephews and nieces to interest her. She even has a little Emma named after her,' I said, looking at the baby. 'I sometimes wonder what is to become of her.'

'Come, George, this is a dim view of things. Emma will fall in love and marry, as we all do. She is only twenty years old, she has plenty of time. She is not averse to matrimony, after all.'

'Very true,' said Isabella loyally. 'She is in favour of it. It was she who arranged the match between Miss Taylor and Mr Weston.'

'That is exactly what I mean! She is full of her own importance, and you do nothing to bring her back to reality. She fancied herself a match-maker, and instead of telling her she was talking nonsense, you all agreed.'

'But it was she who brought them together,' protested Isabella.

'Miss Taylor and Mr Weston did not need anyone to bring them together. Why should they? If two sensible, mature people cannot make a match between themselves without the assistance of a sixteen-year-old girl – for that is what Emma was at the time – then things have come to a pretty pass. And with no friends of her own age to tease her out of her self-importance, it grows at an alarming rate.'

'It is true, that is an evil,' said John. 'It cannot be pleasant for her to be always mixing with people who are so much older than she is. She has had no other young ladies around her ever since I brought Isabella to London.'

'It *is* a pity she has no friends of her own age,' Isabella agreed. 'Miss Fairfax is at Highbury so little—'

She broke off as the tower of bricks fell down with a clatter.

'But what of you, George?' asked John. 'It is high time you were married. Time does not stand still. You are thirty-seven years old. You should be thinking of taking a wife.'

'I have thought of it, but I have seen no one who takes my fancy, and I do not intend to marry for the sake of it,' I replied.

'But think of Donwell. You must have an heir.'

'I will leave it to Henry,' I said.

'Then I hope you are keeping it in good repair!' said John. 'I do not want my son inheriting a ruin. I expect him to come into the property without any disadvantages.'

I told him of the new works I was undertaking, and of the repairs I had in hand. I told him about the crumbling masonry on the front of the Abbey, and my plan to build a bridge across the stream.

We were still talking of the Abbey after dinner. I told him about the leaking roof in the stables, and he was interested, as always, in everything I had to say. So engrossed were we that I was surprised when the clock chimed eleven and it was time to retire.

I found my room as always, with its familiar decorations, its comfortable bed, its reading-desk and its wing-chair. As I closed the door, I thought about John's happy family, hoped I might have the same one day.

Friday 25 September

I finished my business earlier than I expected, and John and I took the eldest two boys into the park this afternoon.

'And how are they getting on with their riding?' I asked.

'They spend little time in the saddle. It is not as easy here as it is in the country,' he said.

'Then bring them to Donwell for the autumn,' I said, trying to persuade him.

He thanked me for the invitation, but he declined it, telling me he had made up his mind to take his children to the seaside.

'You will at least come to Surrey for Christmas?' I said. 'Come, John, give me your word. Emma and her father are anxious to see the children. If you leave it any longer, they will have grown beyond recognition.'

'Very well,' he said.

I am looking forward to it. There is nothing I enjoy so much as a family Christmas.

Saturday 26 September

I tended to business this morning, and then I joined John and Isabella for lunch.

'Has John told you I have made him promise to come to Surrey for Christmas?' I asked Isabella.

'He has, and I am very glad of it. I wish we could have been there for Miss Taylor's wedding as well, but John could not take two holidays so close together, and Mr Wingfield has entreated me to take the children to the seaside before the winter sets in.'

'Never mind. You will be able to visit the new Mrs Weston when you come to Surrey for Christmas.'

'Would you mind very much if we stayed with my father, instead of staying at the Abbey?' said Isabella.

'I thought you would say that,' I remarked.

'He is an old man, and finds travelling difficult,' said Isabella, pleading her case.

'He worries too much,' said John. 'If he is not worrying about the carriage overturning, he is worrying about the horses!'

Isabella ignored his short temper.

'It will make it easier if we stay at Hartfield,' she said.

'Do you not think the children will be too noisy for your father?' I asked.

'Emma and I will take care they do not disturb him.'

'Very well. I have no objection. I would rather you stayed at the Abbey, but I knew how it would be.'

I dined with my friend Routledge at my club this evening, and he asked all about Highbury.

'You do not regret leaving Highbury?' I asked him.

'Not at all. I have been in London a year, and I have found it a great help to my business, as well as expanding my circle of friends. But you know how I like to hear about everyone in Surrey, and I rely on you to tell me all the news.'

We passed the evening very pleasantly, and I returned to Brunswick Square in time to talk to John for an hour before retiring to bed.

Tuesday 29 September

John invited a number of his friends to dinner this evening, and I was pleased to meet them again. There are some very sensible people amongst them. Talk naturally turned to the war after dinner, once the ladies had withdrawn. I wish the fighting would soon be over. It is not good for anyone.

After we joined the ladies in the drawing-room, two of them sang for us. I tried to view them as possible wives. The first, Miss Larch, was a very pretty girl with a graceful neck who sang very well. The second, Miss Keighley, was not beautiful, and her playing left much to be desired, but she was lively and amusing when I spoke to her afterwards. But neither of them awoke within me the slightest real interest, or any desire to see them again.

OCTOBER

Thursday 1 October

Bella entranced us all with her antics this afternoon. It is a good thing John has a second daughter in little Emma, or he would be in danger of spoiling Bella, so that in twenty years she would become exactly like her aunt: self-satisfied and complacent. It is Emma's failing, but I do not despair of her growing out of it. She will be a fine person if she does, for she has a pleasing face and figure, and an affectionate disposition.

Friday 2 October

After the noise and grime of London it is good to be home. I was struck anew with the beauty of Donwell Abbey, with its low, sheltered situation, and its avenues of timber. I left my horse in the stables and walked through the meadow and down to the stream. The light was fading, but there was still enough to see by and the low sunlight sparkled on the water. I thought of happy years spent fishing there with John, and I watched it as it trickled along.

I turned and walked back to the house, and was warmed by the sight of it. The west front was catching the last rays of light, which gleamed on the spires and arched windows. They brought out the detail in the carvings of birds and fruit, and I thought of the craftsmen who had made them centuries ago. After John's town house, I welcomed the Abbey's ancient walls, and its familiar sprawl.

I noticed that some of the furniture was becoming shabby, but I could not bring myself to think of changing it. Besides, the furniture in the drawing-room and dining-room is well enough, and visitors do not penetrate further than those two rooms.

I ate my dinner in solitary splendour, and afterwards I walked to Hartfield to give Emma and her father all the London news.

I found them about to play backgammon, but they abandoned their game as I entered the room. Mr Woodhouse fussed about my health, and the damp and the dirt, but I did not pay him much attention. Instead, I let my eyes wander to Emma.

I was struck at once by the difference in her. With her governess in the house, Emma had always seemed like a schoolgirl, but with Miss Taylor gone, she seemed more like a young woman. Miss Taylor's absence will be good for her.

She was taking her new condition well. She could not but miss the company of Miss Taylor, but she was making an effort to be cheerful. Her face broke out in a smile when she saw me, and it elicited an answering smile from me.

She asked about her sister, and her nephews and nieces.

'Did Isabella like the baby's cap?' she asked.

'Very much. She said it had come just in time, as Emma had outgrown the last one.'

'And did the boys and Bella like their presents?'

'Yes, they did. John complained there was no present for him.'

'I will have to make him a cap the next time you go to London!' Emma said.

'And how did the wedding go?' I asked.

'Ah! Poor Miss Taylor!' sighed Mr Woodhouse, who, I fear, will be lamenting the marriage 'til Doomsday. 'She will miss us, I am sure.'

'We all behaved charmingly,' said Emma. 'Everybody was punctual, everybody in their best looks: not a tear, and hardly a long face to be seen. We all felt that we were going to be only half a mile apart, and were sure of meeting every day. Besides, it had an added matter of joy to me, and a very considerable one – that I made the match myself.'

So she is still claiming to have made the marriage, despite everything I can say to give her a more rational view!

'My dear, pray do not make any more matches, they are silly things, and break up one's family circle grievously,' said her father.

I could not help giving a wry smile at this novel view of marriage!

'Only one more, Papa; only for Mr Elton. Poor Mr Elton! You like Mr Elton, Papa. I must look about for a wife for him.'

I shook my head at her delusions.

'Depend upon it, a man of six- or seven-and-twenty can take care of himself,' I told her.

Nevertheless, I find myself half-hoping she will attempt it. I cannot make her see sense, but when she fails in this new endeavour, it will teach her that her powers are nothing out of the ordinary, and that she had better leave other people to manage their own affairs!

Friday 9 October

I rose early, as my few days away from Donwell have left me with much to do. I began the day by calling on Robert Martin at Abbey Mill Farm. If all my tenant farmers were as industrious and well organized as Robert Martin, I would be very happy, for never a more sensible or hardworking young man drew breath. He has managed splendidly since his father died, and the farm was looking prosperous as I arrived.

I called at the farmhouse and I found the whole family there. Robert invited me into the parlour, a clean and bright room which was a credit to his mother. She and his sisters were all cheerful and well-dressed, and Robert himself was at ease.

Mrs Martin invited me to take tea with them, and I was pleased to accept. It was a happy scene. The Misses Martin had a school-friend with them, a young girl by the name of Miss Harriet Smith. She seemed very fond of them, and they of her. It was easy to see why. She was a beautiful girl, with a naïve yet cheerful disposition, and it was soon apparent that she was the sort of girl who was eager to please and be pleased. It was not to be wondered at, for being a parlour boarder at Mrs Goddard's school, and the natural daughter of no one knew who, she had no family of her own. She was not the only gainer, for it was clear her presence brought a great deal of pleasure to the Martins.

Whilst we waited for the tea, we talked of the farm, and the conversation turned to the cows.

'The little Welsh cow is very pretty,' Miss Smith said, in the manner of one who had never lived on a farm.

I believe she took it for a pet.

The Martins, however, were not displeased by her naïvety, indeed they seemed to like it. Mrs Martin, in her motherly way, said: 'Then, as you are so fond of it, we will call it *your* cow.'

This small piece of good nature was well received by all. Harriet expressed her thanks very prettily; the Misses Martin said what an excellent idea it was; and Robert Martin smiled with all the good nature of a man who liked seeing pleasure bestowed.

When we had taken tea, Robert and I retired to talk business. We talked of the harvest, which was brought in early, and we agreed that the apples were the best crop we had seen, for the weather has been just right and has given them ripeness and sweetness. Then he talked of his plans to extend the farm buildings next year, and he wanted my advice as to where a new barn should be built.

We discussed the matter and decided it would be best at the bottom of the long field.

As I came away, I felt that Abbey Mill Farm was in good hands.

The afternoon was spent going over the accounts with William Larkins. Because of the splendid harvest, I was able to tell him that we will conduct extensive repairs to the estate over the winter. There will be much to see to, and I hope to make a start before the end of the month.

Saturday 10 October

As I took my early-morning ride, I decided I must do something about finding a pony for John's children. The last time they were here they rode Blossom, but they will need a more lively mount this time.

I set out for Kingston after breakfast, and on my way I called on Miss Bates. I was concerned to make sure she had enough fuel, and I knew that the only way to find out was to call. If I asked her it would do no good. She would only say that she had plenty, thanks to the generosity of her friends, whether it was true or not. But I was pleased to see that there was a good fire when I went in, and that there was a bucket full of coal in the grate.

I asked her if there was anything she would like me to get in Kingston for her, but her reply was as usual: 'I am much obliged to you, but I believe there is nothing we need.'

I then asked after her niece, in the hope that Miss Fairfax would soon be visiting Highbury, so that Emma would have a young lady of her own age to talk to.

'Jane? Quite well, thank you,' she replied. 'We heard from her a few days ago. At Weymouth. I was only saying to mother how good the sea air would be for dear Jane, and Mrs Otway said that she had been to Weymouth as a girl, very refined, just the sort of place one would expect the Campbells to visit – Mrs Weston had a letter from Frank Churchill, complimenting her on her marriage, and it was sent from Weymouth – good enough for the Churchills – so kind of the Campbells to take Jane.'

'Since she lives with them, they could hardly leave her behind,' I remarked. 'Do you expect a visit from Miss Fairfax? It is a long time since we have seen her in Highbury.'

'I am very much obliged to you, but no, she does not speak of a visit. I was saying to Mrs Goddard only yesterday – she had called to see how mother was getting on, and was telling us of Miss Smith – staying with the Martins, has been with them all summer, invited by the Miss Martins who were at school with her, you know, and will not be back at Mrs Goddard's until the end of the week. You will have seen them all together at church, in the same pew, when our dear Mr Elton gave us another wonderful sermon. It is a shame he does not marry, but who would be good enough for him in Highbury?' She paused for breath, then asked: 'What were we talking of?'

'We were talking of Kingston, but if you have no commissions for me, then I must be on my way.'

I managed to get away at last, and went on to Kingston. It is a pity that Jane Fairfax is not to pay us a visit. Emma could learn a good deal from her. Miss Bates's niece is as refined and intelligent a young woman as it would be possible to meet, but Emma has never taken to her. I suspect Emma does not feel comfortable with someone whose accomplishments are superior, and who might put her in the shade, but if she could put such considerations aside, I think the friendship would be beneficial to both of them.

I rode into Kingston and examined a number of ponies, but none of them was quite right. The animal needs to be mild enough for young children, and yet at the same time it needs some spirit.

I said as much to Emma when I met her at Ford's on my return.

'You should take up riding again,' I continued, as we stood at the counter, she to buy ribbon, and I to buy gloves.

'I am an indifferent horsewoman,' she remarked. 'I am convinced that horses do not like me, and I am not very fond of them.'

'Because you never ride. You would soon become more proficient if you went riding every day. You would grow accustomed to horses, and they to you.'

'Thank you, but I prefer to walk. It is much quicker to put on my cloak than it is to have a horse saddled. I can have walked to Randalls, paid my visit and be home again by the time that is done.'

'You mean you do not think you look well on horseback,' I said, knowing her real reason.

'You have found me out,' she said. 'I could never acquire a good seat. I look far more graceful on foot.'

'Then I cannot convince you. Perhaps you will change your mind when your nephews and nieces can all ride, and you are left behind.'

'Perhaps. But as Emma is only six months old, I am in no hurry.'

I accompanied her back to Hartfield.

'You will join us for dinner tomorrow?' she asked, as we parted at the gate.

'Willingly,' I said. 'Pray give my compliments to your father.'

I watched her go inside, and then I returned to the Abbey, where I found William Larkins and the account book waiting for me.

Monday 12 October

A frustrating evening. I was looking forward to taking dinner at Hartfield, but when I found Miss Smith there I found myself growing impatient. She was accompanying Mrs Goddard, but she was so overawed by Miss Woodhouse of Hartfield that she hung on Emma's every word.

Miss Smith is a sweet-natured girl, but she will not do Emma any good. Her conversation is silly and ignorant, and she cannot teach Emma anything. Worse still, she gives Emma such flattering attention that it can only add to Emma's conceit.

I hope that, as Miss Smith is unlikely to dine at Hartfield very often, the friendship will not go any further.

Tuesday 13 October

I saw Emma in Highbury today, and Miss Smith was with her. I was disappointed that Emma had pursued the acquaintance, but I bade them both good-morning. They were on their way to see Mrs Weston, and I left them to continue on their way. I spent the rest of the day going round the farms, and this evening I went to the Crown for my Tuesday whist club.

The usual gentlemen were there. Weston, Elton, Cole and I all sat down to play at one table. As Weston dealt the cards, we talked over parish matters, and we all agreed that not enough was being done for the poor. Elton promised to take measures to improve their lot, which we all agreed to support. With winter coming, it will be much easier for us to guard against hardship than it will be for us to alleviate it once it has already arrived.

Weston was the overall winner at cards. He is sure his luck will last until next week, but I have promised him I will have my revenge.

Wednesday 14 October

Emma was about to go out with Miss Smith when I walked over to Hartfield this morning. We exchanged compliments and then they set off for Randalls.

I hope their friendship is not going to become a settled thing, for as well as Miss Smith giving Emma an inflated idea of her own powers,

Emma will give Miss Smith a distaste for the society she truly enjoys. The poor girl will be left between two worlds, being ill-suited for one, and dissatisfied with the other.

Thursday 15 October

I could not help thinking about Emma and Harriet Smith this morning, and I decided to consult Mrs Weston. I was sure her good sense, coupled with her knowledge of Emma, would make her as uneasy as I was, but I found that the reverse was true.

'I have been seeing their intimacy with the greatest pleasure,' she told me. 'I can imagine your objection to Harriet Smith. She is not the superior young woman which Emma's friend ought to be. But on the other hand, as Emma wants to see her better informed it will be an inducement to her to read more herself.'

'Emma has been meaning to read more ever since she was twelve years old,' I returned. 'Where Miss Taylor failed to stimulate, I may safely affirm that Harriet Smith will do nothing.'

I did not realize until I had said it that my remark seemed to reflect badly on Mrs Weston's abilities as a governess, and so I redeemed myself by telling her I thought she was much more suited to being a wife.

'Though I am afraid you are rather thrown away on Weston,' I remarked, 'and that with every disposition to bear, there will be nothing to be borne. We will not despair, however. Weston may grow cross from the wantonness of comfort, or his son may plague him.'

'I hope not *that*,' she returned. 'It is not likely. I had a very well-written letter from him on my marriage.'

She gave it to me and I read it, but although I said it was very fine, I privately thought it was a poor substitute for a visit. He should have paid her that courtesy on her marriage, and not all the obstacles in the world should have prevented him.

'He was very sorry not to be here,' she said, 'but Mrs Churchill was not well, and insisted on his accompanying her to Weymouth. Her physician felt the sea air would be beneficial to her health.'

I managed no more than a harrumph! Though the Churchills took him in when his mother died and made him their heir, Weston being ill-eqipped to care for a two-year-old son, and though he had taken their name, I still felt that, if his character had been what it ought, he would have made a point of calling on his new stepmother on her marriage.

She seemed to read my thoughts, for she said: 'We will not argue about him.'

'No, indeed. I have not come to plague you about your stepson. Rather, I have come to plague you about Emma, and I have not half done. I cannot agree with you in thinking this friendship a good thing. Miss Smith knows nothing herself, and looks upon Emma as knowing everything. How can Emma imagine she has any thing to learn herself, while Harriet is presenting such a delightful inferiority? And as for Miss Smith, I will venture to say that *she* cannot gain by the acquaintance. Hartfield will only put her out of conceit with all the other places she belongs to.'

'I either depend more upon Emma's good sense than you do, or am more anxious for her present comfort; for I cannot lament the acquaintance,' said Mrs Weston. 'Emma must have a friend of her own age to talk to.'

I said no more, and our conversation turned to other matters, but I still feel an anxiety about Emma and I will be glad when the friendship has run its course.

Saturday 17 October

I visited Hartfield this morning, and had the good fortune to find Emma alone. Moreover, she was reading a book. Feeling somewhat heartened by this, I asked her how her plans to educate her little friend were getting along.

'I have drawn up a programme of reading,' she said. 'We mean to study all the great authors.'

'This is most impressive,' I said, as she handed me the list.

It was beautifully laid out, and was written in the most exquisite hand. A great deal of thought had gone into selecting the list, and a lot of care had gone into its presentation.

'I wanted Harriet to have a feel for the beauty of our language, and so I thought I would guide her through some of our greatest works,' she said, pleased with my praise.

'And which of these have you started?'

'All of them.'

'All of them?' I asked in surprise.

'Yes. We mean to finish them by Christmas.'

'An ambitious plan,' I said. 'You will need to read a book every week. Do you not think it would be better to read half as many books and devote twice as much time to each?'

'We can always read them a second time, in a more leisurely manner, later on, but Harriet is eager to make up for the deficiencies of her education as soon as possible. I do not say that Mrs Goddard has been lax,' said Emma graciously. 'Quite the opposite. She has given Harriet sound basics. But it is up to me to further her education, and make it equal that of a young lady.'

I did not know whether to scold her for her pomposity or tease her for her conceit, so instead I sought to open her eyes to her friend's capabilities.

'My dear Emma, Harriet has no interest in literature. She was happy at the Martins' farm, marking her height on the wall and claiming a pretty cow.'

'Which is why I must take her in hand, for then she will add an appreciation of literature, music and art to her repertoire of interests.'

It was useless to argue with this misguided notion, particularly as I am convinced that the programme of education will last no longer than any of her previous programmes. It will start in an excess of zeal, and end in the plans being laid aside in favour of a walk into Highbury.

I saw a way that that could be turned to my advantage.

'Have you visited Miss Bates lately?' I asked.

'Not lately,' she said lightly, but she looked uncomfortable.

She knows that I think she should visit Miss Bates more often than she does.

'She always thinks it an honour when you call, and being situated as you are, in a position of comfort and ease, and with Miss Bates being situated as she is, in a position of dwindling income, you should not be remiss in your attentions,' I reminded her.

'Very well, I will call on her this afternoon. I will take Harriet,' she said, brightening. 'We will be ready for a break from our studies by then.'

It is as I thought. A visit to Miss Bates is far more welcome to her when it is an alternative to study!

Monday 19 October

I dined with my friend Graham this evening. We were a small party, just Graham, the Coles, Elton, and Graham's widowed sister.

'My sister, Mrs Lovage, has joined me from Bath,' said Graham, as he introduced us.

I wondered if here could be the woman I was looking for. She impressed me at our first meeting with her beauty and her good manners, followed closely by her good sense. I asked her about Bath, and Elton joined in the conversation.

'Do you know Bath?' she asked him.

'I know it very well. I visited there with my sisters only recently,' he said.

'Your sisters are not Mrs Winchester and Miss Catherine Elton?' asked Mrs Lovage.

'Yes, indeed they are.'

'But this is famous!' cried Mrs Lovage. 'I know them well. We often take tea together.'

There were the usual congratulations, and Mrs Lovage spoke sensibly about their mutual acquaintances, whilst the Coles added their experiences of Bath to the conversation.

'You must also know the Framptons,' said Mrs Lovage. 'Miss Frampton has newly become engaged to a Mr Bradshaw.'

'I am very pleased for her,' said Elton. 'I believe the other Misses Frampton will not be far behind their sister. They are beautiful girls, with twenty thousand pounds apiece.'

From the way he spoke of them it was clear he was intimate with them, and if I do not miss my guess, he has thoughts of marrying one or other of them.

'Nothing lifts the spirits so much as a wedding,' said Mrs Lovage. She turned to me. 'Do you not think so, Mr Knightley?'

'They are generally thought agreeable.'

'I hear you have had a wedding of your own here recently?'

'Yes, Mrs Weston is newly married.'

'Then I must pay her my respects tomorrow,' she said.

After dinner, we talked of more serious matters and I found that Mrs Lovage was able to hold an intelligent conversation on a variety of subjects. She expressed an interest in old buildings and we talked of the Abbey at some length. I was about to invite her to visit, when Elton broke into our conversation, mentioning more of his Bath acquaintance, and the moment was lost.

I would like to see Emma become as well-informed as Mrs Lovage, but as she does not mix with the Grahams, and would consider them quite beneath her, it is unlikely she will make Mrs Lovage's acquaintance. She will grow out of this false sense of superiority, I hope. It is all very well to preserve distinction of class within reason, particularly if inferiority of station is mixed with inferiority of mind, but where there is only a slight disparity it is nonsense, and I hope that one day Emma will see it.

Mrs Lovage was very agreeable for the rest of the evening, but when I returned home I was disappointed to realize that I had no particular desire to see her again. But perhaps my feelings will change on further acquaintance.

Tuesday 20 October

We had a storm overnight, and some of the fences blew down. I toured the estate with William Larkins and gave instructions for repairs to be carried out.

This evening, I had my revenge at the whist club, and came home the overall winner. Elton would have done better if he had spent less time telling us of the heiresses he knew, and more time in thinking about his cards.

Wednesday 21 October

I went to Hartfield this morning, to see if the storm had done any damage there, and whether Mr Woodhouse needed my help in organizing repairs. I was also curious to see Emma, and to discover whether she had tired of Miss Smith's company. Unfortunately, I found that she was even closer to Miss Smith, and that Harriet, for so Emma calls her, was staying at Hartfield.

'Look, Papa, here is Mr Knightley,' said Emma as I entered the room.

'You have not walked over in all this wind?' he asked in alarm. 'My dear Mr Knightley, you should not be venturing out in this weather. Such a howling in the chimney-pots last night, was there not, Emma? I thought they were going to come crashing down.'

'But they did not, Papa,' said Emma soothingly. 'We were just saying how fortunate it was, that the storm did us no damage. How did you fare at the Abbey, Mr Knightley?'

'Not so well. A number of fences have blown down, and they will have to be repaired.'

'Emma, my dear, you and Harriet must not take a walk today, but must stay indoors. See, it is not safe to be outside. Mr Knightley's fences have blown down, and if you venture out, you and Harriet will surely be blown down, too.'

'Very well, Papa, Harriet and I will go no further than Randalls.'

'Even that is not safe,' he said.

'I believe it is,' said Emma. 'Do you not think so, Mr Knightley?'

Thus appealed to, I soothed her father's fears and secured Emma her walk. It is not easy for her, being tied to such an old man, but she bears it cheerfully.

'We must not be remiss in our attentions, Papa,' Emma went on, to convince him of the necessity of the walk. 'Mrs Weston will like to know we are all safe after the storm.'

'Ah, poor Miss Taylor. If she had only stayed here she would have been safe. We have escaped, though the wind howled in the chimneys, but I fear that Randalls is not so well-built. I hope their roof may not have blown off.'

I told him that I had passed Randalls on my way, and had seen no such calamity.

'Poor Miss Taylor, she would have been much better here with us,' sighed Mr Woodhouse again.

Emma took out a drawing she had been doing, by way of turning her father's thoughts away from the numerous disasters that might have befallen his friends.

'A very pretty drawing,' said Mr Woodhouse. 'Emma draws very well. Emma does everything very well.'

'Papa,' said Emma reprovingly, but pleased none the less.

What hope is there for her, with such flattery around her?

I pointed out its flaws and, though she had the goodness to admit that the tree was too tall in relation to the shrubbery, she showed no inclination to put it right.

'Harriet, show Mr Knightley your drawing,' she said.

Harriet shyly held out her drawing. It was a typical schoolgirl effort, but I found something to praise and some suggestions to make.

I asked Harriet what books she had been reading, and it was as I suspected. Many had been started but none finished. However, overall I found her improved. She had lost her schoolgirl giggle and, if her understanding was not good, at least it was better than formerly. There was nothing of vulgarity in her, and Emma had sought to build on her better qualities with some success.

I believe Mrs Weston might have been right when she said the friendship would provide Emma with much needed company. Perhaps it will do no harm after all.

'We have had a letter from Isabella,' said Emma.

She went over to the table, as Harriet listened patiently to Mr Woodhouse's account of his fears for poor Mrs Weston in the storm.

I followed her, and took the letter she offered me. It was from Southend. Isabella praised the weather, the neighbourhood and the sea.

'So Isabella went bathing after all,' I said.

'Yes, though before she went she protested she would not venture into the water.' She glanced at her father. 'I have not mentioned it to Papa. He would only worry. He does not approve of the children getting their feet wet.'

'If I remember, you were always getting your feet wet as a child,' I said. 'I recall you paddling in the stream at Donwell—'

'And receiving a fine scolding for it when Miss Taylor found me!'

'It was the mildest of reproofs, especially as you had escaped from your lessons and gone outside on the pretext of sketching the Abbey.'

'It was not a pretext! I took my pencils and my sketchbook—'

'And abandoned them as soon as you were out of sight.'

'Unfair!' she cried, adding saucily: 'I abandoned them *before* I was out of sight.'

'Incorrigible girl! If you had applied yourself more, you might now be a mistress of your art, instead of abandoning your portraits, half-finished, in a portfolio.'

'They are not half-finished!' she declared, then she had the goodness to laugh, and to add: 'Not all of them, anyway. I finished the portrait of John. It is my best work, I think, and deserves its place in the drawing-room. Mrs Weston thought it a good likeness.'

'Though Isabella did not.'

She did not like my remark, and said: 'Isabella is partial. No one could have captured John's likeness in a way that would have suited her.'

'And Mrs Weston, too, is partial,' I told her. 'She would have thought it a good likeness however it had turned out.'

'Perhaps I need more practice. I think I might draw you, Mr Knightley,' she said with an arch smile.

'I seem to recall you doing so—' I reminded her.

'—and abandoning the attempt,' she admitted.

'I did not say so.'

'No, but you were about to. You seem to make no allowance for the fact that I was sixteen years old at the time.'

'Quite old enough to finish it. But it is not too late. Perhaps you should take it out and finish it now,' I said.

'I think not. You are the worst person in the world to sketch, for you are never still. You are worse than the children in that respect, for I am sure little George stays in one place for longer than his namesake.'

'A convenient excuse,' I told her.

'Not at all. If you will promise me a day when you will sit in a chair, I will promise you a finished portrait.'

'I thought you had done with taking likenesses? I seem to remember you saying so, when you received a cool reception for your portrait of John,' I teased her.

She smiled up at me. 'I believe I have changed my mind.'

It was a pity that, at that moment, Mr Woodhouse called to us. I do not have enough opportunities to talk to Emma alone. Of all my acquaintance, she is the one whose company I most appreciate, despite her perversity and sauce!

Friday 23 October

I visited Miss Bates this morning, and found her well.

'Oh, Mr Knightley, we're honoured I am sure. Mother was just saying we have not seen Mr Knightley since the storm, we hoped you were well – yes, thank you, Mother and I are both well, though Perry did not like the look of Mother the other day, however it was nothing, just a chill, which is not to be wondered at as the weather has turned cold. What was I talking about?'

'Have you had many visitors lately?' I asked her, wanting to see if my hint to Emma had gone home.

'Oh, yes, ever so many. Mrs Cole came, she is so fond of Mother, and so kind and obliging, asking if there was anything she could do. And then Mrs Goddard called. What do you think, she has had a goose from the Martins. Was that not kind of them? And Mrs Goddard said it was the best goose she had ever eaten. She had it dressed and then Miss Nash, Miss Prince and Miss Richardson all supped with her, and then what do you think? She brought the legs for Mother and me. We are so fortunate in our friends.'

She told me of Elton and Mrs Cole; of Graham and Mrs Lovage; in short, it seemed that everyone in Highbury had been to visit her. And then, at last, she mentioned Emma. I was pleased, and finally took my leave in good spirits.

I dined with the Otways, and found that Mrs Lovage was there. We enjoyed a lively conversation after dinner, and then she sang. She has an agreeable voice, and I believe I may grow to like her very well in time.

Saturday 24 October

Estate business occupied me this morning, but I called at Hartfield this afternoon. I found Emma and Harriet just returning from a walk. It is as I suspected! They are no further on with their reading than last time I spoke to them. Studying has given way to walking to Randalls and talking to Mrs Weston, or walking to Highbury and talking to Miss Bates. Emma defended their negligence by saying that she thought they ought to take their exercise whilst it is fine, for there will be many poor days over the winter when they will be glad to stay inside and read.

'You have an answer for everything,' I told her.

'You should be pleased. You are always telling me you would like me to be better informed,' she said, smiling up at me with that peculiar combination of innocence and mischief which has plagued me for years. 'If I have an answer for everything, I have surely exceeded your expectations!'

I could not help laughing.

'Emma has always been very clever,' said her father.

'That is undeniable, but cleverness must be put to good use, not bad,' I remarked.

'And when, pray, do I ever put it to bad use?'

'I am sure Emma would never do such a thing,' said her father anxiously. 'She has never done anything bad. She has been a good daughter to me, a very good daughter, indeed I do not know a better one, unless it is Isabella.' He shook his head. 'Poor Isabella!'

'Mr Knightley is teasing me, Papa,' Emma said.

'I do not quite like that way he has, my dear,' said her father, as Emma went over to him. 'It is very rough to my ears.'

'Come, now, you know Mr Knightley is a good friend to us. How often have I heard you say that you do not know where you would be without Mr Knightley to write your letters for you? And I am sure I do not know where I would be without him to read the paper to me in the evening.'

'That is true, very true, for I am just a sad invalid and could not manage it, my dear. The print is so small it hurts my eyes, and I am sure I am very grateful to Mr Knightley for reading to us.'

I left Emma soothing him and spoke to Harriet, and by the time the tea was brought in he was content again.

Afterwards, I was able to write some business letters for him. I would have liked to stay to dinner, but my accounts needed looking into and I spent the evening with my books.

Monday 26 October

One of the trees in the wood was damaged by the storm and it is unsafe. I have given instructions for it to be felled. The timber is not of a good enough quality to be sold, and so I have ordered it cut up for firewood. I have given Wiliam Larkins instructions to have some of the logs sent to Miss Bates, and to distribute the rest amongst the poor.

Friday 30 October

Emma continues to make much of her little friend. When I arrived at Hartfield this evening, I found Harriet still there, and Elton was in attendance. Emma brought Harriet forward and set her at her ease, encouraging her to speak to Elton, and to answer questions he had asked. It was kind of her, for it will increase Harriet's confidence and give her more facility with conversation. Elton good-naturedly humoured Harriet, whilst Emma looked on benignly.

I am not sure whether she sees herself as Harriet's fairy godmother, or as Lady Bountiful, but I am convinced that Harriet sees her as a mixture of the two.

Later, I played a game of backgammon with Emma whilst the others entertained Mr Woodhouse, and then I walked part of the way home with Elton. He was full of Emma's praises, saying how well she spoke, and how intelligent were her ideas.

Elton is another one of Emma's friends who is easily pleased, to add to her growing collection! I only hope my presence will be enough to counteract the harmful effects of all this adulation.

NOVEMBER

Tuesday 3 November

At last I had time to think about the footpath to Langham. I have been meaning to re-lay it for some time. At present, it cuts through the meadow, which I do not like. I want to move it so that it skirts the meadow instead. I told William Larkins of my plan, and he approved of it, but I have decided to wait until John has seen it before going ahead with the work, in case he has any better suggestion to make.

After spending the day on Abbey matters, I dined with Graham and discovered that his sister had returned to Bath. Graham had a friend staying with him, a Mr Longridge; a quiet and gentlemanlike man. The three of us spent a pleasant evening with the Otways and Coles, who were also of the party. It was not as enjoyable as an evening spent at Hartfield, but it was very agreeable none the less.

Friday 6 November

I had to see Mr Weston about a matter of business and so I called on him this afternoon. He was out, but I found Mrs Weston and Miss Bates in the drawing-room. Miss Bates was in a state of great agitation.

'She said nothing about it in her letters, but then she has never liked to worry us – so considerate – but Mr Churchill – oh yes, indeed it must be so, but what do you think, Mr Knightley?'

I had no idea what she was talking about, and so I could not answer her question, but Mrs Weston explained that she had had a letter from her stepson Frank Churchill, and that, in it, he had mentioned that he had been a member of a boating-party. There was nothing in that, except that he had recounted an incident which had occurred when he had gone out on the sea. There had been an accident, or almost an accident, and a young lady, who was also a member of the party, had nearly been dashed from the vessel. Someone had caught her, and so no harm had been done, but the strange thing was, that the young lady who had nearly been swept overboard was Miss Fairfax. Churchill had happened to meet her party whilst at Weymouth, and they had both happened to form a part of the boating-trip.

'Mrs Weston thought I must have heard of it – was sure Jane would have mentioned it in one of her letters – but I had never heard anything about it. And now I am not easy about dear Jane,' Miss Bates said. 'Do you think I should tell her to come home to Highbury at once, Mr Knightley? Only the Campbells have been so kind in asking her to stay, even though Miss Campbell is married and gone to live in Ireland, that I think she will not like to offend them, but I cannot bear the thought of them taking her on another boating-expedition and poor Jane being drowned!'

I protested at this terrible speculation, and asked her when Jane was due to leave Weymouth.

'She has already left,' said Miss Bates. 'I had a letter from her only the other day, and in it she distinctly told me they were leaving Weymouth on the morrow, so that by the time I received the letter she would be back at home again. Oh, poor Jane!'

'Then I should not worry any more about it,' I told her. I added: 'There is no reason why you should not invite her to Highbury, though, if you think the Campbells can spare her.'

Not only would it set Miss Bates's mind at ease, but it would give me great pleasure to have Miss Fairfax here. Emma could not fail to see the difference between Miss Fairfax and Miss Smith, and I am persuaded that, even with her prejudice, she would soon learn to value Miss Fairfax's company.

'I have already asked her to come to us,' said Miss Bates.

'And have you received a reply?'

'Yes. Alas, she cannot oblige us. She has already promised the Campbells to spend Christmas with them,' said Miss Bates.

I was disappointed, but it could not be helped.

Miss Bates's alarm gradually faded, and by the time Mr Weston came in, she was calm once more.

He and I retreated to his study to talk business. When we had done, I mentioned the letter and I found that he had not yet seen it.

'What! Frank! Saved Miss Fairfax!' said he, highly gratified. 'Never was a man more fortunate in his son. You should have one yourself, Knightley. Marry! Take a wife! Mrs Lovage would be willing,' he added.

'Mrs Lovage has returned to Bath,' I said.

'She would come back quickly enough, if she thought there was hope.'

'Can no one think of anything but marriage?' I exclaimed. I did not mean to speak so brusquely, but I was disappointed that I had not been able to feel anything for Mrs Lovage. 'You and John are trying to find me a wife, and Emma—'

'Emma?' he asked.

I had no intention of disclosing her plans to find Elton a wife, for they would not please Elton if he came to hear of them. He might be deferential in his behaviour towards her because of her standing in the neighbourhood, but even that would not reconcile him to the idea of her meddling in his affairs.

'Emma is keen to make another match, after claiming to have made yours.'

'Perhaps she did,' he said jovially.

'She thought of it, that is all!' I rebuked him.

'If she wants to make a match, she should make one for you!' he returned.

'Hah! She knows me better than to think I would have someone of her choosing,' I said.

'She chose very well for me.'

I saw there was no arguing with him, and I said no more. Let him think Emma arranged his marriage if he wishes! It can do no harm, as long as he does not say so to her.

Saturday 7 November

This evening, Miss Bates was still talking of her alarm over Jane's accident, and she recounted the incident over dinner at Graham's. Mr and Mrs Cole said everything necessary to reassure her, and she exclaimed that she did not know what she would do without such good friends.

'A fine woman,' remarked Mr Longridge of Miss Bates, once the ladies had withdrawn. 'She reminds me of my dear wife.'

He blew his nose, and became quiet.

I thought he had been recently bereaved, but I later learnt that his wife died twenty years ago. However, he still speaks of her with great affection.

The talk after dinner was of politics and business until we joined the ladies, whereupon Mrs Weston sang for us. I joined her, and I felt it was an evening well spent.

Thursday 12 November

I walked in on a pretty scene this morning when I called at Hartfield. Emma was netting a purse, and Harriet was hemming a handkerchief.

'You find us usefully employed,' said Emma.

'I do indeed.'

Both girls were in good spirits. I could not begrudge Emma her friendship when I saw how happy she was, though I still wished Harriet was a more suitable companion.

Harriet was sewing very prettily, however, and spoke to me sensibly about her work. If she became vague when I asked her what she had been reading, I did not hold it against her. Emma's plan for her education was very grand, and never likely to succeed.

I talked to Mr Woodhouse, attending to some papers that had been troubling him, and stayed at Hartfield for luncheon. Mr Woodhouse was alarmed at the quantity of meat I ate, averring it would do me no good and begging me to join him in a bowl of gruel, but Emma distracted him by talking of Isabella's forthcoming visit, and I was able to finish my meal in peace.

Saturday 21 November

The plans for the new barn at Abbey Mill Farm are coming on well. When Robert Martin called at the Abbey to speak to me about them, we looked at them together.

I happened to mention that I had seen Miss Smith at Hartfield, and he said that his sisters would be glad to hear it. He said that he was going to Kingston after leaving me, and let slip that he intended to buy a book she had recommended.

'What is it?' I enquired, wondering whether it was a book on Harriet's reading list.

He went red and fingered his cravat, then told me its name rather shamefacedly.

I could not help smiling. Emma may not have been able to induce her friend to read Shakespeare, but Harriet has managed to persuade Robert Martin to read *The Romance of the Forest!*

Wednesday 25 November

Of all the evenings it is possible to spend, a companionable evening with friends is the best. I spent one such evening at Hartfield today. Mr Woodhouse was in high spirits, having been assured by Perry that his health was good, and Emma was sitting by the fire, sketching. Harriet was copying some pictures from a fashion journal. I was reading the newspaper, and reading out such things as I thought might interest them.

After a while, I laid my newspaper aside and went over to look at Emma's work. I saw that she had been sketching her father.

'So you are serious about resuming your sketching?' I said.

'I am. I felt an urge to take a likeness of Harriet,' she said, 'and I wanted to refresh my hand.'

I found myself hoping she would persevere with the undertaking, for it had a spirited style, but alas! I thought her likeness of Harriet would probably join the other half-finished sketches in her portfolio.

As I walked back to the Abbey I was well pleased with life. The weather was fine, I had the pleasure of a visit from John and Isabella to look forward to, and in the meantime I had many more evenings to spend at Hartfield.

Thursday 26 November

When I visited Hartfield this evening, I found Emma sitting with her father, Harriet and Elton. As I walked into the room, I saw that Harriet was entertaining Mr Woodhouse, whilst Emma talked to Elton.

'Harriet looks very well this evening,' I heard her say, as I sat down and began looking at the newspaper.

'Yes, indeed,' replied her companion.

'I thought she was looking rather pale this morning, so I suggested we take a walk. I believe it has brightened her complexion.'

'Admirable!' he said. 'A walk! Exercise! Just the thing.'

'Do you not think her complexion has been brightened by it?' she pressed him, as he did not follow up her hint.

It was at this moment I began to suspect her motives for encouraging him to notice her friend, and to think that she wanted to make a match between Harriet and Elton!

I did not know whether to feel annoyance or pity. Emma had mistaken her man if she thought Elton would marry a parlour boarder, a young girl without name, birth or dowry to recommend her.

Elton had no suspicion, however, and was, as always, eager to defer to Miss Woodhouse of Hartfield.

'Indeed I do. I noticed her complexion particularly. *Why, it has been brightened by fresh air and exercise!* I thought as I came into the room. It was just what she needed to bring out her beauty. So good of you to take the trouble!'

'I am sure it was good of Harriet to take the time to walk with me,' she said, firmly turning the conversation back to Harriet's advantages.

Hah! I thought in amusement. *Now, Elton, turn that into a compliment to Emma if you can!*

I continued to be amused by them, as they carried on at cross purposes for the next quarter of an hour, Emma trying to make a match between a glove and a mitten, and Elton to raise his standing in the village by flattering Miss Woodhouse. I waited for them to grow tired of it, but as they showed no signs of doing so, at last I emerged from my newspaper and forced them to engage in more general and rational conversation.

Friday 27 November

Emma's matchmaking continued today and Elton, poor man, had no idea of what she was about.

She asked him outright what he thought of her little friend. It was impossible to make anything of his convoluted answer, for although he said how much she had improved, and how she had now acquired the polish she had been wanting, his every remark reflected well on Emma: it was Emma who had improved her; Emma who had given her polish.

As the evening wore on, I began to have a suspicion that Elton was doing more than flattering a well-connected young woman. I began to think he was lifting his eyes to Emma herself.

Perhaps I was imagining it, but there seemed something more than an ill-judged civility in his words, perhaps the admiration of a man who hoped to be admitted as a suitor?

The latter would be interesting indeed! He has no hope of succeeding, but the very idea of his assuming that he has a chance of success will teach Emma a lesson in humility which I can never hope to surpass.

What, Miss Woodhouse of Hartfield to marry Mr Elton! She would be horrified if she knew.

I mean to pay them close attention, and see how things develop!

DECEMBER

It seems that Emma's present interest in sketching is to last for a little longer, at least. I found her taking Harriet's likeness, as she had intended, when I called on her this morning. Elton, as is usual these days, was in attendance.

Mr Woodhouse and I withdrew for a time as I helped him to write some letters of business, and then we both returned to the drawing-room. We found Emma and her friend hard at work. Harriet was posing, and Emma's sketch was already well-developed.

Elton was standing behind Emma, fidgeting, and not knowing what to do with himself.

He spoke to me when I entered the room, seemingly glad of something to say.

'Miss Woodhouse has decided to paint her friend full-length, like the portrait of Mr John Knightley.'

I went over to Emma and looked at what she had done. Mrs Weston was watching the progress of the drawing, too, and her eye had not failed to see that Emma's portrait was flattering.

'Miss Woodhouse has given her friend the only beauty she wanted,' she said to Elton. 'The expression of the eye is most correct, but Harriet has not those eyebrows and eyelashes. It is the fault of her face that she has them not.'

'Do you think so?' he replied 'I cannot agree with you. It appears to me a most perfect resemblance in every feature. I never saw such a likeness in my life. We must allow for the effect of shade, you know.'

Something had to be done to counteract this flattery, and so I said: 'You have made her too tall, Emma.'

I could tell by her expression that she knew she had, but she would not admit it.

'Oh, no! certainly not too tall; not in the least too tall. Consider, she is sitting down – which naturally presents a different – which in short gives exactly the idea – and the proportions must be preserved, you know. Proportions, foreshortening. Oh, no! it gives one exactly the idea of such a height as Harriet's. Exactly so indeed!' said her would-be suitor.

'It is very pretty,' said Mr Woodhouse, always ready to praise his daughter. 'So prettily done! Just as your drawings always are, my dear. I do not know anybody who draws so well as you do. The only thing I do not thoroughly like is, that she seems to be sitting out of doors, with only a little shawl over her shoulders. It makes one think she must catch cold.'

'But, my dear Papa, it is supposed to be summer; a warm day in summer. Look at the tree.'

'But it is never safe to sit out of doors, my dear,' said he.

His is a nervous disposition indeed. It not only objects to people sitting out of doors, but it objects to them being drawn as if they were out of doors, when in reality they are sitting inside by a fire!

Elton plunged in again.

'You, sir, may say any thing,' he cried, 'but I must confess that I regard it as a most happy thought, the placing of Harriet out of doors; and the tree is touched with such inimitable spirit! Any other situation would have been much less in character. The naïvety of Harriet's manners – and altogether – Oh, it is most admirable! I cannot keep my eyes from it. I never saw such a likeness.'

I did not know whether to be amused or exasperated by his nonsense, any more than I knew whether to be amused or exasperated by the way Emma received it. She took it all as compliments for her friend, little perceiving that the flattery was all for her. I am sure of it: Emma is Elton's object.

If she was not so young, and so dear to me, I would be amused and nothing else, but I am dismayed on Emma's behalf. She thinks she has only to throw Elton and Harriet together, and Harriet's pretty face will do the rest. But Elton will settle for a pretty fortune, rather than a pretty face, and oh! Emma, what will you think, when you perceive the truth?

'We must have it framed,' said Elton.

'Oh, yes, the very thing,' said Emma. 'It must be done well. I owe my friend no less.'

'Can you not ask Isabella to have it done in London?' asked Mrs Weston.

This Mr Woodhouse could not bear.

'She must not stir outside in the fogs of December. She will take cold. I am surprised at your thinking of it,' he said to Mrs Weston reproachfully. 'You would never have thought of such a thing if you had stayed here with us at Hartfield.'

Mrs Weston was admonished. I was about to offer my services, as I had to go to London, when Elton stepped in and offered to take it himself.

'You are too good,' said Emma, smiling all the while. 'I would not think of troubling you.'

'It is no trouble.'

'If you are sure, then it would be a relief to have someone of superior taste to undertake the commission,' she said, and I saw a look of pleasure cross his face. 'I would undertake to wrap the picture very well, so that it will not give you too much trouble.'

'No trouble is too much. That is to say it is no trouble, no trouble at all,' he said. Then finished with a sigh, saying: 'What a precious deposit!'

I thought he had gone too far, and I was sure Emma would balk at that, but though she looked rather surprised she said nothing.

I almost said something, but I decided against it, for no doubt the muddle will be cleared up soon. Harriet will take no hurt from it, for I am sure Emma will not have raised false hopes by mentioning her scheme to her friend – that would be going too far, even for Emma! – but there will be a reckoning with Elton, and I hope Emma will be chastened. Once she stops trying to live Elton's life, I hope she might put more effort into living her own.

Thursday 3 December

I was more pleased than ever that Emma had given a little polish to
Harriet, and that she had removed some of her schoolgirl habits, for I have
had a very interesting visit from Robert Martin today. He called at
Donwell Abbey this evening and he asked if I could spare him ten
minutes. I told him that I could spare him as much time as he needed,
thinking he had come to speak to me about the farm. I was much
surprised, then, when he stood in front of my desk without any of his
usual confidence, indeed much like a schoolboy standing in front of the
desk of his master. He turned his hat in his hand as if he did not know
where to begin, and I was astonished to see a slight flush spring to his
cheek. The cause of his agitation soon became clear.

'I've come to ask for your advice, Mr Knightley,' he said.

'I will give you whatever help I can, Robert, you know that,' I said.

'Yes, I do.'

'What is the matter?' I asked him, to help him on his way.

'It is this way,' he said, then added, not very helpfully: 'I trust your judgement, Mr Knightley. You've helped me many a time in the past, and I hope
you can help me now.' He cleared his throat, and I wondered if he would
ever get to the point. 'I am before hand with the world, and doing well with
the farm. My mother and sisters want for nothing, I've seen to that.'

I said nothing, wondering where all this was leading.

'Well, Mr Knightley, the thing is this. I am of an age to marry, and
being so well set up with the farm, and after seeing Harriet – that is, Miss
Smith – and her being so pretty and well spoken, and being a good friend
of my sisters, and a favourite with my mother – that is, I am not marrying her for my mother or my sisters but for myself, because a man needs
a wife and I am a man—'

He stopped, having tied himself in knots, and I could feel some sympathy for him. I remembered how it was with John, when he proposed to
Isabella. He, too, was like a schoolboy when he left the Abbey that morning. His air of address had completely deserted him.

'You do not need my permission to marry, Robert,' I said, as he paused.

'No, Mr Knightley, I know that, I need no man's permission, but I was just wanting a bit of advice. I was wondering what you would think of me marrying so young, and whether you think I would be wrong to ask Miss Smith, as she is so young, too. And then . . .' He went as red as a turkey-cock. 'The thing is, Mr Knightley, Miss Smith being a friend of Miss Woodhouse's, and being so pretty and all, I was wondering if she wasn't too far above me?'

I was astounded! A penniless girl with no name, being above an honest farmer? A man with a comfortable living and a good name in the neighbourhood?

'Not at all,' I told him. I felt I should offer a word of caution. 'As long as you are sure you can afford it?'

'Oh, yes, I've been into all that, and I've talked it over with my mother and sisters, too. They're as eager for it as I am.'

'Then I advise you to marry Miss Smith, with my blessing. She is a pretty young woman with a very sweet nature and, moreover, she seemed to be very contented when I saw her at Abbey Mill Farm. I am sure you will be very happy together.'

'Thank you, Mr Knightley,' he said, with a smile spreading across his face. 'She's the prettiest thing I've ever seen, and she has such a taking way with her. I'll be a lucky man if she'll have me.'

And she will be a lucky girl when she marries you, I thought as he left the room.

It is a very pleasing solution to the situation! Emma's influence has improved Harriet, and made her more worthy of such a good and solid man, and once Emma knows her friend is to marry Robert Martin, all her nonsensical thoughts regarding Elton will be nipped in the bud. Neither Elton nor Harriet need ever know of the fate she had arranged for them.

Mrs Weston was right and I was wrong. I worried about nothing. This is a most happy conclusion to events.

Saturday 5 December

I cannot believe it was only yesterday that I was convinced a happy end was in view for Harriet: a poor girl, deposited in a school by unknown parents, to end up, not as an old maid, but as a happy and prosperous wife. And yet it has come to nothing. Because of Harriet? No, because of Emma! I have never been so out of charity with her in my life.

I called on her and her father this morning and, as her father went out for a walk, I felt I could give her an intimation of the good fortune about to befall her friend. To my astonishment, if not to say anger, she informed me that she already knew of it, and that Harriet had refused him!

I saw Emma's hand in it and, when challenged, it became clear that it was she who had been, not just a false advisor, but the principal in the affair.

'Mr Martin is a very respectable young man,' she said coolly, 'but I cannot admit him to be Harriet's equal.'

'Not her equal!' I exclaimed. 'No, he is not her equal indeed.' She could not see that Robert Martin was superior to Harriet in both sense and situation. 'It crossed my mind immediately that you would not regret your friend's leaving Highbury, for the sake of her being settled so well,' I went on. 'I remember saying to myself, "Even Emma, with all her partiality for Harriet, will think this a good match." '

'I cannot help wondering at your knowing so little of Emma as to say any such thing,' she returned. 'What! think a farmer a good match for my intimate friend!'

'You had no business making her your intimate friend,' I returned angrily.

'You are not just to Harriet's claims,' she went on. 'Mr Martin may be the richer of the two, but he is undoubtedly the inferior as to rank in society. The sphere in which she moves is much above his. It would be a degradation.'

A degradation! For Harriet Smith, an illegitimate girl, to marry respectable Robert Martin! Emma has never been so foolish. If only I could think it was her youth that was to blame, but she is not a child any more, she is a young woman. She should know better.

'Till you chose to turn her into a friend, her mind had no distaste for her own set, nor any ambition beyond it,' I said angrily. 'She was as happy as possible with the Martins in the summer. You have been no friend to Harriet Smith, Emma. Robert Martin would never have proceeded so far, unless he had had encouragement.'

She did not reply, but I could see my words had given her pause. Good! It was a grave day's work, to separate two people who would have been happy together. And why? Because she thought Elton would offer for Harriet.

I felt sorry for her. She was unaware of the damage she was doing, because she was too confident of her powers, and did not know that she still had a lot to learn. I was worried at how much damage she might do before she saw her mistake, and I felt I had to give her a word of warning.

'As you make no secret of your love of matchmaking, it is fair to suppose that you have views, and plans, and projects, and as a friend I shall just hint to you that if Elton is the man, I think it will be all labour in vain.'

'I have no idea of Harriet's marrying Mr Elton,' she returned.

'Elton is a very good sort of man, and a very respectable vicar of Highbury, but not at all likely to make an imprudent match. He knows the value of a good income as well as anybody,' I said, to make sure she was under no illusions about him.

She disclaimed all thoughts of such a match, but from her uncomfortable manner, I could tell that that was what she had been hoping for. Foolish girl! With no more than twenty summers, to try to counsel a girl of seventeen! Better to say nothing and let Mrs Goddard counsel Harriet, rather than apply her own influence so badly.

I felt sorry I had encouraged Robert Martin to propose. If I had known he would meet with rejection, I would not have done so. And to think that Emma was the cause of such unhappiness!

In an effort to put my ill-humour behind me I walked to Randalls. I hoped to see Weston as I had a matter of business to discuss with him, but he was not at home. Mrs Weston, however, bade me stay. Hardly had the tea been poured when Mrs Weston asked me what was the matter.

'What is always the matter?' I said. 'Emma! I knew how it would be. She has turned Harriet's head. She has filled it with nonsense, and now the poor girl has turned down a perfectly unexceptionable offer of marriage in the hope of marrying Mr Elton.'

'Mr Elton!' exclaimed Mrs Weston, astonished.

'Absurd, is it not! As if Elton would look at a parlour boarder, an illegitimate girl with no name, no connections and no dowry. Misery will be the end of it all.'

'Come, come,' said Mrs Weston. 'It surely cannot be as bad as that. If, as you say, Mr Elton will not look at Harriet – and I believe you are right – then Emma will soon see it.'

'And what of Robert Martin?'

She looked surprised, and I explained the whole. She was thoughtful, but then said: 'Mr Martin is a sensible man. If he truly loves Harriet, he will not be deterred by one setback.'

I was not so sanguine.

'A man has his pride,' I said. I drank my tea. 'If Emma could but meet someone who would interest her, she would forget all about Harriet Smith's prospects and start thinking about her own.'

Mr Weston came in, and after the three of us had taken tea together, Mr Weston and I retired to his study to discuss some business we had in hand. When we had done, I began to ask him about his son.

'Is there any news from Frank?' I asked.

'We had another letter only yesterday. He is very desirous of paying us a visit, but his time is taken up by Mrs Churchill. She rules the household with an iron hand, governing her husband entirely, and governing Frank, too.'

'So there is no news of his coming here yet?'

'He keeps hoping it will be possible, but something always happens to put the visit off. He is such a favourite with Mrs Churchill that his time is not his own. But I hope to see him here before long.'

Unfortunately, I doubt it. If Churchill cannot pay a visit to his father when his father marries, he must be a self-indulgent wastrel indeed, and I pity poor Weston his son.

Sunday 6 December

I saw Emma at church today, and we exchanged a few words. She remarked on my absence from Hartfield, and I told her I had been busy. She did not appear to have got over her schemes, for after the service she went to congratulate Elton, telling him how much Miss Smith had enjoyed it. Elton did not know where to look or what to think. Hah! A fine muddle they are making of it all.

Tuesday 8 December

I was glad to go to my whist club this evening. I had no inclination to go to Hartfield, and watch Emma make a fool of herself and her friend. Longridge was there, as well as Elton, Cole, Otway, Weston and the others.

'And how are you liking Highbury?' I asked Longridge, as the cards were dealt.

'Very much, thank you kindly. I have been thinking of leaving London for some time now – it has not been the same since my wife died – and Highbury seems a very agreeable place to settle. There is a deal of pretty countryside round about, some fine houses, and superior company. I think I might settle here.'

The game began, and we gave our attention to our cards.

Afterwards, we discussed parish business, and I came home well pleased with my evening. There is *some* sensible company in Highbury, at least.

Wednesday 9 December

It was a bright but frosty morning and my ride round the estate was invigorating. The avenues were looking particularly attractive, with their branches coated in frost. It is a time of year I particularly like.

I noticed several things which needed attention, and I spoke to William Larkins about them. He wanted to postpone the work, as it was not urgent, but I wanted to have it done before Christmas.

I do not want John to think I have been neglecting Henry's inheritance, for it seems more and more likely that I will leave the Abbey to my nephew.

Thursday 10 December

I still had no inclination to go to Hartfield today, and watch Emma making a fool of herself and her friend, so I was doubly pleased to accept an invitation from Graham.

It was impossible to forget Emma, however, for no sooner had we sat down to dinner than Graham said: 'By the by, I have a charge for you all. I saw Perry this morning, and he told me that Miss Woodhouse and her young friend Miss Smith are making a collection of riddles. Mr Woodhouse is very interested in the collection, too, and has asked Perry to spread the news so that the young ladies might have some more riddles for their book.'

The ladies were immediately interested, and Mr Longridge said: 'My wife had a very pretty hand, and made a riddle book many years ago. Let me see if I remember some of them. I have it:

When my first is a task to a young girl of spirit
And my second confines her to finish the labour—
Tum-te-tum-te-tum-te-tum. . . .

Something about "she escapes." ' He went on reflectively:

'When my first is a task to a young girl of spirit
And my second confines her to finish the labour—'

'No, not labour,' said Miss Bates, then looked flustered when all eyes turned to her. 'Oh, forgive me, Mr Longridge, it is just that I knew that riddle as a girl:

When my first is a task to a young girl of spirit
And my second confines her to finish the piece.
How hard is her fate! But how great is her merit,
If by taking my all she effects her release!'

'Bless my soul! That was it!' said Mr Longridge, much struck. 'Now, what was the answer?'

The table fell to musing, and Miss Bates supplied it: 'Hemlock!'

There was a murmur of approval and congratulation from around the table, and Miss Bates went pink. It was good to see her triumph, for she does not have many opportunities to appear to such advantage.

'You must give it to Miss Woodhouse the next time you see her,' said Graham, and Miss Bates promised she would.

'So, have you decided whether you will settle in Highbury?' asked Graham of his friend Longridge, when talk of riddles had died down.

'Yes, I have made up my mind,' he said. 'There is such good company – I have not enjoyed an evening so much since my wife died. It will be an upheaval, mind, and I will have to find a house—'

'We can help you with that,' said Mrs Cole.

'Yes, indeed,' said Mrs Otway. 'There are many fine houses hereabouts. Three Chimneys will be available after Christmas. The Dawsons are going back to Cornwall.'

'I thought they liked it here?' asked Mrs Weston, much struck.

'So they did, but Mr Dawson's brother has died, and Mr Dawson has inherited a sizeable house on the coast.'

There was much interest in this, but when it had been fully discussed, the conversation returned to the subject of Three Chimneys.

'I heard the roof leaks,' said Mrs Cole.

'Not at Three Chimneys. Barrowdown has the leaking roof, and anyhow, it is not available, as the Pringles have decided not to sell.'

Two more houses were dismissed in short order, Lowreach because it was too small, and Melrose because it was damp, but at last the ladies had decided on a list of five properties he should arrange to see. They were keen for Longridge to visit them right away, but he said that he did not mean to look at anything before the New Year. That did not prevent the ladies from talking about it for the rest of the evening, however.

Friday 11 December

Robert Martin called on me today to discuss the farm. I did not mention his suit as I had no wish to embarrass him, but the subject was there in both our thoughts, and after our business was concluded he addressed it manfully. Simply, and with great nobility, he told me that his suit had not prospered. I offered my condolences and we parted with the subject finished.

Robert Martin is my idea of a man. He does not shirk uncomfortable duties, but faces up to them. If Robert Martin was Frank Churchill, I am persuaded that he would have paid a visit to his new stepmother by now. He would have found time, even if he had had to travel overnight to do so. He is a sad loss to Harriet, whatever Emma thinks. He would have made her an estimable husband. And she would have made him, if not an estimable, then, at least, a pretty wife.

With these thoughts in mind, I was again in no mood to walk to Hartfield after dinner. I looked over my accounts, and then read a book instead.

Saturday 12 December

I called on Miss Bates this morning on my way into Kingston, and assured myself that the logs had arrived. I found Graham there with his sister, Mrs Lovage, who had joined him again from Bath.

I thought of what Weston had said, and I made sure I was no more than polite when greeting her, as I did not want to raise hopes that I had no intention of satisfying.

After exchanging civilities, I was, however, heartened by something Mrs Lovage said.

'I saw a young friend of yours yesterday. She is very good. She was taking relief to the poor.'

'What young friend do you mean?'

'I mean Miss Woodhouse, and Miss Smith was with her.'

'Oh, yes, Miss Woodhouse is always so good,' said Miss Bates.

'How did you come across her?' I asked.

'I happened to be walking along Vicarage Lane and I passed them going in the opposite direction. Miss Woodhouse was walking along with a little girl from one of the cottages. The child was carrying a pitcher for soup, and Miss Woodhouse was bearing her company. I thought it very good of her, for it must have been much pleasanter for her if she had walked ahead with Miss Smith and Mr Elton.'

'Mr Elton!' I exclaimed.

'Such a good man,' said Miss Bates. 'Always so helpful!'

'Yes,' said Mrs Lovage, smiling at Miss Bates. Then she turned again to me. 'Whether he had joined them in their charitable venture, or whether he had met them by chance, I do not know. He seemed very attentive. He slowed his pace as he tried to wait for Miss Woodhouse, but she remained behind with the child.'

'Did she indeed?' I asked.

My good humour left me. So Emma had still not abandoned her plan of throwing Harriet and Elton together. But perhaps I am misjudging her. Perhaps her charity had been prompted by a desire to do good, and not by a desire to show her friend in an amiable light.

'And what of you, Mr Knightley? How have you been spending your time since I last visited Highbury?'

'Looking after the Abbey,' I said.

'You must have had some pleasure as well.'

'Oh, yes, Mr Knightley, you must have some pleasure,' said Miss Bates. 'So good to everyone else, and never thinking of yourself.'

'I think of myself a great deal. I have my whist and my visiting, and when I am at home I have my books. A man must be very hard to please if he wants more.'

'But have you never longed to go to Bath?' asked Mrs Lovage.

'I have already been, and found nothing there that was so very extraordinary.'

'But the people . . .' she said.

'I like the people here,' I said. To my dismay, she appeared to take my remark as a compliment, and so I quickly disabused her of the notion by adding: 'The Bateses, the Westons and your brother are my oldest friends.'

'Ah, good, I am glad you like my brother,' she said satirically.

She smiled at me invitingly, but I did not prolong the conversation.

Many men would have found her attentions flattering, but as I knew I could not return them, they made me uncomfortable, and I found myself wishing to resume my evenings at Hartfield instead.

Sunday 13 December

I watched Emma closely at church this morning, and from the looks that passed between her and Harriet, I was convinced that she had told Harriet of her plans for a marriage with Elton. I found myself growing angry, for it will only lead to disappointment and humiliation for the girl.

Emma caught my eye as we waited for the service to begin, and she turned away hastily. As well she might!

I gave my attention to the rest of the congregation. Graham was there with his sister and Mr Longridge. The Coles and the Otways were there, and the Westons, of course. There was still no sign of Frank Churchill, and I found myself beginning to wonder if we would ever see him in Highbury.

Elton had not forgotten his duty as vicar of Highbury, even if he had forgotten his sense, for he led Mrs Bates and her daughter to the vicarage pew when they arrived. Miss Bates was overcome by the kindness.

'So kind! – Mother finds it hard to hear, a sore trial to her, as well as to the rest of us, and dear Jane has even mentioned it several times – a letter? Yes, yesterday, not so well, I thank you, she has a cold which will not go. However Mrs Campbell is being very kind – I am sure mother did not expect such attention. I never expected to find myself sitting in the vicarage pew, and I know I can speak for my mother when I say we are both overwhelmed.'

Unfortunately, I saw Elton glance at Emma as he performed this office, and although the kindness was not done for her benefit, he certainly was not sorry to have it witnessed. It won him smiles from Emma and Harriet, then Emma said something to her friend, and Harriet blushed, and glanced at Elton, and he went up into the pulpit as though he was walking on air.

I have resolved not to interfere. I have warned Emma, I can do no more.

I returned to the Abbey in a vexed state of mind, and found myself wishing Elton would marry Mrs Lovage. Then Emma could see her mistake, we could make our peace, and go back to our old, familiar ways. I miss my evenings at Hartfield, and, for all her vexatious ways, I miss Emma.

Monday 14 December

At last I have found a pony for the children. Henry in particular will need to be a good horseman if he is to inherit the Abbey.

Tuesday 15 December

Our whist evening was well attended. Cole was particularly cheerful.

'We are having a new dining-room,' he said, as we met at the Crown. 'Mrs Cole has been wanting to hold dinner parties for some time now, and I have promised her a new dining-room for Christmas.'

'My wife used to enjoy giving dinner parties,' said Longridge. 'She was always so talkative and so gay. She brightened my life, Mr Cole. A man needs a wife to bring sunshine into his home.'

'We hope you will join us,' said Cole, then included all of us in the invitation.

'Delighted,' said Longridge.

'A splendid idea,' said Weston. 'Nothing better than company. No point in sitting at home, unless friends are there, and every reason for going abroad.' He looked at me and laughed. 'Knightley does not agree.'

'I like company well enough, but I am equally happy with my own,' I said.

'I hope you will honour us with a visit?' Cole said, a shade anxiously.

Not so very long ago, Cole was living in a modest style, before success brought him larger ideas. I could not help thinking of Emma, and how she would be horrified to think of the master of Donwell Abbey taking dinner with Mr Cole. I smiled as I thought of her nonsense.

'Delighted,' I said.

Thursday 17 December

John and Isabella arrived from London today, and I dined with them at Hartfield. When I went in, Emma was dancing little Emma in her arms in such a delightful way that it was difficult to decide which was prettier, the eight-month-old baby, or Emma herself. They both looked sweet and innocent, and it was a sight to melt away much of my anger. It was further melted by the fact that, as I walked in and Emma's eyes turned towards me, I detected a look of uncertainty on her face. It told me she was not as happy with her own behaviour as she professed to be, for if she had been confident about it, then she would have greeted me with sauciness.

'You are well?' I asked her civilly, but without my usual warmth, as the memory of Robert Martin's disappointment was still in my mind.

'Very well. And little Emma is well, too, are you not, my dear?' she asked the infant.

Little Emma gurgled in reply.

As I took the baby from her, she said to me, in a spirit of mischief, but still with some uncertainty: 'What a comfort it is, that we think alike about our nephews and nieces. As to men and women, our opinions are sometimes very different; but with regard to these children, I observe we never disagree.'

She wanted to make friends, that much was clear, and I told her, in friendly fashion, that if she would only let herself be guided by nature when she was esteeming men and women, as she was when she was esteeming the children, we would always think alike.

'To be sure, our discordances must always arise from my being in the wrong,' she said, her good humour restored.

'With good reason,' I said with a smile. 'I was sixteen years old when you were born.'

'A material difference then, and no doubt you were much my superior in judgement at that period of our lives; but does not the lapse of one-and-twenty years bring our understandings a good deal nearer?'

'Yes – a good deal *nearer*,' I said.

'But still, not near enough to give me a chance of being right, if we think differently,' she said saucily.

I smiled.

'I have still the advantage of you by sixteen years' experience, and by not being a pretty young woman and a spoiled child. Come, my dear Emma, let us be friends and say no more about it.' I turned to the baby. 'Tell your aunt, little Emma, that she ought to set you a better example than to be renewing old grievances, and that if she were not wrong before, she is now.'

She agreed, and we shook hands. I liked the feel of it. There is something very agreeable about being with Emma.

John entered, and whilst Mr Woodhouse played with the children, and Emma and Isabella made sure they did not tire him too much, John and I caught up on the news. He was as eager as ever to hear about Donwell. I told him about the tree that was felled, and the new path I am planning, and one or two interesting cases that have come before me as the local magistrate.

I was just beginning to enjoy the evening when the usual arguments about health began.

'I cannot say that I think you are any of you looking well at present,' said Mr Woodhouse.

'I assure you, Mr Wingfield told me that he did not believe he had ever sent us off altogether, in such good case,' said Isabella, who cites Mr Wingfield as a fount of all knowledge, in the same way that Mr Woodhouse cites Perry. 'I trust, at least, that you do not think Mr Knightley is looking ill.'

I glanced at Emma, and she at me. We both of us knew where this would lead.

'Middling, my dear; I cannot compliment you. I think Mr John Knightley very far from looking well.'

I tried to talk loud enough to drown out the remark, but John heard it.

'What is the matter, sir? Did you speak to me?' he cried.

'I am sorry to find, my love, that my father does not find you looking well,' said Isabella.

'Pray do not concern yourself about my looks. Be satisfied with doctoring and coddling yourself and the children, and let me look as I choose,' said John testily.

The arguments about health subsided, but then arguments about the seaside began.

'You should have gone to Cromer, my dear, if you went anywhere,' said Mr Woodhouse. 'Perry was a week at Cromer once, and he holds it to be the best of all the sea-bathing places.'

'But, my dear sir, the difference of the journey; only consider how great it would have been. A hundred miles, perhaps, instead of forty,' said Isabella.

Mr Woodhouse was equal to the protest.

'Alt, my dear, as Perry says, where health is at stake, nothing else should be considered; and if one is to travel, there is not much to choose between forty miles and an hundred. Better not move at all, better stay in London altogether than travel forty miles to get into a worse air. This is just what Perry said. It seemed to him a very ill-judged measure.'

'I have never heard Perry saying anything of the sort!' I said in an aside to Emma, and she smiled.

John, already goaded earlier in the evening, could bear it no longer.

'If Mr Perry can tell me how to convey a wife and five children a distance of an hundred and thirty miles with no greater expense or inconvenience than a distance of forty, I should be as willing to prefer Cromer to Southend as he could himself,' he said sarcastically.

I felt it was time to intervene.

'True,' I said. 'Very true. That is a consideration, indeed.'

'The expense must be acknowledged,' said Emma.

And between us, Emma and I set about restoring the peace.

'I think the evening passed off as well as could be expected,' I said to her, when it was all but over.

'Perhaps better,' she said. 'John has always been quick tempered, and my father worries so much about everyone that he often says things without thinking.'

'An explosive combination.'

'But at least we are not exploding. How good it is to be friends again. No, do not tell me that it is my own fault, for I am sure you must bear your share of the blame. You stayed away from Hartfield when you should have come for my father's sake, if not mine. He missed you.'

'And you? Did you miss me?'

'I will not tell you, for fear it will make you vain,' she said mischievously.

'I am not so reticent. I will tell you, knowing it cannot make you vain, for you are vain already.'

'For shame!' she cried. 'And so you missed me?'

'I missed my visits to Hartfield. I would rather spend an evening here than anywhere else.'

'And that must do as a compliment, I suppose, for I shall never get one better. I am glad we are friends again,' she said.

I returned to the Abbey in good spirits, and I am looking forward to resuming my daily visits to Hartfield.

Friday 18 December

John arrived at the Abbey early this morning, bringing with him his two eldest children. They ran wild in the garden as John and I talked. I told him of my concerns about Elton raising his eyes to Emma.

'Elton and Emma? That would be a dreadful marriage,' he replied.

'There is no danger of a match. She has enough awareness of her own worth not to throw herself away on Elton,' I said.

'Then what is the danger?' John said.

'I think she may be headed for a very unpleasant scene. If I do not miss my guess, he is getting ready to declare himself.'

'And what do you want me to do about it?'

'I want you to observe them, and see if you think I am right. And then, if I am, I want you to tell me whether I should give Emma a hint of it.'

'Very well. I will keep my eyes open. Have you spoken of this to anyone else?'

'No. I know of no one who would take it seriously, or if they did, they would worry about it.'

'You may rely on me.'

'And now, come and see the pony.'

We walked round to the stables and John looked the pony over with a critical eye, then pronounced himself pleased. The boys were delighted, and John and I gave them turns at riding.

I did not know who enjoyed it more: the boys; John and I; or old Hayton, who said he remembered when John and I were that age, and that Henry and John were just like us.

We returned to Hartfield for luncheon, and we found Mr Woodhouse playing with Bella. Emma was playing with the baby, and George was looking at a book.

Mr Woodhouse was alarmed to learn that the boys had been riding on such a cold morning, and we all joined in assuring him that they had been well wrapped up against the cold.

John remarked: 'Your friend Perry thinks riding a healthful kind of exercise. It is just the sort of thing for young boys. They find the fresh air invigorating, and they learn to do something of importance. It would be a sorry man who could not ride.'

Before an argument could ensue, Emma called John to join her, and I occupied Mr Woodhouse with an account of the plans I had for the home farm.

Saturday 19 December

Isabella amused herself this morning by visiting all her friends in Highbury and showing off her children, and when she had done, John brought the eldest two boys to the Abbey for another riding lesson.

When we returned to Hartfield, we found that Harriet and Elton were also there. I was pleased, as I knew it would give John a chance to observe them and decide whether Elton was partial to Emma, or to Harriet, or whether he was partial to neither, but was simply indulging in an excess of civility to the ladies.

For myself, I could see no sign of preference for Harriet in Elton's looks and conversation, but I could see a great deal of preference for Emma. As she and I talked of our fondness for spruce-beer, Elton was determined to like it also.

'Spruce-beer – the very thing for this season,' he said.

'Do you like it, Harriet?' asked Emma, involving her friend in the conversation.

'I hardly know. I do not believe I have ever drunk it,' she said.

'You must give me your recipe,' said Elton. 'I will write it down.'

He took out a pencil, but as soon as he began to write, he discovered it had no point. He scratched and scraped at the paper, until I thought he would wear it through!

'Surely your pencil is not making any mark?' asked Emma.

He looked sheepish, then brightened. 'I have my knife – a moment! – I will mend it,' he said.

He was as good as his word and took out his knife, but by the time he had sharpened it, there was no pencil left.

'Pray, do not concern yourself, I am sure my recipe is no better than any other,' said Emma.

But Elton would not give it up.

'I would so value it – I am sure it must be superior,' he said with a simper.

I snorted, and took up my newspaper. How could the man bear to make such a fool of himself? He continued with his antics, however, feeling in his pocket for another pencil, and it was as good as a farce. If not for the fact that Harriet might be hurt by the tangle, I would have laughed at his goings-on.

Emma, meanwhile, saw her opportunity for furthering the cause of her friend.

'Harriet, do you not have a pencil that you could lend to Mr Elton?'

Harriet blushed and found one, handing it to Emma.

'Pray, give it to Mr Elton,' she said.

He stopped patting his pockets and looked at it as though it was a priceless object, instead of a pencil. He took it from Harriet, but looked languishingly at Emma.

I wondered if I was making too much of it, and if it would come to nothing in the end, but when I spoke to John as he walked back to the Abbey with me, I found that he thought as I did, that Emma was Elton's object.

'Shall I warn her?' I asked him.

He said that, if the opportunity arose, he would mention it himself.

Monday 21 December

I walked over to Hartfield today, and when I arrived I found the house looking festive. Emma and her friend had spent the morning decorating the banisters with greenery, and the children had helped them. They had decorated the pictures and mirrors in the drawing-room with sprigs of holly, which were thick with berries. The portrait of Harriet, elegantly framed, and hanging above the mantelpiece in the sitting-room, had been similarly adorned.

The children had been infected with the holiday atmosphere. They were playing boisterously, and Emma and her sister were trying to protect their father from the children's high spirits.

Further excitement had been caused by a flurry of snow. Unluckily for the children, the flurry soon stopped, and Henry spent the rest of the afternoon asking when it would start again.

The subject affected everyone variously: Isabella was so keen to please her children that I think she would have caused a snowstorm if she could; Mr Woodhouse was worried that snow would cause all manner of accidents, and decided that the only thing to do if it snowed would be to stay indoors; Emma shared her time between hoping for snow with the children and hoping for a lack of snow with her father. Harriet helped with the children, keeping them away from Mr Woodhouse, except in small doses. This endeared her to Isabella, and the atmosphere was a happy one.

Even so, I could not help wishing that Harriet was at the Martins'. Everyone was kind to her at Hartfield, but at Abbey Mill Farm she would have been someone of consequence, particularly if she had been betrothed to Robert Martin. She would have had a place in her own right, instead of being there as someone's guest.

Tuesday 22 December

An invitation came from the Westons, inviting me to dinner at Randalls on the 24th. I was about to answer it when John arrived.

'I would have been here earlier, but Isabella has been showing the children to all her friends, and I could not have them until they had returned to Hartfield. It is a pretty thing, when a man may not have his children until his wife has done with them!' he said.

The boys were eager for their riding lesson, and whilst John and I encouraged them, we talked of the Westons' party.

'Isabella and Emma have managed to persuade their father to accept the invitation,' he said.

'Have they indeed? They have done well. He does not like to go out at the best of times, and at Christmas, with his family at Hartfield, and snow threatening out of doors, I thought they would find it impossible.'

'The Westons have consulted his feelings in everything. The hours are early and the guests few. Besides, I said that if he did not care to go, then Isabella and I must go without him, for we could not snub the Westons. He became so agitated at the thought of treating the Westons with less than their due that he was persuaded, particularly once Isabella had pointed out to him that there would be no difficulty in conveying everyone, as we had our own carriage at Hartfield.'

'I mean to go, too.'

The boys had finished their lesson, and we walked down to the stream. It had been so cold overnight that it had frozen over. The boys delighted in skating on it in their shoes, and we have promised them that, if the weather holds, we will skate properly tomorrow.

'Do you not miss all this?' I asked John.

'I do, but I would miss my business more, and it holds me in town. I cannot have both, so I am content with visiting you whenever I can.'

By the time we returned to Hartfield the boys were exhausted, and they were able to sit and play quietly by the fireside.

'What good children they are,' said Mr Woodhouse contentedly.

'When they have had Uncle Knightley to wear them out!' said Emma. 'It is a good thing he invited them to the Abbey, where they could run about.'

'They are lively children. They need to use up their energy, and where better than at their uncle's house? And what have you been doing?' I asked Emma.

I looked at the drawing by the fire and picked it up. I noticed that it had not been done by Emma, but by her niece.

'This is good. This is very good,' I said teasingly to Emma. 'I think it is your best work'

Emma laughed.

'I cannot aspire to such greatness. That is Bella's picture.'

'Did you do this?' I asked Bella.

She nodded.

'And what is it ?' I asked, looking at the squiggle on the paper. 'Is it a castle?'

She shook her head.

'Is it a horse?'

She shook her head again,

'What then?'

'Papa!' she cried.

I looked at it from every direction, and discerned an eye and a mouth. 'A very good likeness. I like it even better than your Aunt Emma's portrait of Papa. You have caught his expression beautifully.'

Bella was delighted, and we settled down to a comfortable family evening. Mr Woodhouse seemed to have accepted our dining at the Westons' as a settled thing, and a few more cheerful conversations on the subject reconciled him to going out on a cold, dark evening.

As I walked home, I found I was looking forward to it.

Wednesday 23 December

I had Horrocks find our skates, so that by the time John joined me with the children, I was ready to take them down to the stream.

John and I showed the boys how to fasten the skates, helping them as they needed it, and then we all ventured on to the ice. The weather was perfect for our enterprise. The air was cold, but not biting, and a weak sun shone down on our faces. The exercise was invigorating, so that we all returned to Hartfield with hearty appetites.

After taking tea, Emma proposed charades. Isabella fell in with the suggestion readily enough. Harriet seemed lethargic, but was compliant.

The children went up to the attic with Emma and Isabella, and came down with an armful of clothes. There was great hilarity as Bella put on an old dress of Isabella's, which was far too big for her, and walked round in her mother's shoes, which were also far too large. In vain did Emma, Harriet and Isabella try to persuade her to part with her treasures, and tempt her with other, more suitable, clothes!

The children were too young to understand much of it, but they liked dressing up, and the rest of the party enjoyed the game.

The first charade took us some time to guess. It began with Isabella and the children sitting down, throwing something through the air. A great deal of laughter was produced by our false guesses, until John guessed that they were fishing, and we arrived, by circuitous route, at 'river-bank'. A moment's further thought showed us the word was simply 'bank'. Emma then came in dressed as a queen.

Mr Woodhouse could offer no guesses, being more concerned with Emma's beauty, and for myself I had to agree, for I have always found her face and form to be more pleasing than any other I have ever seen.

I could not immediately see the significance, until I thought again of the first syllable, and realized the word was 'bank-note', with Emma being a woman of note.

By the time the game was over, it was obvious why Harriet was so lethargic. She was suffering from a cold. She said that she must return to Mrs Goddard's, and Emma would not hear of it, saying she could not allow her friend to leave the house. But Harriet begged to be allowed to be nursed by Mrs Goddard, so the carriage was sent for, and Harriet was conveyed home.

Mr Woodhouse was anxious all evening, hoping Harriet might not take a turn for the worse, but offering tragic tales of colds that had turned to pneumonia, leading to early graves. Isabella watched her children anxiously, lest one of them should have also taken cold. She and her father argued about the cures recommended by their respective physicians, and Emma sensibly decided to take the children up to the nursery. John and I retreated behind our newspapers, and let Isabella and her father have their argument in peace.

Thursday 24 December

John had an opportunity to warn Emma about Elton's attentions today, though whether she has taken the hint he does not know. He chanced to meet them both this morning, when he was returning from the Abbey with the boys. Emma seemed very solicitous of Elton, John told me, which alarmed me, until I had heard the full tale. She had tried to persuade him that he had a cold, and that he should not go to the Westons this evening as he was not well enough.

'Elton did not know what to say,' said John. 'He had no sign of a cold that I could see, yet he did not want to contradict her.'

'I see her purpose! She wanted him to spend the evening thinking of her little friend, and perhaps calling in at Mrs Goddard's to ask after Miss Smith, instead of dining at Randalls.'

'I thought you said that Elton was in love with Emma, not Harriet?' asked John with a frown.

'Not *in love*. I said his *ambition* tended in that direction. But they are at cross-purposes. Emma's ambitions are in a different quarter. She thinks that he will marry her friend.'

'What! The parlour boarder?'

'Yes.'

'Has Emma taken leave of her senses?' he asked.

'The girl is pretty.'

'And so are a hundred other girls. He has only to go to Brighton, or Bath, to find plenty of *well-born*, pretty young ladies with a handsome dowry, who would not turn down a handsome vicar.'

I brought him back to the point, asking if he had warned Emma, and learning that he had.

'And what did she reply?' I asked.

'That I was mistaken. That she and Mr Elton were friends and nothing more.'

'Foolish girl! Well, she has been warned. If he proposes now, at least it will not take her entirely by surprise.'

'He will not get a chance tonight,' John said. 'I have offered to take him in my carriage. And once at the Westons he will get no time alone with her.'

I was reassured. Even so, I had followed Emma's progress with such interest, for so many years, that I was curious to know what the evening would bring.

When I arrived, the first party from Hartfield was already there. Isabella and Mr Woodhouse were sitting by the fire, waiting for Emma, Elton and John.

Emma's party soon followed, and Emma greeted Mrs Weston fondly. I have always been glad of the affection they share.

Emma took a seat, and Mr Elton sat next to her. He was very solicitous, asking her if she was warm enough, asking if her father were comfortable, and crowning it by calling attention to some of her drawings, which hung in Mrs Weston's drawing-room.

'Remarkable,' he said. 'Such a way with line. Quite exquisite. You are fortunate to have them, Mrs Weston.'

Mrs Weston agreed, but Emma looked uncomfortable. I guessed that Elton's flattery was not to her taste. Either that, or my brother's caution had given her pause, and she was now considering whether he could be right, and whether Mr Elton's object could be herself.

She did not have long to think of it, however, for the subject of Frank Churchill was soon raised.

'We want only two more to be just the right number. I should like to see two more here, your pretty little friend, Harriet, and my son, and then I should say we were quite complete,' said Weston. 'I believe you did not hear me telling the others in the drawing-room that we are expecting Frank?' he went on, growing expansive as he addressed Emma. 'I had a letter from him this morning, and he will be with us within a fortnight.'

'Oh, yes, that would be perfect,' said Emma with genuine enthusiasm.

She, along with the rest of Highbury, has long been wondering about Frank Churchill.

'He has been wanting to come to us, ever since September,' said Weston, 'but he cannot command his own time. He has those to please who must be pleased, and who (between ourselves) are sometimes to be pleased only by a good many sacrifices. But now I have no doubt of seeing him here about the second week in January.'

Emma spoke of his son at length to Weston. She could not say too much to please him.

After dinner the ladies withdrew, and Mr Woodhouse went with them. He has no interest in business or politics, and sees his attendance as a compliment to the ladies.

When they had departed, we talked of the parish and the war, our farming troubles and our hopes for the coming year. Weston was convivial, resisting any effort to break up the gentlemen by passing the port again. He liked nothing better than to have a group of friends round his table.

I saw Elton looking at the clock once or twice, but otherwise he bore his separation from the ladies well. At last, Weston could delay us no longer, and we left our seats.

'I am going to take a walk,' said John, as we left the dining-room. 'I need some fresh air after Weston's good food. Do you care to join me?'

'No, thank you,' I said.

Truth to tell, I wanted to see how Emma got on with Elton.

The other gentlemen demurred, and John set out.

On arriving in the drawing-room, I was not surprised to see Elton making for Emma, and, with scarcely an invitation, he seated himself between her and Mrs Weston. He began to speak of Harriet at once, saying he hoped that Emma would not risk catching a cold from her friend.

Really, he was as bad as her father, with his talk of colds! She quickly gew weary of his attentions, and I became sure of one thing: she was finally convinced that she was his object, and not Harriet. No matter how many times she tried to turn the conversation back to her friend, he would not have it. Everything he said was about her.

'So scrupulous for others,' said Elton to Mrs Weston, 'and yet so care-less for herself! She wanted me to nurse my cold by staying at home today, and yet will not promise to avoid the danger of catching an ulcerated sore throat herself! Is this fair, Mrs Weston? Judge between us. Have not I some right to complain? I am sure of your kind support and aid.'

Mrs Weston looked astonished, as well she might. This was going beyond anything I had so far heard, and assumed an intimacy that plainly was not there. I wondered that Emma could endure it, though by her look she could not do so easily. I almost stepped in, but knowing her to be equal to Elton, I left her to fight the battle herself.

She turned on him a quelling look, and I did not know whether to pity them or laugh at them: Emma abusing her powers and creating a muddle where there had been none, and Elton, blinded by ambition, mistaking the matter so badly he was about to make an even bigger muddle than the one already made.

There was no time for any more of Elton's chivalry, however, as John returned from his walk. He came in, rubbing his hands and speaking briskly, breaking like a whirlwind into the room.

'This will prove a spirited beginning of your winter engagements, sir,' he said to Mr Woodhouse heartily. 'It will be something new for your coachman and horses to be making their way through a storm of snow.'

I wished he could have been less dramatic in his entrance. Mr Woodhouse was so distressed he was struck dumb, but a regular hubbub broke out from everyone else.

'Snow? I would not have thought it,' said Emma.

'No, indeed,' said Elton. 'Who could have guessed?'

'How deep is it?' asked Weston.

'Do you think it will lie?' asked Mrs Weston.

'I admired your resolution very much, sir, in venturing out in such weather,' continued John to Mr Woodhouse, 'for of course you saw there would be snow very soon. Everybody must have seen the snow coming on. I admired your spirit; and I dare say we shall get home very well. Another hour or two's snow can hardly make the road impassable; and we are two carriages; if *one* is blown over in the bleak part of the common field there will be the other at hand. I dare say we shall be all safe at Hartfield before midnight.'

To him, the snow was a matter of novelty and excitement. There are times when he reminds me of his children! To Weston, too, it was a source of satisfaction, or at least the concealment of it was.

'I knew it was snowing all along,' said Weston. 'I saw it as I crossed the hall, but said nothing for fear of breaking up the party. I could see that it was nothing, a mere dusting, and nothing to worry about. There will be no difficulty in anyone getting home. A pity! I wish there would be, then you could all stay the night. We would love to have you, would we not, my dear?' he said to Mrs Weston.

She hardly knew how to look, and I was not surprised, as there are only two spare rooms at Randalls, and she had six guests.

'What is to be done, my dear, Emma? What is to be done?' said Mr Woodhouse, over and over again.

Leaving them to their worries, I went outside to judge the situation for myself. John had exaggerated. There was very little snow, nothing but a fine covering, and it was not likely to cause any difficulties in getting home. I went beyond the sweep, and walked some way along the Highbury Road, to make sure, but it was nowhere more than half an inch deep, and in many places it was hardly there at all.

I looked up. A few flakes were falling, but the sky was clearing, and I felt it would soon abate. I spoke to James, and he agreed with me that there was nothing to worry about.

I returned to the drawing-room and set everyone's minds at ease, but Mr Woodhouse had been so worried that he did not recover.

'Your father will not be easy; why do not you go?' I said to Emma.

'I am ready, if the others are.'

'Shall I ring the bell?'

'Yes, do.'

I think she was not sorry to be leaving Elton. Once back at home, she would be free of his attentions.

Between us, we managed to soothe Mr Woodhouse until the carriage was brought round. I saw him to his carriage, and Isabella and he stepped in. I stood back, and John, forgetting that he had not come with his wife, followed her into the carriage. I was about to remonstrate with him, when the carriage pulled away.

What did it matter which carriage he took? I thought, until I remembered that Emma would now be left alone with Elton.

I was just about to suggest that I went with her, when I saw that both she and Elton had climbed into their carriage, and that it was already following the first up the drive.

I consoled myself with the though that Elton was a gentleman. Though he had partaken freely of wine I did not fear for Emma's safety. But as to what he might say to her. . . .

On reflection, I felt it was perhaps as well that things should come to a head. I could not stand to see him dancing attendance on her any longer, and the sooner she made her feelings plain to him the better.

I went back inside.

'So, we have lost the rest of the party,' said Mr Weston. 'You will stay a while longer?' he asked me.

He was looking dejected at the sudden break-up of his party, and I agreed. The conversation turned once again to his son, and we spent an hour talking of Frank Churchill, Mr Weston's delight in being about to see him, and Mrs Weston's desire to meet her new stepson.

As we spoke, however, I could not help wondering what was taking place in the carriage.

'You seem tired,' said Mr Weston, noticing my abstraction at last.

'No,' I said, rousing myself.

'The children have been wearing you out,' said Mrs Weston with a smile.

I let her think it. It was better than have her worrying about Emma.

I left them at last, and, thanking them for a very enjoyable evening, I returned to the Abbey.

I took up a book, but it would not do.

What was Elton saying to Emma? What was she saying to him? And would I ever learn anything of it? I wondered.

Probably not. She had not admitted her mistake to me, and probably never would. But I should know by her manner if something had happened, even if she said nothing.

Friday 25 December

When I woke up this morning, there was a brightness about my chamber, and I could tell at once that it had snowed heavily in the night. On pulling back the curtains, I saw that a blanket of snow lay over everything. The gardens were thick with it, and the meadows beyond, and the drive was covered so effectively that I knew there would be no travelling by carriage today.

I walked out before breakfast, enjoying the briskness of the exercise and the crispness of the air, then returned to a hot meal before setting off for church. I did not expect to find the Hartfield party there, but one or two hardy souls had braved the walk. Graham was there, with his sister.

Mr Longridge was there, also. He told me that he had looked in on the Bateses on his way, and had found them both well. They had had a good fire, he told me, and the smell of cooking had been coming from the kitchen.

'Miss Bates would have come to church – I offered her my arm – but she would not leave her mother. A wonderful woman, Mr Knightley,' he said. 'Always thinking of others, and never of herself. And always interested in the world around her. My wife was another such woman. I was busy with business, but I never minded, because my wife always brought the world to me. I knew what our friends were doing, because she told me. And now that I sit by myself, my business days being behind me, I like to hear a woman's voice telling me all the news again.'

I thought how kind he was, and I was pleased he had entered into our ways already. It was very good of him to look in on Miss Bates, and to say how agreeable he found her chatter.

Miss Nash was there, and I took the opportunity of asking her how Harriet did.

'Very poorly, thank you for asking,' she said. 'The poor girl has a shocking cold and a sore throat. She has kept to her bed since returning from Hartfield, and will not be out of it for several days.'

The service began, and I thought Elton looked subdued, though it could have been my imagination, for afterwards, Miss Nash said she thought the service had been particularly good, and Mr Longridge declared it the best service he had been to for a long time. He left me with the intention of calling on the Bateses on his way home, so that he could tell them all about it.

I walked to Hartfield, and found the family indoors. Mr Woodhouse had recovered from his shock of the night before, and was sitting by the fire with Isabella, the baby on his knee. Little Emma was looking placid and contented.

Her namesake, my Emma, was playing with the other children. She looked up as I entered the room, but she could not meet my eye.

So! Elton had spoken, I thought, but I did not plague her by mentioning it.

Mr Woodhouse was shocked that I had walked over to Hartfield in all the snow, and he was even more alarmed when I said that I had been to church. Isabella asked about the service, but Emma made no enquiries. Instead, she became absorbed in Henry's blocks, and did not look up until the conversation had moved on to other things.

John was cheerful, having worked off his ill-humour yesterday evening, and was enjoying his children. Despite Mr Woodhouse's protests, he ordered Henry and John wrapped up warmly, then he and I took them out into the garden. They delighted in walking through the snow, trying to step in our footsteps.

When we returned to the house, we exchanged presents, and I enjoyed seeing Emma's face when she unwrapped the gloves I had bought her. I rejoiced in her present to me, a pen-wiper, which was to replace the one she made for me ten years ago.

'It is much better made than the last one,' I remarked.

She smiled, and said she hoped so.

Her spirits improved as she watched the children unwrapping their presents, and then she encouraged them to sing for me. They had already sung for the others. To begin with, the children stood mute before us, Henry and John looking bashful, Bella giggling, and George trying to do what his brothers and sister did. Isabella gave them encouragement, and Henry began to sing. The others, emboldened, joined in with:

Rejoice our Saviour he was born
On Christmas day in the morning

Or so I took the words to be, for they came out with a lisp and a stutter that was perfectly charming. Their efforts were heartily praised, and each was rewarded with an orange.

After dinner, when the children were in bed, Emma suggested we play at bullet pudding. John declared that he was too old for such a game, but when the mound of flour was brought in, with the bullet set on top of it, he joined in with as much enthusiasm as anyone. Isabella was the first to let it fall, and when she had retrieved it with her teeth, her face was covered completely in flour. She looked such a strange sight that we all burst out laughing, and Isabella had to wipe her face quickly for fear of the flour choking her if she started to laugh, too.

John was next to let it fall, by cutting the flour too finely, and when he emerged with the bullet held triumphantly between his teeth, his face was worse than his wife's had been. Emma was the next to let the bullet fall, and Mr Woodhouse worried about her until she had restored the bullet to its place at the top of the shrinking pyramid and wiped her face clean. I, too, came in for my share of flour, and ended up with a great deal on my coat as well as my face.

Our evening did not end there. Emma played the pianoforte and we sang carols, and then Isabella played and Emma and I had an impromptu dance. It ended only when she declared her sister must have her share of the fun, and she sat down at the pianoforte herself.

So ended a very enjoyable Christmas Day. Mr Woodhouse entreated me to stay the night, rather than face the walk home, but I would not be persuaded.

As I walked home through the freezing night, I felt I had never liked a day more in my life.

Saturday 26 December

Another snowy day. I walked over to Hartfield and spent it with my family. A cheerful sight met my eyes as I arrived. John was in the grounds, with John and Henry. The boys were wrapped up warmly and were running about.

We went into the house together. The smell of spices lingered on the air, and the fires sent it round the house.

Emma seemed in better spirits, and before long we were playing hunt-the-slipper with the children. Isabella was as pleased as could be, playing with her children, and John joined in.

He is a lucky man to have five such fine sons and daughters. I thought again of my hope to marry, and I was sorry that I had not managed to find a suitable wife.

I passed the day most agreeably, regardless. I spent the time with the children, and when they were in bed, the adults played charades.

Mr Woodhouse entreated me to stay the night, as he did yesterday, for he feared something might happen to me on the walk home, but I would not give in. I returned to the Abbey. There is nothing better than a crisp walk through the snow on a moonlit night, at the end of a happy day.

Sunday 27 December

I went to church this morning, but I was not surprised to find that Emma and her father had not ventured out, for the snow was still lying thickly on the ground. There was some good to come out of the weather, however, for it would delay John and Isabella's departure. I said as much to Emma when I walked over to Hartfield after church.

'To be sure, that is a happy thought,' she said.

We took the older children out into the snow without, however, letting her father know.

'Papa worries so,' she said. 'It is better not to draw attention to our absence. He will be happy sitting by the fire.'

After a while, Isabella brought Bella and George out to join us. She had been torn between maternal solicitousness, not wishing the children to get their feet wet, and a desire to please her younger children, who had begged to be allowed to join us, Bella with words, and George by walking over to the window and looking longingly at the snow.

'You must be thinking of marrying soon, Emma,' said Isabella.

'I shall never marry,' said Emma firmly. 'What could marriage offer me that I do not already have? I could not have a better house, or a higher place in the neighbourhood, or more agreeable company, and no one could ever love me more than Papa.'

'But they would love you in a different way,' said Isabella, 'and you would have your children.'

'I do not need any children, when I can play with yours.'

Isabella was torn between an urge to see her sister with a family, and a belief that Emma's children could not be any dearer than her own.

'I only wish you did not have to leave us so soon,' said Emma.

'I do not know how we will return to London in all this snow,' said Isabella.

'We must do it if we can,' said John, joining us. 'I have to be in London on the twenty-eighth.'

'Business will not continue in this weather, surely?' I said.

'It will if it is at all possible.'

We returned to the house, where we drank mulled wine, much to the concern of Mr Woodhouse, who thought it bad for our constitutions, and tried to encourage us to take a bowl of gruel. I was almost in a mood to humour him, so well at ease did I feel with my world.

Almost!

Monday 28 December

John and Isabella were to have departed for London today, but the roads were still impassable, so they remained.

John was fretful, but the children lifted him out of his ill-humour. Isabella was pleased to be still at Hartfield, and Mr Woodhouse went so far as to say that he hoped it might snow again tomorrow, so that he would have the pleasure of his family for a few days longer.

Emma was glad of her sister's company, and I was glad for her.

'It is not easy for you, having no one of your own age to talk to,' I said, as I sat down beside her and watched her doing some embroidery.

'I have Harriet. I am lucky to have found her. She is the best friend I could wish for. She is good humoured, and I have the added enjoyment of feeling I am doing her good.'

'She is not the right companion for you,' I said. I could see she was about to argue, so I added: 'She is three years younger than you.'

'She is not my only friend,' said Emma. 'I have you.'

I was gratified, but I said: 'I am so much older than you.'

'Yet for all your superiority, I have yet to see you embroider a handker-chief,' she said archly, and held out her work for me to examine.

'Perhaps I should learn!'

'What? And neglect your work at the Abbey? William Larkins would never forgive me. He looks at me darkly as it is, when I pass him in Highbury. I am sure he thinks you spend far too much time here.'

'Do you think so?' I asked her.

'You can never spend enough time here for Papa and me.'

For some reason, the answer did not satisfy me as it should have done. I am becoming as uneven-tempered as my brother!

Wednesday 30 December

John and Isabella were at last able to leave for London. They left with many good wishes, wrapped around with blankets, and with hot bricks at their feet. Mr Woodhouse insisted they took a hamper, in case they were delayed on the road, and he had his housekeeper pack it with so many good things that they will have enough to eat for three days!

At last they set off. Emma and I walked to the edge of the estate, cutting off a loop of road, so that we could wave to the coach as it passed us again. The children returned our waves, their faces aglow.

'And so they are gone,' said Emma. 'The time went so quickly, it does not seem two minutes since they arrived.'

I was as disappointed as she, and I found myself already wishing for their return.

'I will try and persuade John to visit us again at Easter.'

'You are luckier than I, for you see them all when you visit London,' she said.

'I do, but it is not the same as having them here in Surrey.'

We watched the carriage until it had shrunk from view, and then we returned to the house. Emma fell behind me, and when I looked round, I saw her walking in my footprints! It reminded me of her antics as a little girl. But she is a little girl no longer. She is turning into a beautiful young woman.

She joined me, and together we walked back to the house.

'Poor Isabella!' sighed Mr Woodhouse. 'I wish she had not had to go back to London. It is so much better for her here.'

Emma set about soothing him.

'She will visit us again before long,' Emma said.

By and by, he accepted their departure, and after playing a game of backgammon with him, I set out back to the Abbey. It was looking very pretty, with the snow still lingering on the branches of the trees. If only it had a mistress, it would be complete. But I have found no one who pleases me, and have no desire to marry for the sake of it.

Thursday 31 December

I walked to Hartfield to see how Emma and her father were bearing the loss of their guests.

'Ah, Mr Knightley, we feel it sadly,' said Mr Woodhouse. 'Everyone is leaving us.'

'Papa, tell Mr Knightley what Perry said of the children,' said Emma. 'He said he had never seen them looking better, did he not?'

'That is because they have been staying at Hartfield, my dear,' he said. 'They should not have left us. And Mr Elton, too, is leaving us, and going to Bath. Young people are always running about.'

'Mr Elton?' I asked.

'He sent me a letter. A very pretty letter, very long and civil, was it not, Emma?' he asked.

Emma agreed, although without much conviction, and when Mr Woodhouse showed me the letter, I could see why. Elton, though effusive in his compliments to Mr Woodhouse, had not mentioned Emma once. I guessed there must have been some unpleasantness, though Emma had not mentioned it, because, if not, his letter would have conveyed his compliments to her. Even so, his neglect to mention her was the kind of bad manners I would not have expected of Elton.

Poor Emma! As I looked up from the letter and found her eyes on me, I did not know whether to be more exasperated by her folly, or more sorry for her at its outcome.

'Emma is talking of walking over to Mrs Goddard's and seeing her friend, Harriet,' said Mr Woodhouse. 'She has not been able to enquire after her because of the snow, and she does not wish to be remiss.'

I could guess why Emma was so eager to visit her friend. Although, eager is not the right word. Say rather, I could guess why she felt it her duty to pay an early call on Harriet: she had to break the news of Mr Elton's true feelings, and admit that his attentions had been for herself and not her friend. And she had to reveal that he had left the neighbourhood. I did not envy her the task, but I hardened my heart, for I sincerely hoped it would prevent her from creating havoc in the lives of those around her in the future.

'Tell her she must not go, Mr Knightley,' said Mr Woodhouse. 'The weather is not fit. She will slip, and take cold, or lose her way.'

'Nonsense,' I said cheerfully. 'The exercise will do her good. She is looking pale from spending too much time indoors. A brisk walk, in this winter sunshine, will put some colour in her cheeks. Perry himself recommends walking, you know, and I am sure he would consider the exercise beneficial.'

I offered to sit with Mr Woodhouse whilst she was gone, and he accepted my offer. I set out the backgammon board, and as Emma left the house, her father and I settled down to a game. He played well, but I managed to beat him. I then offered to help him with some letters of business, and remained with him until Emma returned.

She did not look happy. But her unpleasant task was behind her, and she had the new year to look forward to.

I returned to the Abbey and began to plan in earnest for the spring.

JANUARY

Friday 1 January

It is the New Year!

I was not surprised to find that Emma had drawn up a list of resolutions. They were written in a fine hand, and exquisitely illustrated. If only she could put as much earnestness into keeping them as she does into making them!

My New Year's resolution is to take a wife, if I can find anyone to suit.

Saturday 2 January

The thaw has left a number of problems in its wake at the Abbey. The stream has flooded, and as the thaw progresses there will be worse to come. I made provision for attending to matters once the water subsides.

I called on Graham this morning to wish him the compliments of the season. He returned the greeting. I soon learnt that he, too, had received a letter from Mr Elton.

'I should not wonder if his visit to Bath was prompted by all this talk of weddings and families,' said Mrs Lovage. 'First with Miss Taylor getting married, then with your brother and his family visiting, then with talk of Mr Frank Churchill paying a visit to Highbury. Mr Elton is at a time of life when he might well be thinking of marriage, and there are one or two families in Bath who would not be sorry to see him there.'

I would not be at all surprised if he returned with a bride. It would soothe his pride, and put an end to the kind of scenes he has recently been a part of. Besides, who is there for him in Highbury? He cannot marry Emma, for Emma will not have him. No other woman is high enough in his estimation, I fear. I had thought, at one time, he might marry Jane Fairfax, and provide her with a respectable home. But now that he has shown his true worth, I would not inflict such a man on Miss Fairfax. She deserves a better man than he.

I wonder . . . I have always liked Jane Fairfax. It remains to be seen if I can like her enough to think of her as a wife.

Monday 4 January

Emma and I have had an argument, and about the most ridiculous thing: Frank Churchill. It began when she told me that he would not be coming to Highbury after all.

'I cannot say it surprises me,' I remarked. 'He has grown proud, luxurious and selfish through living with the Churchills.'

'What nonsense!' said Emma, laughing at me.

'Why else would he keep putting off his visit? If he had wanted to see his father, he would have contrived it between September and January,' I said.

'You are the worst judge in the world, Mr Knightley, of the difficulties of dependence,' she said.

It is true I have never been dependent. But even so, I am sure I should never have been slow in doing my duty, and so I told her.

'Besides, we are for ever hearing of him at Weymouth, or some other such place,' I went on. 'This proves that he can leave the Churchills.'

She allowed the point, but maintained that his time was only his own when his aunt allowed it.

'We shall never agree about him,' she said. 'But that is nothing extraordinary. I have not the least idea of his being a weak young man: I feel sure that he is not; but I think he is very likely to have a more yielding, complying, mild disposition than would suit your notions of man's perfection.'

For some reason, I did not like to hear her praising him.

'He can sit down and write a fine flourishing letter, full of professions and falsehoods, if that is what you mean by a complying disposition,' I said scathingly, for she seemed to think very well of a man she had never met. 'His letters disgust me.'

She looked surprised at the strength of my feeling, but why should I not have strong feelings?

'You seem determined to think ill of him,' she said.

'Not at all. I should be as ready to acknowledge his merits as any other man; but I hear of none, except what are merely personal; that he is well-grown and good-looking, with smooth, plausible manners.'

'Well, if he should have nothing else to recommend him, he will be a treasure at Highbury,' she said mischievously. 'We do not often look upon fine young men, well-bred and agreeable. We must not be nice and ask for all the virtues into the bargain.'

'If I find him conversable, I shall be glad of his acquaintance,' I remarked disdainfully, 'but if he is only a chattering coxcomb, he will not occupy much of my time or thoughts.'

'My idea of him is, that he can adapt his conversation to the taste of everybody, and has the power as well as the wish of being universally agreeable.'

'And mine is, that if he turn out anything like it, he will be the most insufferable fellow breathing!' I said irascibly.

'I will say no more about him,' cried Emma, 'you turn everything to evil. We are both prejudiced; you against, I for him; and we have no chance of agreeing till he is really here.'

'Prejudiced! I am not prejudiced,' I exclaimed, although I knew, even as I said it, that I was.

'But I am very much, and without being at all ashamed of it,' she said. 'My love for Mr and Mrs Weston gives me a decided prejudice in his favour.'

'He is a person I never think of from one month's end to another,' I remarked with vexation.

But, in fact, I did not speak the truth. For some reason, I have taken a dislike to Frank Churchill, and I do not want Emma to like him, either.

It is a good thing Churchill has put off his visit. I find myself wishing he might never come to Highbury at all.

Tuesday 5 January

There was a discrepancy in the accounts, and it took me all afternoon to trace it and correct it, so I was glad to go to my whist club this evening. It was an escape from the irritations at Hartfield and the annoyances at the Abbey.

Once there, I found that a new subject of conversation had arisen, and one that had thankfully put Frank Churchill out of everyone's mind.

'This is good news,' said Otway, when I entered the Crown. 'Jane Fairfax is to visit her aunt and grandmother. I have not seen Miss Fairfax for years. A taking little thing she was, when she was a girl. She will be a young woman now, of an age with Miss Woodhouse.'

'It will be good for the two of them to have each other. Mrs Weston is very pleased,' said Weston.

'And so am I,' I said. At last, Emma will have some refined company. After the disappointments of recent weeks, I hope she will value it for what it is worth. And I . . . perhaps I will find what I have been looking for. 'Nothing would give me greater pleasure than to see Miss Fairfax and Emma become friends.'

'It's a sad situation,' said Cole. 'Poor girl. It was very good of Colonel Campbell to raise her when her parents died—'

'A lot of men would have conveniently forgotten that Jane's father had saved their life,' agreed Weston.

'—or regarded it as a duty to do something for the infant, making a contribution to their upkeep, perhaps, but nothing more,' said Cole. 'But not Colonel Campbell.'

'I suppose he thought he might as well take her in, having a girl of his own. It gave both children a playmate, his daughter being an only child.'

'I dare say that played its part, but it was still good of him to give Jane a home and all the benefits of an education.'

'Something her aunt could not have afforded,' agreed Weston.

'But it is a double-edged kindness,' I said. 'Now that Miss Fairfax is a woman, she has to earn a living. It will not be easy for her to move from a world in which she has had a great deal of pleasure, to one in which she will be little better than a servant.'

'I would like to help her, but what can we do?' asked Cole.

'Nothing but make her welcome in Highbury, where we can show her the attentions she deserves, and make her feel that here there will always be a place for her,' said Weston.

As he spoke, I thought that I might be able to do something more.

Tuesday 12 January

Business brought me to town, and after it was concluded, I dined with my friend Routledge at the club.

'What news from Highbury?' he asked.

I began by telling him about the Abbey and the farms, and then we talked of my neighbours. I told him about Mr Longridge and Mrs Lovage.

'Mrs Lovage?' he asked.

'She is Graham's sister, and she has been to stay with him several times.'

'Does her husband not object?' he asked. 'He seems to be unusually compliant if he allows her to stay with her brother so often – unless, of course, he goes too?'

'She is a widow.'

'Ah, I see. It is a recent bereavement? Is that why she stays so often with her brother? She is in need of consolation, I suppose.'

'Not so very recent. Her husband has been dead for five years. She stays with her brother because she enjoys his company, not because she is grieving.'

'I see. She is old, I take it? Graham must be thirty-five, so his sister is about forty, I collect, with several children?'

'Forty!' I said. 'She is no such thing. She is his younger sister, and cannot be more than seven- or eight-and-twenty. As for children, I have never heard them mentioned.'

'I believe you said she was ugly?'

'No, she is rather beautiful,' I remarked. 'In fact, she is very beautiful.'

'And?'

'And what?'

'And, if she is a young and beautiful widow, who is the sister of your friend, have you not thought of marrying her?' he asked.

'Yes,' I admitted. 'I have. But I could not bring myself to think of her in that way. She would always be wanting to go to Brighton, or Bath, or London, or Weymouth, and I like to spend my time in Highbury.'

'That is the worst reason for not marrying a woman I have ever come across! You surprise me, Knightley. I did not think you would be so easily defeated. Surely some agreement could be reached?'

'If I loved her, yes. But I have no feelings for her. I did not miss her when she returned to Bath for a spell and that told me that she was not important to me.'

'Why should you, indeed? You had plenty to do. You could not be expected to pine for her like a lovesick schoolboy.'

'I was never a lovesick schoolboy. The notion of love, in my youth, struck me as ridiculous, but I always miss Emma when I am away from Highbury, no matter how much I have to do.'

'Do you?' he asked thoughtfully.

'Yes, I do. I often resent an evening spent in London, because I cannot walk over to Hartfield after dinner and discuss the day's news.'

'And is there no one else you have seen who might interest you? No woman who has caught your fancy, or entertained you, or intrigued you?'

'My brother has introduced me to several young ladies, but the idea of an evening with one of them is not as enticing to me as the idea of five minutes with Emma,' I said shortly.

'And have you met no great beauties?'

'A few. But I prefer to look at Emma.'

'And what does all this tell you?' he asked me,

'That I have not yet met the right woman, and that there is no use my marrying unless I find someone I like as well as Emma,' I said.

He laughed, though I did not know why. There was nothing very amusing in what I had said.

'I have a feeling you will be married before the year is out,' he told me.

I could not agree with him, but for the sake of peace I did not contradict him and our conversation moved on to other things.

Friday 15 January

I returned home from London, and spent the evening at Hartfield. I enjoyed myself so thoroughly that I was convinced I would be foolish to exchange such company for something less agreeable. I would like to marry, but I would rather remain single than give up my evenings with Emma and her father.

Wednesday 20 January

The new path at the Abbey is proving troublesome. First we could not lay it because of the snow, then because of the flood that followed, and now there is such a thick frost that work cannot go ahead. I would like to have it finished for the spring, and I am chafing at the delay. However, it is only January, and I do not despair of some milder weather soon.

Weston called this morning to discuss a matter of business, and as he was leaving he told me that Miss Fairfax had arrived.

I took the first opportunity to call on Miss Bates, so that I could pay my respects.

Somehow the Bates's apartment seemed shabbier today than usual, though I could not think why. It was still in the same house, belonging to the same people in business. It still occupied the drawing-room floor. It was still of a moderate size. Mrs Bates was still sitting in the corner with her knitting, and Miss Bates was still ready to make me welcome.

And then I realized it was because of Miss Fairfax. Whether it was because her presence provided novelty, and therefore made me look at the room anew, or whether it was because everything seemed shabby in comparison with her beauty, I could not say. But shabby it seemed.

My first impression of Miss Fairfax was very favourable. She was even more beautiful than I remembered her, and I moved forward to greet her.

'I am very glad to see you in Highbury again, Miss Fairfax,' I said to her.

'Thank you,' she replied.

As I saw her in a better light, I noticed she was thin and pale.

'Your aunt tells me you have been ill?' I remarked, as I took a seat beside her.

'It is nothing. A cold, that is all,' she said.

She seemed listless and out of spirits.

'But you have had it for several months?' I asked.

'It is hard, over the winter, to rid oneself of a cold,' she said quietly.

'Now we have her back at Highbury, she will be well again in no time,' said Miss Bates. 'Our good Highbury air will restore her, depend upon it, Mr Knightley. Mr Perry is convinced of it. I spoke to him only this morning. He called to see Jane – so good! So obli-ging! We are so grateful to him – and he says that now she is back home, she will no doubt recover. Our friends have all been so kind, sending anything they think Jane might enjoy. Only this morning Mr Longridge sent some calves'-foot jelly! Mr Woodhouse has sent us a beautiful piece of pork, and Mr Graham sent some bottled pears. I told him we could not think of taking them, but he said he had had such a glut of pears this year that we would be doing him a kindness in taking them. I am sure we will have her better in no time.'

I could tell from her expression, though, that she was worried.

Various remedies were discussed; and then, seeing that Miss Fairfax looked upset at all this talk of her health, I talked about the Abbey, about John, Isabella and the children; in short, anything that I thought would lift her spirits.

She smiled a little when I spoke of Henry and John skating on the stream, for she met them as very small children when she visited us two years ago.

'Oh, yes, Jane was so pleased to hear about the children. We had a visit from Miss Woodhouse, and she was so obliging as to tell us all about them,' said Miss Bates.

Her remark pleased me. I had been going to call at Hartfield and suggest that Emma visit Miss Fairfax, but I was glad that her own good sense had already prompted her to call.

I spent a little while longer with the Bateses, then I went on to Hartfield, pleased with my visit. I was eager for Emma's opinion of Miss Fairfax, and I was both surprised and happy to discover that, for once, Emma seemed to be fully aware of Miss Fairfax's merits.

It made me glad of Emma's friendship with Harriet which has, I believe, served as a useful counterpoint, in showing Emma how to value Jane Fairfax.

'She is certainly handsome; she is better than handsome!' were Emma's first words to me.

I was very gratified to hear them

'I had forgotten how elegant Miss Fairfax is,' she went on. 'A very pretty height, and a graceful figure, though I thought she looked a little thin.'

'So did I!' I joined in, pleased to know that, for once, we thought alike. 'But then, she has been ill.'

'Yes, so her aunt told me. A cold, I believe. It is strange for a cold to last so long,' she added thoughtfully.

There was something in her eye as she said it, and I feared mischief, but I found it was nothing worse than a desire to be useful, after all, for Emma continued: 'I do not like to think of her going as a governess, for so much elegance and beauty will be wasted in the schoolroom. It is a pity there is no young man in Highbury who could rescue her from that fate.'

'Matchmaking again?' I asked her, but I was not displeased. A husband would be the very answer to Miss Fairfax's situation, and relieve her from the unappetizing life before her – a life which, I believe, is troubling Miss Fairfax, and ruining her health.

Friday 22 January

Today was busy. I rode over to Kingston this morning and visited the bank, and then visited my tenants. The recent heavy rain had caused damage to the roofs in several of the farm labourers' cottages, and repairs were needed. I have arranged for them to be done as soon as there is a dry spell.

So busy was I that I was almost late arriving at Graham's. After exchanging civilities, I sat next to Mr and Mrs Cole, and the conversation turned to Jane Fairfax. We all expressed our sym-pathy for her fate, our concern for her health, and our pleasure in having her amongst us once again.

After dinner, as soon as the ladies had left us, the conversation moved on to business. We spoke of the war, and of Napoleon, and hoped the hostilities would soon be at an end.

When we rejoined the ladies, Mrs Lovage played and I joined her at the pianoforte. We sang together, and then she relinquished her place to Miss Cox, who played a sonata.

I returned to the Abbey, and I found an invitation to dinner at Hartfield waiting for me. I was pleased. I wanted to see Emma and Miss Fairfax, and to see how they got on together.

I cannot marry Miss Fairfax if she does not get on with Emma.

Saturday 23 January

I had high hopes of the dinner party at Hartfield, and I was not disap-pointed. I wished to see a further intimacy developing between Emma and Jane Fairfax, and I was gratified to see that it was so. Emma was polite, Jane was graceful, and they seemed to enjoy each other's company.

Emma was an excellent hostess. She drew Miss Fairfax out by talking of Miss Fairfax's friend, Miss Campbell, and Miss Campbell's new husband, Mr Dixon. He sounded to be a gentlemanlike man, and it seemed that Miss Campbell had been fortunate in her choice.

Emma also drew forth some information about Frank Churchill. He was at Weymouth in the autumn, at the same time as Miss Fairfax, and so Miss Fairfax had made his acquaintance. This fact was of great interest to our fellow-guests, not all of whom had heard of it, and it made the conver-sation particularly gratifying to the Westons, who were eager to hear further details about him.

Miss Fairfax said little, being still in low spirits, but what she said amounted to the fact that he was a very gentlemanlike man with agreeable manners, and was a general favourite.

I was surprised, but pleased, that Emma did not want to know more about him. She seemed more interested in the Dixons. Indeed, her questions were so pointed that I suspected some mischief but what mischief could there be in her asking about Jane's newly married friend? It was just a woman's curiosity, I suppose, as to how Miss Campbell and Mr Dixon met, and how often Miss Fairfax was with them.

Thursday 28 January

January has proved to be busy both for me and for Highbury. I have had a great deal to do at the Abbey, and when I called in on Cole this morning, I heard that Elton was to marry! Cole showed me the letter. It was short and to the point.

> *My dear Cole, You must congratulate me. I have been so fortunate as to win the affection of a most beautiful young woman by the name of Augusta Hawkins. She is a goddess! We met quite by chance, and soon afterwards sat next to each other at a dinner party. I was taken with her straight away, but she was so far above me, her sister being married to Mr Suckling of Maple Park, that I hardly dared hope – and yet her looks, her smiles! We met again, and my heart took flight! She is the embodiment of my dreams. My dear Augusta! An heiress, a beauty, and soon to be mine!*
> *Your friend,*
> *BE*

Poor Emma! I had better warn her of it, so that she is prepared when it becomes generally spoken of. It will give her a chance to prepare her little friend as well. If it were not for Harriet, I would be glad that this has happened. It will make intercourse between us all much easier, and smooth over any problems that might have arisen. Otherwise, embarrassment and coldness must have been the result of Emma's misunderstanding. But Elton's forthcoming marriage will provide so much to talk about, that the past will be forgotten. Any change in his habits will be attributed to his new situation. He will no longer be expected to dine at Hartfield so much, which will be a blessing both for him and for Emma.

For Harriet, though, the news must hurt. I comforted myself with the thought that it will hurt her pride only. I do not believe she was ever in love with Elton, or that she would have thought of him at all if Emma had not put the idea into her mind.

Perhaps now she may be allowed to go back to her own life, and to marry Robert Martin, as she should have done in the first place.

As for Emma, there will be some humiliation for her, but she will take no lasting harm from it.

Besides, she has other things to occupy her mind.

I was pleased to see her being so friendly to Jane Fairfax yesterday. If I do not mistake my guess, the two of them are well on the way to becoming friends, and a far more suitable friendship it will be than the ones Emma has so far indulged in.

I went round to Hartfield after leaving Cole, to persuade Mr Woodhouse that he really must build a new hen-house, and then I was free to talk to Emma.

'It was a very pleasant evening yesterday,' I said. 'I think everyone thought so.'

'Once, I felt the fire rather too much; but then I moved back my chair a little, a very little, and it did not disturb me,' said Mr Woodhouse. 'I like old friends; and Miss Jane Fairfax is a very pretty sort of young lady, a very pretty and a very well-behaved young lady indeed.'

I was pleased to have the subject of Jane Fairfax introduced, and I could not agree more with Mr Woodhouse. Jane Fairfax is very pretty indeed.

'You and Miss Fairfax gave us some very good music,' I said to Emma. 'I was glad you made her play so much, for having no instrument at her grandmother's, it must have been a real indulgence.'

'I am happy you approved, but I hope I am not often deficient in what is due to guests at Hartfield,' she said, rebuking me.

I let it pass. I encouraged her to talk of Jane Fairfax, saying that she had seemed pleased with Miss Fairfax..

'I was pleased with my own perseverance in asking questions, and amused to think how little information I obtained,' she returned saucily.

I was disappointed she had not liked Jane more.

'She must have found the evening agreeable, Mr Knightley,' said Mr Woodhouse, 'because she had Emma.'

'And Emma because she had Miss Fairfax.'

I was gratified to hear Emma say: 'She is a sort of elegant creature that one cannot keep one's eyes from. I am always watching her to admire; and I do pity her from my heart.'

I was so warmed by this generous tribute that I was reminded of my news, and I resolved to speak at once, so that I could prepare Emma for the shock, but at that minute Miss Bates and her niece were announced and my chance was lost.

I had to listen as Miss Bates said : 'Oh! my dear sir, how are you this morning? Yes, very well, I thank you. My dear Miss Woodhouse – I come quite overpowered. Such a beautiful hindquarter of pork! You are too bountiful! Have you heard the news? Mr Elton is going to be married.'

And so Emma heard about the death of her schemes, along with Miss Bates's health and a discussion of a hindquarter of pork. She was surprised; she blushed; but she took it well.

'There is my news: I thought it would interest you,' I said to her.

The subject furnished our talk for the rest of the morning. Elton was described to Miss Fairfax, who said very little, and I began to realize why Emma thought her reserved. But I think her merely quiet. It is a result, no doubt, of her present unsettled situation. Her poor health can, I am sure, be attributed to the same cause.

Fortunately, Emma did not appear unduly distressed, and this led me to believe that news of Elton's marriage was not wholly unexpected. She must have already known that he would never marry Harriet, and I found myself wondering again what exactly had happened in the carriage on Christmas Eve. Had he said so? Had he been horrified at the suggestion? Had he proposed to Emma? I wished I knew.

Meanwhile, Miss Bates was still talking of Elton.

'I always fancied he would marry a local young lady, some young lady hereabouts; not that I ever – Mrs Cole once whispered to me – but I immediately said, "No, Mr Elton is a most worthy young man – but"— In short, I do not think I am particularly quick at those sorts of discoveries.

I do not pretend to it. What is before me, I see. At the same time, nobody could wonder if Mr Elton should have aspired—'

Emma was growing more and more uncomfortable, and at last Miss Bates perceived it.

'Miss Woodhouse lets me chatter on, so good-humouredly. She knows I would not offend for the world.'

And indeed she would not, but her tongue is so rapid, she blunders before she knows what she is saying.

I looked at Emma, but she merely smiled, as though nothing untoward had been said.

It cannot have been easy for her to listen to Miss Bates suggesting, in her artless way, that Mr Elton had aspired to her hand. It must have been even harder for her to think that the whole village knew of it. But she bore it well. Bravo, Emma!

Miss Bates herself realized the conversation was not well-chosen and started another thread, only this one was unfortunately no more happy than the last.

'How does Harriet do?' she asked. 'She seems quite recovered now.'

Emma said that she was, but I pitied her, as I saw from her blush that she remembered her folly with regard to her friend.

And then at last Miss Bates hit on a topic that could not fail to please everyone in the room.

'Have you heard from Mrs John Knightley lately? Oh! those dear little children. Jane, do you know I always fancy Mr Dixon like Mr John Knightley? I mean in person – tall, and with that sort of look – and not very talkative.'

Elton was forgotten, and before long Miss Bates was rising to leave. I encouraged her. I felt that Emma had suffered enough for one morning.

Miss Fairfax being tired, I offered her my arm, as I, too, was leaving. She took it gladly.

I barely felt her weight, she is grown so thin. I am glad that Perry has seen her, to make sure there is nothing more seriously wrong with her than a cold. I must redouble my efforts to help her. I would not see her fade away for the want of a friend, and, perhaps one day, I might be something more.

I escorted her and her aunt back to their home, which we reached just as it was coming on to rain, and Miss Bates pressed me to go inside until it stopped. I was happy to do so.

I took the opportunity of talking to Miss Fairfax about books, about music, about her friends the Campbells, in short about anything and everything, but she said very little. It was much more difficult for me to converse with her than it was for me to converse with Emma, but allowances must be made for shyness. She has only just returned to Highbury, after all.

Once the weather improved I set off for the Abbey, and having some business at Ford's, I passed through Highbury. I had almost reached the shop when I saw an interesting thing. Harriet Smith emerged from the door and set off towards Hartfield. Not a moment later, Robert Martin appeared and ran after her. They talked for a minute, and then Harriet set off in a different direction, taking the road past Mr Cole's stables. From the hesitations and embarrassment apparent on both sides it seemed they were not comfortable with each other, or perhaps it would be more accurate to say that they were not comfortable with the situation. With each other, if left to their own devices, I think they could be very comfortable indeed.

Friday 29 January

I called at Abbey Mill Farm today. Robert Martin was not at home, but Mrs Martin made me welcome and asked me if I would wait. I said I would, and after the usual pleasantries and comments on the farm, I remarked that it had been fortunate for Miss Smith to see Robert the previous day, as he had been able to warn her away from the flooded path. Mrs Martin was at first rather cold, saying she hoped her son always remembered his manners, but she soon warmed to her theme and it became clear that she was still very fond of Miss Smith.

'Such a nicely spoken young lady, and so well-read,' remarked Mrs Martin. 'She recommended *The Romance of the Forest* to us, and we've all read it, even Robert. I am reading *Children of the Abbey* at present, another book Miss Smith recommended. I've not been able to get near it until now, because my daughters have all been reading it, though Robert bought it before Christmas. "What a coincidence, it being about an abbey," my oldest girl said. "And here are we, living at Abbey Mill Farm. We could be the children of the Abbey". We all laughed at that. It was a pity Miss Smith wasn't here, she would have enjoyed the joke.'

Yes, I believe she would.

When Robert Martin returned, we took a tour of the farm and he showed me the improvements he intends to make. The farm is flourishing, and he hopes to make it more profitable next year. After hearing about his plans, I think he will succeed.

Saturday 30 January

A bright day. After the snow and the rain, it made a welcome change to see the sun. I fancied a break from my labours, and so I walked over to Hartfield to see Emma and her father. Perry was there, and whilst he sat with Mr Woodhouse, Emma and I took a turn in the garden.

'Your little friend is not with you, I see,' I remarked.

'No. She had some shopping to do, and I did not like to leave my father. The bad weather has depressed his spirits, and I played backgammon with him to pass the time until Perry arrived.'

'I saw her the other day, outside Ford's.'

I thought Emma stiffened, but she replied coolly enough: 'Oh?'

'Yes. She was just on her way to Hartfield, I think. She set off to go by the nearest route, but Robert Martin followed her out of the shop and recommended she take another way because the path was flooded.'

'That was very good of him,' she said lightly.

'Yes, it was. But then Robert Martin is a good man.'

'I am sure he is. But not good enough for Harriet,' she said.

'And how are your efforts to educate your little friend coming along? How is her sketching, her reading and her music?'

She coloured.

'You have abandoned them, I see. I am not surprised. Harriet was not made for music and sketching, but Miss Fairfax was. You should invite her to Hartfield. Together you can sketch and read, and play the pianoforte. She would be a proper companion for you.'

'She is so thin I do not like to trouble her,' said Emma awkwardly.

'You mean you do not like to trouble yourself! You were never fond of practising your music, even as a little girl. You were always eager to escape.'

'Well, and what if I was? There was always something more interesting to do!' she said with an arch smile.

'You will never be truly accomplished if you do not practise.'

'I am accomplished enough for Highbury,' she said.

'It is a pity you do not go to London more.'

'You know I cannot leave Papa. Besides, you always listen to me, despite my wrong notes!'

'I hope you are not passing these standards on to Harriet,' I said. 'You will never improve her if you are.'

She had the grace to blush.

'You have not forgiven me for trying to improve her,' she said.

'Improvement is a good thing, in general, but it should not be allowed to interfere with real life, and real prospects.'

We were back to Robert Martin.

I said no more, for I believe she is capable of continuing with her misguided notions to prove that she is right, whereas if I leave her to herself, in time I hope she will admit that she is wrong.

I am less worried about Harriet than I was. I am beginning to think she and Robert Martin will make a match of it, despite Emma's best efforts to keep them apart.

FEBRUARY

My attentions to Miss Fairfax have produced an unforeseen complication. As I was dining at Otway's this evening he said to me: 'This seems to be a season of marriages. There must be something in the air. First Weston, then Elton, and if I do not miss my guess, you will be next.'

'I?' I exclaimed, surprised.

'You are very attentive to Miss Fairfax,' he said.

I coloured.

'I am sensitive to her situation, and having known her since her childhood, I feel an interest in her welfare. I mean to do everything I can to assist her, but marry her? – no,' I returned.

It may be that I will marry her, but until I am certain, I must be careful of her reputation, and make it clear that I intend no such thing.

'I beg your pardon,' said he, colouring slightly also. 'I meant no offence.'

'None taken. Indeed, you have done me a service. If you have misinterpreted my actions, then others might have misinterpreted them as well. I must be more circumspect.'

I would not damage Miss Fairfax for anything. She is a beautiful young woman, elegant, refined and cultured. In short, she is the kind of woman any man would be proud to marry. But there is something reserved about her, and I am not sure if I could ever feel towards her as a man should feel towards his wife. I could imagine her very well as a guest at the Abbey, but I am not certain I could see her as its mistress. She would greet my guests politely, but there would not be the warm welcome for them that there is at Hartfield, where Emma makes everyone feel at home.

I am very willing to fall in love with Jane Fairfax, but so far, love eludes me.

Friday 12 February

I dined with Graham this evening. Miss Bates was there with her mother and Jane. Mr and Mrs Cole were also there, as well as the Otways. Mrs Lovage, however was not there.

'She has gone to Bath to visit a cousin,' said Graham.

Graham's friend, Mr Longridge, was also there.

'A wonderful party,' said Mr Longridge. 'Just the sort of party my wife would have liked. So much good friendship and good cheer.' He blew his nose.

'There is nothing like good friendship,' said Miss Bates. 'I do not know where mother and I would be without it. I often say to her, "Mother, where would we be without such friends?"'

'Very true,' said Mr Longridge, with much feeling.

'We lack for nothing,' went on Miss Bates. 'I do believe if we were the richest people in the kingdom, we could not be better off than we are. Mr Woodhouse sent us such a piece of pork, mother and I could not stop talking about it. "Why, this is the finest piece of pork I've ever seen," said Mother. And so it was, for we had some nice cutlets fried, and I do not know when I have tasted better. And Mr Knightley can never pass our door without asking if we have enough apples, or if we need any more logs for the fire. . . .'

As Miss Bates and Mr Longridge continued to talk, my attention was claimed by Mrs Cole, who wanted to talk to me about Elton's engagement. I knew I could not escape the subject, but it was wearing thin. He seems to have rushed into an engagement in an effort to show that he can do better than Emma's Harriet. I doubt if there is any true feeling there, on either side. He and his fiancée cannot have known each other more than four weeks, and very possibly less.

'It seems like a great match,' Mrs Coles said. 'Miss Augusta Hawkins is an heiress with a dowry of ten thousand pounds. She is very beautiful, and the most accomplished woman Mr Elton has ever met. I had a letter from Mr Elton this morning, telling me so.'

'It must be very agreeable for him to be marrying such a paragon,' I remarked.

'Indeed it must. She is very well connected. Her brother-in-law, Mr Suckling, lives at Maple Grove.' She seemed to have a moment of doubt, and asked: 'Have you heard of Maple Grove?'

'I have not had that pleasure,' I said.

'Oh, well it is a long way away, to be sure, so I am not surprised. He – Mr Elton – will be returning soon to tell us all about it. I am expecting him any day. Mr Cole and I will be holding a dinner party in his honour. Do say you will come.'

I said I would be delighted, though I fear the evening will not interest me. But Elton must be congratulated, and I may as well do it sooner as later.

Monday 15 February

I met Elton at the Coles' dinner party tonight. He was looking very pleased with himself, and could speak of nothing but his dear Augusta.

'My dear Mr Elton – so propitious for you to return to us the day after St Valentine's day,' said Miss Bates. 'I declare it is so romantic, is it not, Jane? I was just saying to mother this morning, what a coincidence it was that Mr Elton should return to tell us of his happy suit so close to St Valentine's day.'

'A very happy suit,' said Elton, all smiles. 'Little did I think, when I quit you all shortly after Christmas, that I would be returning as an affianced man. But as soon as I saw my dear Augusta, I knew she must be mine.'

'Ah, that is how it was with me and my dear wife,' said Mr Longridge, wiping a tear from his eye. 'As soon as I saw her in that blue satin frock, I thought, that's the girl for me.'

'Oh, I have always thought blue satin most becoming,' said Miss Bates.

'I remember Jane had a blue satin gown once, did you not, my love? Colonel Campbell bought it for her. He has always been very good to Jane.'

'I am sure he was not the loser by it,' said Mr Longridge with courtly manners. 'My dear wife always loved a pretty young girl. We hoped for a daughter ourselves, but it was not to be.'

He wiped his eyes with his handkerchief again.

'But come, Mr Elton, tell us all about your fair Augusta,' said Mrs Cole. 'Is she very beautiful?'

Mr Elton smiled.

'It is not for me to say. You must pay no attention to me. I am a man in love, after all. But I think she is the most beautiful woman I have ever seen,' he said.

'Has she any brothers or sisters?' asked Mrs Cole.

'One sister.'

'And do they live in Bath?'

'No, and there is the wonder of it. They live in Bristol. But Augusta visits Bath every winter. A most agreeable place at that season, I might say. There is so much to do, and the people are of the first elegance. I am very fond of Bath.'

'Her parents, no doubt are delighted?'

'Alas, her parents are dead. She lives with an uncle, a very respectable man in the law line.'

'And when will we see her?' asked Mr Cole.

'I have persuaded her to name the day, and I am to return to Bath for the wedding. Just as soon as all the arrangements can be made, Augusta will be mine.'

'And then you will be bringing her back to Highbury?'

'I will indeed. I wish I had something better to offer her than the Vicarage – she has been used to very fine things at her brother-in-law, Mr Suckling's seat, at Maple Grove – but she is not interested in finery. She is a woman who knows how to value the real things of life.'

'Ay, my wife was just such a woman,' said Mr Longridge.

There was more in this vein, and it was a relief when the evening was over. Poor Emma! I wonder how she will endure it, having to listen to nothing but Elton and his betrothal, and then Elton and his wedding, and then Elton and his bride.

Wednesday 17 February

Mrs Weston gave a dinner party this evening for Elton. His betrothal has excited much interest, and I had to listen to his further recitals of Augusta's perfections.

Emma was one of the party, and I watched her as Elton poured forth the details of his happy love affair. He could not refrain from several triumphant glances in Emma's direction, and I believe she had an uncomfortable time of it.

'We met by accident – quite by accident,' Elton was saying. 'I shudder to think what might have become of me had I not come across my dear Augusta quite by chance. It was a happy fate that took me to Bath. I was much taken with Augusta, and I could not forget her, so you can imagine my delight when we met, again by chance. It was at Mr Green's – Green is an estimable fellow, who keeps a very fine table. I was looking forward to my evening, but for one thing: I could not forget the face of the lady I had encountered by accident the day before. And then, who should be announced but Miss Hawkins, and she was the lady I had seen!'

There was a murmur of surprise and approval.

'Not such an unlikely coincidence, considering you were both in the same town,' said Weston good-naturedly.

'But to be there on the same day?' said Elton. 'When I think that I might have missed her by one evening – the whole course of my life would have been different.'

And so he went on.

'And what do you think of this betrothal of Elton's?' I asked Emma, when I could find her alone.

I wondered if she would admit to trying to catch him for little Harriet. She has never told me so. Indeed, when I mentioned it, she declared quite the opposite. But I am convinced it was so. I wondered, too, if she would admit that he made love to her in the carriage on Christmas Eve.

But she admitted nothing. She said only: 'From all he says, Miss Hawkins seems to be a handsome and accomplished woman. I wish them both very well.'

Well done, Emma! I thought with admiration.

Elton's triumphant glances in her direction, his dwelling on his beloved's dowry and her connections at Maple Grove, had all been intended to humiliate her, but they had not done so. She had risen above them, and behaved perfectly. Not even such a shameful display on Elton's part had been enough to make her petty-minded, or to prompt her to say something rude about Augusta Hawkins.

And that is why, though I am frequently exasperated by her, and often despair of her, I always find Emma endearing.

Saturday 20 February

Elton has at last departed for Bath, and we are left in peace. It is a busy time of year at the Abbey with the sheep. The weather is not propitious, as we have had more snow, but my shepherds know their job, and I hope we will have a good number of lambs this year.

Monday 22 February

I called on Miss Bates this morning as business took me into Highbury, but she was out, and I found that old Mrs Bates was alone. It was difficult to talk to her, as she is growing rather deaf, but I gathered that Miss Bates was helping Mr Longridge to choose a house, and that Miss Fairfax had gone with them.

Mr Longridge had wanted a woman's opinion, it seems, as he knows little about the arrangement of kitchens and so forth, and Miss Bates had been happy to oblige.

I am sure his motive in asking for her help was kindness: Miss Bates, with her own small establishment, knows little of houses.

I liked him even more when I discovered that he had prevailed upon

Miss Bates and Miss Fairfax to agree to dine with him afterwards, at a small country inn, in company with the Otways and the Coles. He would have taken Mrs Bates as well, but she had preferred to remain indoors, knitting by the fire.

And so, he had arranged to provide Miss Bates and her niece with an enjoyable day, and with a meal into the bargain.

It is a pity that I did not see Miss Fairfax, but as she is to be with us for some time, there will be plenty of other opportunities for me to speak to her.

Tuesday 23 February

The weather grows worse, and it was with difficulty that I managed to walk to Hartfield after dinner this evening, but I did not want to neglect my friends. I found Emma and her father sitting with Harriet.

I have grown used to finding Harriet there, and it was welcome this evening, as it meant that Emma and I could play backgammon without worrying that her father would be bored. He had Harriet to sit with him, and she read him Isabella's latest letter again: little George had a cold, the baby was growing rapidly, and Henry was making good progress with his reading.

'I called on Miss Bates this morning,' she said.

'And you are wanting me to praise you for it,' I said.

'No. If I want flattery, I know I must look elsewhere!'

We began to play.

'And did you find Miss Fairfax at home?' I asked her.

'I did. She had just returned from the post office. If I had called half an hour sooner I would not have seen her.'

'And did you still find her reserved?'

'Yes, I did. I found it very difficult to have a conversation with her. she listened politely to everything I had to say, and she answered every question I put to her, but she volunteered nothing.'

'Perhaps she had nothing to volunteer.'

'Nothing to volunteer, when she has been away from us for two years?

What of all her news? Talk of her friend and her friend's wedding? Of the Campbells, and her life with them? Of her time at Weymouth, and her adventure on the boat? I am sure that could occupy half an hour at least.'

'I thought she had told you something of her friend's wedding a few days ago?'

'She did, but only when I asked her outright for information.'

There was something in her tone which gave me pause.

'What mischief are you brewing now?' I asked.

She looked at me innocently.

'You are a very suspicious man, Mr Knightley. What makes you think I would be brewing mischief?'

'Experience,' I remarked.

'It is sometimes very inconvenient to talk to someone I have known all my life,' she said playfully. 'It is also very unfair. It gives you an advantage. You know all about my childhood freaks, and I know nothing about yours.'

'That is because I never had any!' I returned.

She laughed.

'What is it, my dear?' asked her father, looking up from the letter.

'Mr Knightley says he had no childhood freaks.'

'I am sure he did not,' said her father. 'I have known Mr Knightley all his life, and he has never suffered from freaks. A better man it would be hard to find. Why, even as a boy he was very well-mannered. I remember him saying to me, when I had had a cold: "I am sorry to hear you have not been well. I hope you are recovered?" and he was only five years old.'

I did not remember this evidence of my childhood virtues, but I said: 'There you are,' to Emma none the less.

'I believe I will ask John about you and find out the truth, the next time I see him,' she returned. 'I cannot believe you led a blameless childhood. I am sure you had your share of mischief.'

'As he is unlikely to visit us before the summer, I am not afraid.'

'Summer will come,' she said, 'and I will be waiting!'

'You are incorrigible,' I told her, and she laughed.

It was a very happy evening, and I came home well pleased with life.

Wednesday 24 February

I called on Miss Bates today, and found Mrs Goddard there. They were talking of Mr Longridge as I was shown in.

'A very fine man,' Miss Bates was saying. 'It was so sad for him to lose his wife. It was twenty years to the day yesterday, he was telling me, and he's never forgotten her, poor man, but so kind-hearted! He came to see if mother and I had enough coal. He is in the way of it, though I am not sure how. I think it was something to do with canals, though what canals have to do with coal I am sure I do not know. Why, here's Mr Knightley.'

I enquired after her health, and the health of her mother and Miss Fairfax.

'Well, I thank you,' she said. 'We are all well.'

I thought, perhaps, Miss Fairfax looked a little better. She was not so pale as previously, although this could have been because she was sitting nearer the fire, and the heat was giving her cheeks a ruddy glow. She was helping her grandmother wind wool.

Mrs Cole was talking about the dinner party she means to give. Ever since her husband provided her with a new dining-room, she has been longing to entertain.

'I have ordered a screen from London, in the hope that Mr Woodhouse might be prevailed upon to join us. I know he does not go out as a rule, but we would be honoured if he would condescend to visit us, and I thought, perhaps, if he was properly sheltered from draughts, he and Miss Woodhouse might accept our invitation,' said Mrs Cole.

So Mrs Cole is planning to invite Emma to her dinner party. It will be interesting to see how Miss Woodhouse of Hartfield reacts!

Thursday 25 February

It was good to dine out again, at the Otways, as problems with the accounts, heavy weather and troubles with the sheep have kept me at the Abbey for some time, except when I have been dining at Hartfield.

There was the usual talk before dinner. Mr Longridge had seen two houses near Highbury, but neither of them had been suitable. Three Chimneys had had a dark hall, and Whitestone had had a very small garden.

'Hardly big enough to put a seat in, let alone have friends round in the summer. I like a garden,' Mr Longridge said.

Weston seemed very happy. He said nothing, but he and Mrs Weston have been married for some months, and I think we might soon have news that another Weston is on the way. Mrs Weston was not there this evening, as she was indisposed, lending credence to my idea.

At the end of the evening, Weston and I walked home together until our paths diverged. He told me he was still hoping to see his son in Highbury, but until such time, he was finding comfort in talking of Frank to Miss Fairfax.

'It was fortunate her meeting him at Weymouth,' he said to me. 'She has been able to tell me how he looked, and what he said and did. She is more nervous than I remember her, though,' he said with a frown. 'Every time I asked her a question she blushed before she answered.'

Perhaps it is just because her spirits are low, but I suspect another reason for her embarrassment. I think it possible that Frank Churchill did not please her. If he is what I think he is, he was probably condescending to her or her friend. She would not wish to say so to Mr Weston, of course, which is why she was embarrassed.

I did not tell Weston what was going through my mind. He might as well think his son is perfect for as long as he can.

Friday 26 February

I have discovered Emma's reaction to the Coles' plan to invite her to their dinner party. I do not know where she heard of it, though I suspect the news came from Mrs Weston, via Weston and Cole, but she has already decided she will not go.

'Who are the Coles?' she asked in a superior voice, as we played chess, whilst her father ate a bowl of gruel.

'They are your neighbours,' I said.

'But of such low origin, in trade!'

'You dine with Harriet every night without knowing anything about her antecedents. I would not be surprised if she had a dozen relatives in trade,' I reminded her, for as Harriet was absent for once, I felt it possible to speak honestly.

'That is quite different,' said Emma.

'How so?'

'Because, as you say, I know nothing about her antecedents. Her father might be a shopkeeper, though I doubt if a shopkeeper could produce such a charming daughter, but he might equally well be a prince,' she said in all seriousness.

'Oh Emma!' I said, shaking my head. 'Not even you can think something so ridiculous.'

'I do not see why it is ridiculous.'

'Because a prince would never leave his daughter at Mrs Goddard's!'

'Mrs Goddard's school is a very refined establishment,' she said mischievously, but she was forced to laugh. 'Well, perhaps not a prince,' she acknowledged, moving her piece. 'Nothing quite so grand.'

'A duke, perhaps?'

'Pay attention to your game,' she admonished me. 'You are about to make a disastrous move.'

'Disastrous for you,' I said, making my move.

'Not a duke, perhaps, but a baron or baronet. I think it only too likely. Someone who has a position to maintain, and enough money to ensure Harriet's happiness.'

'I hope you are not filling her head with this nonsense,' I remarked.

'I am encouraging her to think well of herself, if that is what you mean. I do not want to see her fade into oblivion for lack of someone to bolster her confidence. A girl with a sweet disposition and a pretty face should be entitled to think well of herself.'

'Have a care, Emma. There is a fine line between confidence and self-deception. If you encourage her to think her father is a baron, and he turns out to be a shopkeeper, what then?'

She looked uncomfortable.

'I am only trying to help her.'

'You are not helping her by filling her head with conceit. I thought you would have learnt your lesson about interfering by now.'

'I want what is best for her, that is all,' she said, but she did not meet my eye.

'Then let her be happy, in her own way.'

She gave a laugh, but she abandoned the subject of her friend, saying: 'But we were not speaking of Harriet, we were speaking of the Coles.'

'Very good, unpretending people,' I returned. 'They are respectable, and well thought of by their neighbours. Their business has prospered, and their style of living is now second only to Hartfield.'

'That is exactly what I mean. What business have they living in such style? It is proof, if proof were needed, that they are only moderately genteel. To have them presume to invite the best families to dinner! If you will be guided by me, you will send them your regrets and you will stay at home.'

'I shall do nothing of the kind, and Weston will not refuse the invitation either.'

'Then it is up to me to show them the error of their ways. Nothing shall tempt *me* to go, and my only regret is that my father's habits are so well known that they might not ascribe my refusal to the real reason; by which I mean to say, they might think it is because Papa does not like to dine out, rather than realizing it is because their invitation is presumptuous.'

I shook my head, smiling.

'The Coles are very respectable in their way, but they ought to be taught that it is not for them to arrange the terms on which the superior families will visit them,' she said majestically. 'Standards must be maintained. I could not possibly go to one of their dinner parties.'

'You need not worry about it. I doubt if they will invite you,' I said, to puncture her conceit.

She looked surprised and then displeased, and I laughed. She did not want to go, because she believed it would be beneath her dignity, but she did not want to be neglected either!

We finished the game. I won, which did not please her, but as she is as good a player as I am, the next time we play, the positions will probably be reversed.

Saturday 27 February

Today was a fine day. After the recent bad weather it was a relief to wake to a blue sky and a stiff breeze, rather than sleet and scattered snow. I received a letter from John this morning and I walked over to Hartfield so that I could share the news.

'Will he be coming to us at Easter?' asked Emma.

'No, he says he is too busy, but he has promised to visit us for an extended spell in the summer.'

'But the children will have grown so much by then!'

Mr Woodhouse sighed and shook his head, murmuring, 'Poor Isabella! She must miss us terribly.'

'You must write back and persuade your brother to spare us a few days,' said Emma.

'I only wish I could. I would like to have the boys here myself.'

'And not the girls?' Emma teased me.

'The girls too!'

'Emma will no longer be a baby the next time we see her. If we wait until the summer she will be more than one year old.'

'But she will not be too big for her aunt to play with,' I said.

'Or her uncle. You are as capable of doting on the children as I am.'

At this Mr Woodhouse broke in anxiously: 'Only sometimes, Mr Knightley, I fear you are too rough. I have seen you throwing them up to the ceiling, and it is very dangerous.'

'Come now, Papa, the children enjoy it,' said Emma.

'Children enjoy all sorts of things that are not good for them, my dear,' he said. 'Once, Henry asked me for a knife, but I told him knives were only made for grandpapas. I could not think of letting him have anything so dangerous.'

Emma wisely changed the subject. We spoke of the Bateses, the Coles and the Westons, and Mr Woodhouse was soon soothed.

I could not stay to luncheon as business called me back to the Abbey but I walked over to Hartfield after dinner and spent the remainder of my evening there.

Once I was settled in my chair, Emma told me she had written to Isabella and begged her to spare her two oldest children for a time.

'I know she will not be parted from the younger ones, but if John finds himself travelling this way on business he could bring the older children with him and leave them here.'

She looked at me.

'Well?' I asked her.

'I thought that you might like to write something similar to John,' she said.

'Hah! Very well. I will add my entreaties to yours, and see if we cannot persuade them between us.'

MARCH

Monday 1 March

Whilst dining with Graham this evening, Mr Longridge spoke of his continuing efforts to find a house in Highbury.

'I have seen so many houses, if I did not have my friends to help me, I would be thoroughly confused.'

'You have been to Brookfield?' asked Mrs Cole.

'Not yet, but I have it on my list, and I am going there tomorrow. I have high hopes of it. I have heard it is an excellent house.'

'It is certainly very conveniently placed, being on the London road.'

'I do not believe I shall be going to London very much, except to visit the shops and theatres from time to time. I like the countryside hereabouts, and I am having a new carriage made, the better to explore it. The springs are deplorable on the one I have at present.'

'Not at all – most comfortable – Jane was only saying so this morning,' said Miss Bates.

As she regaled Mrs Cole with an account of Longridge's carriage, I spoke to Miss Fairfax, trying to draw her out on the subject of the carriage, but after answering my questions with one word she relapsed into silence.

'I like my friends to be comfortable, and I like to be comfortable myself,' said Mr Longridge.

After talk on the comfort of carriages died away, Mrs Goddard said that she had had a visit from the Miss Martins.

'They are the sisters of your tenant farmer, Mr Robert Martin, I believe,' said Graham.

'Yes, I know the family. Mr Martin is an excellent tenant, and his family are very agreeable,' I said.

'They were great friends with Harriet when they were all at school together, but they have not seen so much of each other recently,' Mrs Goddard said, determined to have her share of the conversation. 'It is a pity, for Harriet enjoyed her visit to them last summer immensely. But now, I hope, their intercourse is to resume.'

'Oh?'

'They all seemed very friendly together. Miss Smith was surprised to see them. She has been so much with Miss Woodhouse and they, no doubt, have been busy at home, but she was soon chatting very pleasantly with them. I said to Miss Smith she must make sure she returned the call, and she said yes, she was looking forward to it. She was very happy at Abbey Mill Farm.'

Mrs Goddard looked at me as she said it, and then looked away. She has been in place of a mother to Miss Smith for many years, and I am sure she would like to see Miss Smith happily settled, as I would.

It remains to be seen if Emma has learnt her lesson and wishes it, too.

Tuesday 2 March

I went over to Hartfield to see Mr Woodhouse on a matter of business and I was hoping to see Emma, but I learnt that she was out.

'She has taken Harriet to see some friends of hers, the Martins. She promised me she will not be long,' said Mr Woodhouse.

My spirits fell. I had hoped Emma would encourage her friend to return the visit, but I was unhappy that she had decided to go with her. I hoped it was an act of kindness on her part, to take Miss Smith in the carriage, but I feared it was because she did not want her friend to stay too long.

I scarcely listened to Mr Woodhouse's complaints about the weather, his infirmity, and the imagined infirmity of all his friends, so busy was I thinking of Emma, but when I heard the name Frank Churchill, I began to pay attention.

'Mr and Mrs Weston were here this morning, with some news about Mr Weston's son, Frank. He is to visit us,' he said.

'I have been hearing of his visit these last six months, but it has never happened yet,' I remarked.

'His time is not his own,' said Mr Woodhouse, shaking his head. 'Mrs Churchill is very ill, poor lady! If only she had Perry to attend her, she would soon see a marked improvement in her condition, but she has to rely on some Yorkshire doctor, who I dare say does not know his business.'

'And when is Frank Churchill to visit?' I asked, feeling out of humour.

'On the morrow.'

'On the morrow!'

I could scarcely believe it. After all the delays, to learn that Frank Churchill was to visit so soon!

'That is what Mr Weston said,' continued Mr Woodhouse. 'They are to see him by dinner-time as a certainty. He is at Oxford today, and he comes for a whole fortnight.'

'A whole fortnight!' I cried.

I could think of nothing worse than a fortnight of Frank Churchill.

When I returned to the Abbey, I found my exasperation leaving me, and wondered why I had become so angry at the idea of his imminent arrival. I had never even met the young man, and to take him in such dislike was absurd. But when I called on Graham this evening and discovered that Frank Churchill had already arrived, my animosity was rekindled.

'Already arrived? But he is not due until tomorrow!' I said.

'He arrived early, as a surprise,' said Graham, well pleased.

'A charming thought,' said Mrs Cole, who had dined with Graham, along with her husband and the Otways.

'An unforgivable one,' I said. 'What, to arrive a day early, when nothing is ready, and to take his hosts by surprise. What if they had been out?'

'But they were not out,' said Graham good-humouredly. 'Mr Weston is delighted with him, and Mrs Weston, too.'

I could say no more, but that did not stop me thinking it. Young men of that age are always careless of the feelings of others. They do not have the steady character that comes later in life. They make very bad sons and even worse husbands. It is a pity Frank Churchill could not have stayed at Enscombe.

Wednesday 3 March

Everywhere I go I hear of no one but Frank Churchill. I called on Miss Bates this morning, thinking I would find a respite, only to discover that he had called on her, and that she could talk of nothing else.

I could not think what he was doing at the Bateses so early in his stay. It was his father's doing, I suppose. Knowing Miss Bates to be in difficult circumstances, he had made sure his son paid a visit at once, as a mark of respect, and I commended him for it. If it had been left to his son, the visit would probably never have been made.

'Such a handsome young man!' said Miss Bates. 'With such an air! Mother was saying we have never seen such a fine young man – a credit to Mr Weston – Mrs Weston so pleased – stayed with us for three-quarters of an hour – sure I do not know what we have done to deserve such a distinction. We were all very pleased with him, were we not, Jane?'

Thus appealed to, Miss Fairfax said that he was a very pleasing young man, but her words were not heartfelt. As she is a woman of discernment and taste, if she has found something lacking in him, then something lacking there must be. I tried to encourage her to say more, but she would not be drawn.

'He called to pay his respects to Jane. He met her at Weymouth. You remember I told you that Jane went to Weymouth? That is where she caught her shocking cold. It was when she was nearly swept overboard, I am sure.'

'No,' Jane murmured, but her aunt would not be silenced.

'You wrote to us not long afterwards, Jane, my dear, and that was when you mentioned you were not feeling well. Mrs Campbell had commented on it, you said. You told us you were in low spirits, and had been glad to leave Weymouth behind.'

I found myself wondering again if he had offended her there. That would account for her low spirits, her relief at leaving Weymouth behind, and it would fit in with my belief of him. Finding her to be elegant and accomplished, he had perhaps mistaken her for a woman of fashion and behaved charmingly towards her, but had then ignored her when he had discovered that she was destined to become a governess. Perhaps he had even flirted with her, or made love to her, before learning his mistake. Seeing her in Highbury must have been a shock to him, and his feeling of guilt probably accounted for his early call.

'It is my belief that that is where she caught such a shocking cold. Mr Perry is in agreement with me,' said Miss Bates.

Miss Fairfax protested that she was well, and I did not add to her distress by saying that she did not look well, but even so, I resolved to send Miss Bates some chickens, in the hope they might tempt Miss Fairfax to eat. More than that I could not do, without arousing the suspicions that Cole had entertained, of my being in love with her.

I begin to think such a sentiment impossible. She is graceful and charming, but there is a lack of warmth in her that I am finding it hard to ignore.

Thursday 4 March

I found the Westons at Hartfield this morning, talking about Frank. I did not want to speak of him, but I could not very well leave, so I took up a newspaper and studied it intently.

'I told you he would come!' said Mr Weston. 'Did I not say that he would be with us in the spring? I knew how it would be. As soon as Mrs Churchill could spare him, he came straight away, and he is very glad he did. He told me so himself.'

Weston turned to Emma.

'He admires you greatly,' he said.

So! He had seen Emma. I gave a harrumph behind my newspaper. It was a remark which could not fail to please her – or to add to her vanity.

'He thinks you very beautiful and charming,' said Mrs Weston.

If anything was destined to make Emma even more conceited than usual, it was the arrival of Frank Churchill! What hope is there for her better nature to develop if she is constantly surrounded by flattery? I am sure the Westons mean Emma to marry him. That was where all these remarks about her beauty and her charming nature tended.

If Mr Woodhouse could have understood the treachery being conducted under his very nose, he would have immediately sent for Perry!

Friday 5 March

I returned to Hartfield this morning, drawn there by a desire to find out what Emma thought of Frank Churchill. She could not speak freely in front of the Westons yesterday, but I hoped that today she would tell me the truth: that he was well enough, in a frivolous sort of way, but not the kind of man to appeal to a woman of sense.

'And what do you make of Frank Churchill?' I asked, as Emma sat down opposite me, adding: 'I half-expected to find him here.'

'He has gone to London,' she said.

'To London?' I asked in surprise. 'There is nothing wrong, I hope? No accident that requires his presence?'

'No.' She had the goodness to look a little ashamed. 'He has gone to have his hair cut.'

I was much gratified.

'Hum! Just the trifling, silly fellow I took him for,' I said, retiring behind my newspaper.

'I hope he returns in time for the Coles' dinner party,' said Mr Woodhouse. 'It would not do to slight the Coles. Emma is going for that very reason. It is good of her, for she cannot want to go out, I am sure.'

'I thought you had made up your mind to refuse their invitation?' I said to her.

'I had,' she said uncomfortably. 'But they expressed themselves so well in their invitation that I changed my mind. I did not wish to disappoint them, and Mrs Weston particularly wished me to go,' she added, with the air of one making an excuse. 'I felt it would be wrong of me to refuse.'

I detected the reason for the change at once.

'And is Mr Churchill to be there, or will he still be having his hair cut?' I asked.

I was surprised at how scathing my words sounded.

'Of course not! And yes, he will be going to the dinner party. At least,' she said, colouring slightly, 'I suppose he will be going. I am sure I do not know. But as Mr and Mrs Weston are going, I suppose I must assume that Mr Churchill will be going, too.'

'I only hope that Emma will not come home cold,' said Mr Woodhouse. 'I have made my excuses. The Coles know that I am a sad invalid, and although they had ordered a screen for me specially so that I would not have to sit in any draughts, I told them I could not go. I have made Emma promise me that if she comes home cold, she will warm herself thoroughly, and that if she is hungry, she will take something to eat.'

I watched Emma throughout this speech, and I saw how uncomfortable she was. If Churchill had not been going to the dinner party, then I am sure Emma would have remained at home.

Saturday 6 March

I was worried about Miss Fairfax walking to the Coles' house in the cold night air, and so I called on Miss Bates this morning and offered to take her and her niece in my carriage.

'Oh, Mr Knightley, you are too kind,' said Miss Bates. 'Is he not, mother? Mr Knightley has offered to take us up in his carriage. I am sure I do not know when I have been shown such kindness.'

'It is nothing,' I said. 'I am going to the party myself, and I have to pass your door; it is no trouble.'

That was not quite true, but nevertheless, Miss Bates accepted my excuse and the time of the carriage was arranged.

Monday 8 March

After a day's work I was ready to enjoy the evening. I arranged for the carriage to be brought round in good time. I would not have taken it for myself, as I prefer to walk or ride, but I was glad to be able to show Miss Bates some attention, and to safeguard the health of her niece.

'Well, this is travelling in style, is it not, Jane?' asked Miss Bates as we drove to the Coles' house.

Miss Fairfax, thus appealed to, said it was, but she continued to be in low spirits. It is perhaps not to be expected that the Highbury air could do her any good in March, but when the weather improves, then I hope to see an improvement in her health.

We arrived. I helped the Bateses out but I did not immediately follow them inside, as Emma arrived just behind me.

As she stepped out of the carriage, I thought I had never seen her look better. Her gown could be glimpsed beneath her pelisse, and I could see that it was new. I noticed that her hair was done in a different style, and I was disappointed to think that it was all in compliment to Frank Churchill.

'This is coming as you should,' she said in her nonsensical way, as she looked at my carriage appreciatively, 'like a gentleman. I am quite glad to see you.'

I shook my head and laughed, saying: 'How lucky that we should arrive at the same moment; for, if we had first met in the drawing-room, I doubt whether you would have discerned me to be more of a gentleman than usual. You might not have distinguished how I came by my look or manner.'

'Yes I should; I am sure I should,' she said serenely.

'Nonsensical girl!'

I could not help my eyes following her as we went in, and I saw that the Coles had gone out of their way to please her. She was received with a cordial respect which could not but gratify her, and she was given all the consequence she could wish for. When the Westons arrived, their brightest smiles were for her, and Mr Weston's son went straight to her side.

I wanted to like him, but I could not. Insufferable puppy! To go to London for a haircut! And then to go straight away to Emma, and ignore the rest of the party!

I did not want to watch the two of them, but I found I could not help myself. He is of an age with her, he is handsome and charming, and what is more, the Westons wish the match. I have long suspected it, and now I am sure of it. They look upon her already as a daughter-in-law. But I cannot abide the thought of Emma being married to Frank Churchill!

To a good man, yes, one who knows her in all her moods, who can laugh at her follies and rejoice in her virtues; who will not allow her to give in to her worst instincts; one who knows her, and who, knowing her, will still love her, and love her as she should be loved.

And that man is not Frank Churchill.

I spent the rest of the evening in an unhappy state and paid little attention to the conversation over dinner. Elton and his interesting situation were talked over; Miss Fairfax's new pianoforte was discussed; and Emma talked all the time to Frank Churchill.

What could he have to say to her that was so amusing? She seemed to value his every word. I heard some mention of Weymouth, but nothing that seemed to warrant such close attention.

I was glad when dinner came to an end. The ladies left us, and the talk turned to politics. Frank Churchill took no part in the discussion. As I watched him, I could not help thinking that there was something unsettled about him, something that did not ring true. He was very taken with Emma, and mentioned her often but I thought his remarks were shallow and immature.

The talk moved on to parish business.

'I can have nothing of interest to add,' he said, standing up, 'and so I will go and join the ladies. Perhaps I might be able to entertain them.'

Weston looked pleased at this gallantry, and Cole remarked, when he had left the room: 'An agreeable young man.'

Hah! That was not my view of him, but I did not say so.

When we had finished with parish business, we moved through to the drawing-room, and I saw that he was sitting next to Emma. On her being spoken to by Mr Cole, however, his eyes wandered to Miss Fairfax. I hoped he might be switching his affections, but no such thing. As soon as Emma spoke to him, he was all attention again.

To turn my thoughts from this gloomy scene, I engaged Harriet in conversation, for she was sitting by herself. I asked her what she had been reading, and she told me she had been reading a romance. She looked nervously at Emma as she said so, and a further question elicited the infor-mation that she had been reading it at Mrs Goddard's and not at Hartfield. She talked about the book intelligently, however, and it was clear she had given it much thought.

I saw Emma glance at me several times, and look concerned. She supposed I was finding her little friend wanting. But Harriet is much improved, and there is a sweetness to her nature that will always recom-mend her to people of sense. She, at least, does not fly off to London for a haircut on a whim.

My attention was caught by a bustle round the pianoforte, and Emma was called upon to sing. I was just enjoying the song when Churchill, the coxcomb, joined her, unasked. Everyone complimented him on his voice, though I could not think it was anything out of the ordinary.

Miss Fairfax then played, and her music was, as always, superior. She played with a perfect mastery of the instrument, and sang with a sweet-ness of tone. But, somehow, I did not like to listen to her as much as I liked to listen to Emma.

I went to sit with Emma, and once the music was over, we fell into conversation.

'I often feel concerned that I dare not make *our* carriage more useful on such occasions,' she said, commending me on bringing the Bateses. 'It is not that I am without the wish; but you know how impossible my father would deem it that James should put-to for such a purpose,' she said.

'It is quite out of the question,' I said, but I was pleased with her kind thought. 'You must often wish it, I am sure.'

Her thoughts seemed to dwell on Miss Fairfax.

'This present from the Campbells – this pianoforte is very kindly given,' she said.

It had been the talk of the evening, that Miss Fairfax had received a pianoforte.

I agreed, but said they would have done better had they given her notice of it.

'Surprises are foolish things. The pleasure is not enhanced, and the inconvenience is often considerable,' I said.

Miss Fairfax and Mr Churchill were still singing, but Miss Fairfax's voice was growing thick, and I had to urge Miss Bates to step in.

Emma did not seem to like my interference, but her displeasure was soon forgotten when singing gave way to dancing, and Frank Churchill claimed her hand.

I was obliged to sit and watch them, and to listen to Mr Cole when he said had never seen anything finer, though I privately thought that Frank Churchill's dancing was remarkably wooden. There was no grace to his movements, and twice he forgot the steps.

Tuesday 9 March

As I was passing Miss Bates's house on my way to Kingston this morning, she hailed me from the window.

I asked after her niece, and cut short her effusive thanks for the use of my carriage by asking if she wanted anything from Kingston. She could not think of anything, but invited me in, and I was inclined to accept her offer as she said that Emma was there. I was just about to go inside when I learned that Frank Churchill was there as well, so I declined.

I had no wish to see the two of them together, nor indeed any desire to see Frank Churchill again.

Wednesday 10 March

I dined with the Coxes this evening. The Coles were there, as were the Bateses, Mrs Goddard, the Otways, Graham and Mr Longridge.

After dinner, there was some sensible discussion about ways to relieve the poor, but as soon as we rejoined the ladies in the drawing-room, the talk was all of a coming ball.

'It was Mr Churchill's idea,' said Miss Cox. 'He and Miss Woodhouse were so taken with the dancing at your house, Mrs Cole, that they wanted to continue it, and so they have decided to hold a ball at the Crown.

Mother and I just happened to pass Mr Churchill when he was hurrying to see Miss Bates, to ask her opinion on the size of the room.'

'Ay, just the person to ask,' said Mr Longridge kindly.

'I do not know when I have been more gratified,' said Miss Bates, taking up the tale. 'Mother and I were just sitting down to a dish of tea when who should walk in but Mr Frank Churchill! I was just thanking him for mending mother's glasses – so kind! So obliging! For mother cannot see without them, and she could not wear them without the rivet, for you know it was quite impossible – what was I speaking of? Oh yes, the ball. Mr Churchill asked me to go and give my opinion and he would not take no for an answer, and Jane was invited, too, of course, for I am sure no one knows more about elegant gatherings than Jane, through having been to so many with the Campbells. I went across to the Crown and told them the rooms were perfectly large enough, and no draughts to be feared, as long as the windows are kept closed. Mr Churchill was so obliging as to secure Miss Woodhouse's hand for the first two dances, so we will all be treated to some dancing of the most superior kind.'

Miss Fairfax looked distressed, and I thought she must be ill indeed if the thought of a ball did not lift her spirits, for I cannot believe her distress was at Emma being singled out in this way. Miss Fairfax is too generous for that.

Miss Fairfax was the only person who was silent, however. Everyone else broke out into conversation. As they discussed the ball, I found myself wondering why Churchill should be asking Emma for the first two dances. It was not his place to do so, though everyone else seems pleased with the idea. I found myself wishing I had asked her first.

However, the ball will very likely come to nothing as he is to return to his aunt in a few days' time. I find myself hoping that he will never come back.

Thursday 11 March

Emma was full of the ball, and my hope that it would not take place proved a vain one. When I visited Hartfield, Emma could talk of nothing else. Frank Churchill had appealed to his aunt, who had graciously declared she could manage without him, with the result that he was to stay for a week beyond his appointed time.

I tried to be generous, for Emma has little enough to entertain her, but my tongue would not do what I wished it to do.

'If the Westons think it worth while to be at all this trouble for a few hours of noisy entertainment, I have nothing to say against it, but they shall not choose pleasures for me,' I said.

'But you will be there?' Emma asked me, with a trace of anxiety.

I almost asked her what it was to her, but I managed to restrain myself just in time.

'Oh! yes, I must be there,' I said. 'I could not refuse; and I will keep as much awake as I can; but I would rather be at the Abbey, I confess.'

'Surely you would rather be at the Crown, instead of sitting at home with your accounts?' she asked.

'I cannot see why,' I answered bad-temperedly.

'Because you will have an opportunity of dancing.'

'I do not care to dance,' I remarked.

'You will at least take pleasure in seeing it,' she said.

'Pleasure in seeing dancing! Not I, indeed. I never look at it. I do not know who does. Fine dancing, I believe, like virtue, must be its own reward. Those who are standing by are usually thinking of something very different.'

I felt annoyed with myself for saying it, but I could not take any pleasure in seeing Emma dance with Mr Churchill.

Emma was quite angry, and I am not surprised. I was being churlish. Moreover, I was implying that her belief that people enjoyed to see fine dancing sprang from the vanity of those who were dancing, and that is not the case. I know it as well as she. And yet I could not be gracious with the thought of Frank Churchill in my mind.

Why I am so opposed to him I do not know. He is young and foolish and has odd fancies, but there is no real harm in him. And yet I cannot like him, do what I may. If Emma had not taken such a fancy to him, then it might have been different, but to hear her constantly talking about him puts me out of temper. He is no different from other young men his age, and I cannot see why she finds him so interesting.

Saturday 13 March

I have been punished for my gracelessness, for I find that Emma's happiness is to be lost. Frank Churchill has had a letter from his uncle saying that his aunt is unwell, and that he must go home. I am sure the letter had more to do with his aunt's selfishness than any illness. She could not bear to think of her nephew enjoying himself, that was all

And I, I am almost as bad, for I could not bear to think of it either. It was a warning to me, indeed, not to let bad temper rule my life.

'I am sorry for you, Emma, truly sorry,' I said, when I joined her and her father for supper. 'You, Emma, who have so few opportunities for dancing, you are really out of luck; you are very much out of luck!'

I could tell how disappointed she was.

'We should not have delayed,' she said. 'We could have held the ball with far fewer arrangements.'

Mr Woodhouse, however, was glad it was not to go ahead. 'I am sorry for your disappointment, Emma,' he began, 'but I cannot think it a bad thing. No, I cannot think it a bad thing at all. Mrs Weston was all for saying there were no draughts, but an inn, my dear, must always have them, and you would probably have taken cold.'

Even in her disappointment, Emma did not grow impatient with him.

'We inspected the inn most particularly, Papa, you know we did,' she said. 'Besides, I have not despaired of holding the ball. Mr Churchill must be with us again soon, Papa, and then it will go ahead.'

She spoke bravely, but I could tell by her tone she did not believe it.

I tried to cheer her by inviting her and her father to the Abbey tomorrow for dinner. Mr Woodhouse goes out so little that Emma is often forced to spend her time at home, but he is familiar with the Abbey, and after a little persuasion, I hoped he might give his consent.

It seemed as though he would do so, but at the last moment he decided that the horses would not like it, and invited me to Hartfield instead.

I was happy to accept. I could not promise Emma a ball, but I could promise her a cheerful evening with her friends, and a chance to talk of her lost ball to her heart's content.

Monday 15 March

I was hoping that, now Frank Churchill is not in front of her, Emma would quickly forget him, but it is not to be. She talked of nothing but him this morning, or so it seemed to me.

The Westons joined us at Hartfield, and they were only too glad to talk of him. They did everything they could to promote his virtues with Emma, and I grew more and more impatient with every word. They have a right to be delighted with their son, but they do not have a right to expect everyone else to be delighted with him as well.

Tuesday 16 March

I do not want to see Emma marry Frank Churchill, and so I said to Routledge this evening when, having travelled to London this morning to deal with a matter of business, I dined with him at the club.

'Churchill is not the man for Emma,' I said. 'He would encourage her rasher ideas, and lead her into temptation. He would be always jaunting off to London to have his hair cut or some other freak, and she would not like it. What is amusing in an acquaintance, and allowable in a friend, is less comfortable in a husband.'

'Nevertheless, it sounds as though it would be a good match,' he remarked.

'It would take her away from Hartfield and all her friends,' I returned. 'Churchill would carry her off to Enscombe in Yorkshire, and separate her from her father and sister as effectively as if he took her off to France. She would not be comfortable there, away from everyone and everything she knows. At the Abbey, she is only sixteen miles from her sister, and close to her father—'

'At the Abbey?' he asked.

'I mean, of course, that at *Highbury* she is only sixteen miles from her sister, and close to her father.'

'But you said the Abbey,' he pointed out. 'Your mistake was revealing. You never seem to talk of anyone but Emma. You told me yourself that you have never met anyone you like better. It is as plain as a pikestaff. I have thought so ever since our last meeting. You should marry her, Knightley.'

'Marry Emma? Nonsense! I have known her all my life.'

'A very good basis for marriage. Think of your brother. He has known Isabella all his life, and I have yet to see a happier couple.'

'No, it would not do. I am too old for her,' I protested.

'Nonsense. You are in your prime.'

'She is too young for me,' I said, shaking my head.

'She is twenty-one. You're a clever man, George,' he said, 'but some-times you cannot see what is under your nose. Emma is the perfect wife for you, and you are the perfect husband for her. I have known it for many months. If you do not ask her yourself, then you cannot complain if some-one else does.'

'Good. I would like to see her married,' I said. 'Just not to Frank Churchill.'

'Jealous?'

'Of course not! Why should I be jealous of a frippery fellow like Frank Churchill?'

He laughed at me, but then he grew serious.

'If she marries, your life would change,' he said. 'There would be no more evenings spent at Hartfield. Her marriage would take her away.'

'She would never move far from her father. She would find a man from Surrey.'

'And would you be able to sit with her every evening, if she did?' he asked.

'A man from Highbury then!' I said impatiently.

'Who? You have already discounted Elton, and quite right, too. She is too good for Elton. But who else is there? She will marry no one related to Highbury – unless she marries Weston's son. He is the right age, and he is a good-looking man, by all accounts.'

'She can do better than Frank Churchill! A man who does not know his duty, who writes flowery letters that deliver nothing but promise every-thing, a weakling who cannot do right when it is under his nose. Such a man will not do for Emma.'

'She might not feel as you do. Women are strange creatures. They like a handsome face, and she must have someone, after all. Besides, on reflection, I think you are right. You *are* too old for Emma.'

'I am not yet in my dotage!' I returned.

'Have it your own way!' he said. 'You are too old for her, and not too old!'

'Perhaps, before you find a mate for me, you should find one for yourself,' I said.

'I might have done.'

I was immediately curious, and encouraged him to tell me about Miss Turner, a young lady he met at a soirée six weeks ago. He confided in me that he meant to marry her, if she would have him.

I retired to Brunswick Square at last. After spending an hour with John and Isabella, I retired to bed.

As I went upstairs, I thought again of what Routledge had said. Marry Emma? Ridiculous!

Thursday 18 March

I thought of Routledge's words again this morning. Marry Emma? Impossible! I am not in love with her, and my dislike of Frank Churchill has nothing to do with jealousy. It is just that I do not think it would be good for her to marry him. Now he is no longer in Highbury, I am sure Emma will think no more about him.

Monday 22 March

Work on the path is at last finished, and I examined it to make sure the work was well done, then went over the costs with William Larkins. We managed to spend more than we had anticipated, but it was well worth doing, and I am looking forward to getting John's approval of it when he visits us.

Tuesday 23 March

Elton has named his wedding-day at last, and will soon be back among us. I heard it first at the whist club, where it produced a variety of reactions.

'Happy man,' said Longridge, blowing his nose. 'It is twenty-five years to the day that my dear wife and I were married. It was a beautiful wedding. Everyone said she was the prettiest bride they had ever seen. She was a wonderful woman, always cheerful, and always with some news to bring me. She took a great interest in life, Mr Knightley, and was a source of much solace to me.' He shook his head sadly. 'The house is too quiet without her.'

Cole was interested in the event in a more practical manner. He told me that Mrs Cole had offered to find Elton a parlour-maid, as Elton would no doubt require more servants, now that he was losing his bachelor status.

Weston said he hoped that Elton would be as happy as he is, but begged leave to doubt it, and then said that he would like to see his son find a good woman and marry, too.

After everyone had ventured his or her opinion on the subject, we settled down to whist. Weston had all the luck tonight, and declared himself blessed, whereupon Longridge offered that his wife had been a keen cribbage-player, and had beaten him on many occasions. Cole hoped that Elton would still visit the whist club once he was married, and we parted in perfect amity.

Wednesday 24 March

I called on Miss Bates as I was passing this morning. I found Miss Fairfax trimming a bonnet for her aunt.

'So good, I am sure it is better than anything Ford's has to offer, or indeed anything from London, Jane has always been so clever – yes, I thank you, well, though growing a little deaf, but Perry says she is remarkable for her age – I was going to trim it myself, some ribbon from Ford's, but Jane had some in her workbasket, just the right shade. . . .'

I was glad to find her in good spirits, and Mrs Bates in health. Miss Fairfax still looked pale and ill. I hope that the better weather might bring an improvement. We had sunshine today, and if it continues, perhaps Miss Fairfax will regain her spirits.

Sunday 28 March

We had our first glimpse of Mrs Elton at church today, and I'll wager that not one woman in the congregation paid attention to the sermon, they all spent their time looking at the newcomer instead.

Very little of Mrs Elton could be seen, save the back of her bonnet. It did not look as well as Miss Bates's bonnet to me, and Emma was amused when I said so.

'It has come from London, depend upon it,' she said.

'It seems as though it could just as well have come from Bath to me,' I said.

'As you are so much older and wiser than I am, I must of course defer to your judgement.'

'Not so very much older,' I said.

'And not so very much wiser,' she said saucily.

I smiled, but would not give her the satisfaction of laughing.

'I may be allowed to be a little wiser, I suppose,' I said.

'You may. But not where bonnets are concerned.'

She teases me and bedevils me, she exasperates and infuriates me, but what would I do without Emma?

Tuesday 30 March

It is two weeks now since Frank Churchill left, and I have fallen back into my routine of regular visits to Hartfield.

'And what do you think of Mrs Elton?' I asked Emma. 'Or have you not yet had time to visit her?'

'Yes, I called on her yesterday,' she said.

I was surprised that she had paid Mrs Elton the compliment of an early visit, but I was also relieved. I am not perfectly sure of what happened between Elton and Emma, but I know her thoughts were not easy on that score, and yet she still performed her duty.

'And did you see her?'

'Yes, I did.'

'Then you had better luck than I did. When I called, she and her husband were out. Well?' I asked, as no comment was forthcoming.

'She was very elegantly dressed,' said Emma.

'In a London bonnet?' I asked her.

'In a London gown.'

'And have you nothing more to say?' I asked in surprise.

'One visit is hardly enough to judge of someone's character,' said Emma, 'but she seemed to be very pleasing.'

She would say no more, but perhaps she might be ready to commit herself when Mrs Elton has returned the call.

I did not meet the lady myself until later in the day, when I came across her at the Westons. I had called to speak to Weston about some hay, but as soon as the Eltons entered the room, everything of that kind was naturally postponed.

I had not been in company with Mrs Elton for more than five minutes when I realized that she was not destined to become a regular guest at the Abbey. Between telling me how fine her brother-in-law's house is; calling Elton by turns her *caro sposo* and Mr E; informing me of her many resources – which, however, she seems determined to ignore now that she is a married woman – and saying that Emma was already a favourite with her; she managed to disgust me in as many ways as she spent minutes talking. How Elton could bear it I do not know, but he simpered and smiled as though he had brought home a jewel.

I was polite, however, and welcomed her to Highbury society.

'I would love to stay all day, but my *caro sposo* insists I return Miss Woodhouse's visit,' said she. 'I am looking forward to seeing Hartfield. Mr E tells me it is very like Maple Grove. Did I mention Maple Grove? My brother-in-law, Mr Suckling's place?'

Mrs Weston assured her she had, and Weston bowed her out of the room.

'A very elegantly dressed woman,' said Mrs Weston.

'Hah!'

She looked at me in surprise.

'That is exactly what Emma said!' I told her.

Mrs Weston had the goodness to smile, and I knew our views of Mrs Elton coincided.

Wednesday 31 March

I was eager to find out about Mrs Elton's visit to Hartfield, and I had an opportunity this evening when I dined with Emma and her father. Whilst Mr Woodhouse fretted that he had not paid Mrs Elton a visit – 'A bride, you know' – Emma reassured him that his health would be his excuse.

I could get very little from her concerning Mrs Elton, and she said no more than yesterday, but that in itself told me everything I needed to know.

'You do not like Mrs Elton,' I remarked. 'So you have been subjected to her talk about her *caro sposo* and Mr E as well, have you?'

'I have, though I think it is very unfair of you to ridicule her for demonstrating her knowledge of Italian – and the alphabet,' she said to me saucily.

'I have no objection to her knowledge of either, but I have a lively dread of her displaying such knowledge in the most vulgar way possible. How Elton can stand it I do not know.'

'He is in love. Allowances must be made,' she said.

'Hah!'

She does not think that Elton is in love any more than I do.

'I am glad to see that your taste, which erred in singling out Harriet, and again in rejecting Miss Fairfax, and yet again in singling out that puppy Frank Churchill – yes, well – your taste, in this case, was not at fault,' I told her. 'Mrs Elton is a vainglorious woman with a small mind who thinks she is bringing refinement to a quiet corner of the country, when she is bringing only change.'

'At last, we think the same on something!' said Emma. 'No, pray do not spoil it,' she said, when I opened my mouth to speak again. 'Let me savour the moment.'

Impossible girl! But out of the goodness of my heart, I let her have her own way.

APRIL

I was glad to find that Miss Fairfax had extended her visit, and would not be returning to London so soon as was expected.

'We are so glad, Mr Knightley,' said Miss Bates. 'We are to have her for a full three months. She still does not look well. No, Jane, my love, you do not, though you protest you are very well indeed. When you were altering my gloves for me – such wonderful gloves, Mr Knightley, quite the warmest I have ever worn, and bought from Ford's, but just a little big around the wrist, and Jane kindly offered to take them in for me, as she was mending Mother's petticoat anyway, and who should walk in but Mr Longridge. A very kind gentleman, Mother is quite besotted with him – yes, you are, Mother, you know you are, for he comes and sits here for an hour or two together, and we are always glad of company, Mr Knightley. He has asked me to give him my opinion on another house, Whitestones, you will know it Mr Knightley, the Dodds have been renting it out but their tenants have left and they have decided to sell it. It seems a fine house to me but it is perhaps a little large for a single gentlemen. And then there is another house I have promised to see next week, Southdean, a pretty house with a stream, you know. I have always liked that house. It is not so grand as Whitestones, but I often used to think, when I was a girl, if I could choose a house to live in, that would be it. I painted it once, though not as well as Jane, she sketched it when she was eleven years old, do you remember, Jane? I believe I still have the picture somewhere, though I cannot remember where. I remember Mother saying to me. . . .'

She paused for breath, and evidently did not remember what she had been saying, which gave me an opportunity to ask Miss Fairfax: 'Will you be joining the Campbells again when your stay in Highbury is finished?'

'Yes for a little while. But I would rather not think of that,' she remarked.

I said no more, as I did not wish to distress her. I wish I could offer her a home at the Abbey, but it is impossible.

'Oh, Jane, I know what I forgot to say. I meant to mention it but Mr Knightley's visit put it out of my mind – so kind of you, Mr Knightley! So obliging! – I sent a reply to Mrs Elton for you, you were out when her message arrived. She asks you to tea. Such an elegant woman! Such refinement! I am sure I never saw a better woman in my life, and it is always good to have a bride in the neighbourhood, is it not, Mr Knightley? Jane must want to be with younger people, and not always shut up with her grandmother and her aunt, though I am sure her grandmother is the best woman in the world—'

'And so is her aunt,' said Miss Fairfax with an affectionate smile.

'Oh, Jane, my love, I am sure I do not know – well – have you finished your sewing?'

And so she went on, spreading goodwill with every word but saying very little. Despite Miss Fairfax's affectionate smile, I could tell that her aunt's constant chatter wearied her.

I did not envy her. A choice of spending an hour with Mrs Elton, or an hour with her relations, was not a happy one.

I only wish Emma would take more notice of her. An afternoon at Hartfield would be far more enjoyable for Miss Fairfax than an afternoon at the vicarage or at home.

Saturday 3 April

There has been a heartening piece of news, one to gladden everybody in Highbury, and one to make me forget my own problems for a while. It is as I suspected. Mrs Weston is expecting a child! The Westons have known for some time, but have told no one. Now, however, they have broken their silence, knowing it could not be disguised for much longer.

Emma was smiling as I met her just outside Randalls. I was coming out of the gate as she, accompanied by Harriet, was going in.

'This is good news!' I said.

'Very good news,' she agreed.

'You will have to make some more caps.'

'I have started one already, and so has Harriet!'

'Very well done,' I said.

Harriet blushed and murmured something I did not catch.

We parted, I to go on business, and Emma to go in to see her friend.

Monday 5 April

Today was like spring, warm and sunny. I rode round the estate with William Larkins and we made sure that everything was in order. The farms were flourishing, and it did my heart good to see them. There is nothing like being in England in the spring.

Weston felt the same. He was very expansive this evening, and was more than usually talkative when I joined him for dinner.

Emma was there, and looking well. We spoke of many things, including Miss Fairfax.

'I wonder that Jane Fairfax spends so much time with Mrs Elton,' said Emma.

'We cannot suppose that she has any great enjoyment at the vicarage, my dear Emma,' said Mrs Weston, 'but it is better than being always at home.'

'Another thing must be taken into consideration too,' I said. 'Mrs Elton does not talk *to* Miss Fairfax as she speaks *of* her. And besides the operation of this, as a general principle, you may be sure that Miss Fairfax awes Mrs Elton by her superiority both of mind and manner. Such a woman as Jane Fairfax probably never fell in Mrs Elton's way before – and no degree of vanity can prevent her acknowledging her own comparative littleness in action, if not in consciousness.'

I tried to do full justice to Miss Fairfax's virtues, because I knew I could never marry her.

'I know how highly you think of Jane Fairfax,' said Emma anxiously. 'And yet . . .' She stopped, as if she did not know how to continue, then went on: 'And yet, perhaps, you may hardly be aware yourself how highly it is. The extent of your admiration may take you by surprise some day or other.'

Although I had had a similar idea myself, I did not want her to know it, so I bent and fastened the button of my gaiter to prevent her seeing my confusion.

'Oh! are you there?' I asked. 'But you are miserably behindhand. Mr Cole gave me a hint of it six weeks ago. That will never be, however, I can assure you. Miss Fairfax, I dare say, would not have me if I were to ask her; and I am very sure I shall never ask her.'

'You are not vain, Mr Knightley. I will say that for you,' Emma replied.

To my surprise, she was not angry that I would not fall in with her plans. She was relieved.

'So you have been settling that I should marry Jane Fairfax,' I said curiously, wondering exactly what had been going through her mind.

'No indeed I have not. You have scolded me too much for matchmaking, for me to presume to take such a liberty with you. Oh no, upon my word I have not the smallest wish for your marrying Jane Fairfax or Jane anybody. You would not come in and sit with us in this comfortable way, if you were married.'

Ah. So that was it. She liked my company, and would miss it if it were gone. I thought of Routledge and his words to me in London. Marry Emma! I had said it was a ludicrous idea, but was it? I had tried to take an interest in Miss Larch, and I had failed. I had tried to take an interest in Mrs Lovage, and I had failed. And I had tried to take an interest in Jane Fairfax, and I had failed. But I had never failed to take an interest in Emma, and I did so without even trying.

Why had I not seen it before? I never thought of anyone but Emma. But then my spirits sank as I realized that Emma could think of no one but Frank Churchill.

I could fiddle with my gaiter no longer.

'Jane Fairfax is a very charming young woman – but not even Jane Fairfax is perfect,' I said. 'She has a fault. She has not the open temper which a man would wish for in a wife.'

The open temper that Emma has.

'You soon silenced Mr Cole, I suppose?' she said.

'Yes, very soon. He gave me a quiet hint; I told him he was mistaken; he asked my pardon and said no more. Cole does not want to be wiser or wittier than his neighbours,' I said, with a wry smile. 'Jane Fairfax has feeling,' I said, to give her her due, for I did not want Emma and Mrs Weston to think I was slighting her. 'I do not accuse her of want of feeling. Her sensibilities, I suspect, are strong, and her temper excellent in its power of forbearance, patience, self-control.' An image of Jane rose before me, and I could not help my real feelings coming through. 'But it wants openness. She is reserved, more reserved, I think, than she used to be: And I love an open temper. No; till Cole alluded to my supposed attachment, it had never entered my head,' I added, for I did not want to harm Jane's reputation by letting anyone know I had thought of marrying her, but had rejected the idea. 'I saw Jane Fairfax and conversed with her, with admiration and pleasure always; but with no thought beyond.'

Emma and Mrs Weston exchanged glances, and I felt I had spent enough time talking about Jane Fairfax. Indeed, I had spent enough time talking altogether, and I soon excused myself, returning to the Abbey, where William Larkins was waiting for me, with the accounts.

Wednesday 7 April

John is to be with us shortly, with his two sons, and it will not be a moment too soon. My only regret is that John cannot stay. He will be here for a day, but then he must go back to London. We must be grateful that he is leaving the boys with us. It will provide us with some welcome company; company, moreover, that is more to my taste than the present Highbury company. I am growing tired of Weston's talk about his son. Never a day seems to go by without him having a letter from his son, or expecting a letter, or wishing for a letter, and with it goes a wish that his son might pay us another visit. He seems to be obsessed with the young man, and Mrs Weston is just as bad!

And if I am not hearing about Frank Churchill, I am seeing the Eltons!

I seem to meet them everywhere I go. The whole of Highbury is giving parties for them. Mrs Elton can do nothing but talk of her sister and her sister's barouche-landau, and if I hear another comment about Mr Suckling and Maple Grove, I am liable to say something I shall regret.

Thursday 8 April

It was a relief to throw myself into Abbey business today and forget about my neighbours.

Friday 9 April

It is a good thing I am in a better temper today! Emma is arranging a dinner party for the Eltons, and of course I must go, and be polite to Mrs Elton. I admire the way Emma is bearing it all. I am sure she does not wish to see them, but she is behaving as though nothing unfortunate happened between her and Mr Elton. I am sure in my own mind that he proposed, or came as close to it as makes no difference. What else would have made him leave Highbury so suddenly after Christmas, if he had not made a declaration and been rejected? So, on the 11th, I must brace myself to hear all about Mr Suckling and Maple Grove.

Saturday 10 April

An unlucky chance has made my brother choose the day of the party for his visit to Hartfield. He is not fond of company at the best of times, and to have to endure it without his wife present, and with a bridal couple who must be made much of, will be a sore trial to him. I can only hope he will curb his temper, and not upset Mr Woodhouse.

Emma is worried because it will put her numbers out, and her father's nerves are on edge because it makes the party bigger than he cares for.

The one good thing is that Harriet has cried off. She does not want to see Elton, I suppose, after Emma put it into her head to think of him.

How the matter of Harriet will resolve itself I do not know.

Monday 12 April

Emma's problems have been solved in an unexpected way. Weston has been summoned to town, and cannot attend the dinner, though he means to call in afterwards, when he returns, so Emma's numbers are now perfect.

All is now settled. John arrives tomorrow. He will be calling here first, and then going on to Hartfield, where he will leave the boys.

Tuesday 13 April

My two eldest nephews are growing apace. They are bright, lively boys, and they chased each other round the garden as John and I took a walk. He told me that Isabella and the other three children were well, and that his business is prospering. I took him to see the new path, and he approved of what I had done.

He did not stay long, but soon went on to Hartfield, with the boys being quieter for their run around. They were much more subdued when they arrived at Hartfield than they had been for most of the journey, he told me when I saw him again at Hartfield just before dinner, and they had not put too great a strain on their grandfather's nerves.

Mr Woodhouse was as courteous as ever, making the round of his guests and paying particular attention to Mrs Elton, which pleased her greatly. He was very conscious of what was due to her as a bride.

John was talking to Miss Fairfax. He feels, as I do, that her lot is a hard one. To be taken away from everyone she knows and loves, and thrust into another family – one which might be disgreeable, with spoilt children and doting parents – is not an enviable fate.

I have asked amongst my acquaintance and tried to find her a position but I have not had any success. If I could know she was going into a well-regulated household, where her talents would be appreciated, I would be much happier.

My brother was very courteous to her, and as he had passed her on a walk this morning, he asked if she had arrived home before the rain. Fortunately she had, but Mrs Elton, officious as ever, declared that Miss Fairfax must not walk to the post office any more; Mrs Elton would have her servant collect Jane's post.

I admired Miss Fairfax for her tact in dealing with Mrs Elton. She did not give any direct reply, but instead skilfully turned the conversation towards the post office's efficiency, and from thence to handwriting, which was a subject much more to her taste, for it meant Mrs Elton could no longer irritate her.

'Isabella and Emma both write beautifully,' said Mr Woodhouse; 'and always did. And so does poor Mrs Weston,' he added, with half a sigh and half a smile at her.

I wonder when he will stop calling her 'poor Mrs Weston'!

'Mr Frank Churchill writes one of the best gentlemen's hands I ever saw,' said Emma, distracting her father's thoughts from the sad fate of the woman who sat there, happy and contented, with her husband and her friends about her.

I would have applauded, yet I do not like this habit she has grown into, of forever praising Frank Churchill. Why no one else can see that he is a wastrel with no sense of duty I do not know. I seem to be the only person who is not blind to his faults, and he has many of them.

'I do not admire it,' I said, determined to speak my mind. 'It is too small – wants strength. It is like a woman's writing.'

Emma did not agree. Perhaps I had gone too far in saying it was like a woman's hand, but really, I do not see what is so remarkable about Frank Churchill's writing.

Mrs Weston was called upon to find a letter, and Emma declared that she had kept a note written by him, and that it was in her writing-desk.

Why has she kept a note written by the man? Is she really falling in love with him? A foolish young puppy, who thinks of no one but himself? Who cannot take the trouble to pay a visit to his own father on his father's marriage? Who indulges in freaks and whims?

I believe my impatience showed in my reply.

'Oh! when a gallant young man, like Mr Frank Churchill writes to a fair lady like Miss Woodhouse, he will, of course, put forth his best,' I remarked.

I saw John look at me in surprise, but I could not help myself. Besides, I did not think it was so very rude, although perhaps it was as well that, at that moment, dinner was announced.

Mrs Elton led the way, as a bride should, and gloried in it, as a bride should not.

Poor Miss Fairfax! I believe she had a great deal to bear after dinner, when the ladies withdrew. When I returned to the drawing-room with the other gentlemen, Mrs Elton was offering to help her find a position as a governess. I should be sorry to see Miss Fairfax take up a position in any household known to Mrs Elton.

I was just thinking that things could get no worse when Weston joined us. As luck would have it – or as bad luck would have it – he brought with him a letter from his son.

I took up my newspaper. I had no desire to listen to any further praise of Frank Churchill's magnificent handwriting.

The letter was even worse than I had expected. A string of promises, a row of false hopes, all wrapped up in insincerity and capriciousness; that was what I had expected. But instead I learnt that the Churchills are to remove to town on account of Mrs Churchill's health, and that Frank is to remove with them. He will be so close to Hartfield – only sixteen miles away – that he will be able to visit easily.

Mr and Mrs Weston were delighted. Emma was delighted. And I was not delighted.

'We have the agreeable prospect of frequent visits from Frank the whole spring,' Weston said.

Agreeable to whom? I thought, rustling my newspaper.

'Precisely the season of the year which one should have chosen for it: days almost at the longest; weather genial and pleasant, always inviting one out, and never too hot for exercise. When he was here before, we made the best of it; but there was a good deal of wet, damp, cheerless weather; there always is in February, you know, and we could not do half that we intended. Now will be the time. This will be complete enjoyment; and I do not know, Mrs Elton, whether the uncertainty of our meetings, the sort of constant expectation there will be of his coming in today or tomorrow, and at any hour, may not be more friendly to happiness than having him actually in the house. I think it is so. I think it is the state of mind which gives most spirit and delight.'

In May, then, I am to have all the pleasure of Frank Churchill's company, as long as I do not expire before then with the promise of so much spirit and delight.

Fortunately, John began to speak of his sons before my bad temper could get the better of me.

'I hope I am aware that they may be too noisy for your father; or even may be some encumbrance to you, if your visiting engagements continue to increase as much as they have done lately,' he said to Emma.

'Let them be sent to Donwell,' I said. 'I shall certainly be at leisure.'

'Upon my word,' exclaimed Emma to me, 'you amuse me! I should like to know how many of all my numerous engagements take place without your being of the party; and why I am to be supposed in danger of wanting leisure to attend to the little boys. If Aunt Emma has not time for them, I do not think they would fare much better with Uncle Knightley, who is absent from home about five hours where she is absent one – and who, when he is at home, is either reading to himself or settling his accounts.'

I smiled at this. She knows me well.

Mrs Elton claimed my attention, but when she had done I went to sit by Emma.

'You will bring the boys over to the Abbey tomorrow? If the weather continues wet, it will give them a chance to run about and be noisy without distressing your father.'

'By all means. Harriet is to call in the morning, and we will bring them together.'

'Must you always be with Harriet?' I asked impatiently.

'That is hardly fair!' she cried. 'I have seen very little of Harriet since. . . .'

'Since Mr Elton returned?' I enquired. I saw her look uncomfortable, but I let it pass. 'Very well, if you must bring her, you must.' I had done with Harriet. 'I want to give the children a chance to ride whilst they are here,' I went on. 'It is not often we have them for such an extended spell.'

'Oh, yes, they are full of high spirits and are bound to enjoy it. But it is perhaps better not to mention it to my father; he will only worry about it. I hope the weather holds.'

'There will be some dry spells, I am convinced.'

'And if it rains tomorrow?'

'Then you and I will have to entertain the boys indoors.'

I am looking forward to it. Inside or out, any time I spend with the boys is well spent, and I would never rather be with anyone but Emma.

Wednesday 14 April

I cannot make up my mind. Is Emma in love with Frank Churchill, or is she not? I sometimes think she is, but then she says something that convinces me otherwise. She seems to welcome his attentions, and yet she has not shown any signs of being in a decline when he is away.

We were talking of Isabella's living in London, and I said to Emma: 'Could you bear to move away from Highbury?'

'If there was a strong enough inducement, then perhaps I might,' she said.

I thought of Frank Churchill. Would he be a strong enough inducement?

'Isabella seems happy enough in London,' she went on, 'but then she is happy wherever her husband is.'

'And when you marry, you will be happy wherever your husband is,' I said, looking at her earnestly.

'I will never marry,' she said. 'Why should I? I already have everything I want at Hartfield. Like you, I have no need of children to interest me, for I have Isabella's children, and like you, I am happiest at home.'

I felt myself grow brighter. It is very comfortable to have Emma so near, and spending my time with her, playing with the children, is my idea of a perfect day.

Thursday 15 April

There has been a delay in the Churchill family's move to London. I knew how it would be! Churchill's letter meant nothing at all. I never put any reliance on it. What! Mrs Churchill, to remove to London from her native Yorkshire? Why should she do such a thing? And even if she thought she might, then why should she go ahead with her plan, when she is as fickle as her nephew?

I said as much to Emma.

'It is hardly Frank Churchill's fault,' she said. 'He is very much at his aunt's beck and call. He will be with us as soon as he can.'

She did not seem unduly worried by the delay, which was heartening, but she defended him, which was dispiriting.

I still do not like the idea of his merely being delayed for a while. Whenever he comes to Highbury, it will be too soon for me.

Wednesday 21 April

I had a most unwelcome shock when I went to Hartfield today. I had promised to collect the boys, so that they could spend a day at the Abbey with me, and when I walked into the drawing-room, I found Frank Churchill there!

He had only come to pay a short visit, in order to say that the Churchills had at last moved to town. His aunt is still very sickly and she could not spare him for longer.

I was very sorry for Mrs Churchill, and, once I knew he was not to visit us, for Frank Churchill, too.

'I believe the idea of Frank Churchill always being at Hartfield, now the Churchills are in London, will come to nothing,' I said to Emma.

She remarked that it would be a pity, but as she then went on to see that the boys were warmly wrapped up, and to soothe her father's fears that they would take cold on the walk to the Abbey, and to tell them to behave, and to remind me that I must not give them too much to eat, I did not think she was very much affected by it.

I begin to think that Frank Churchill is not so bad, after all. Perhaps I have been too hard on him: a young man who has to pay constant attention to a sick aunt must be forgiven the odd indiscretion.

In fact, if he remains in London, I believe I will like him very well indeed.

Thursday 22 April

The day was cold and wet. I attended to business this morning, and this afternoon, Emma called with the two little boys. I was delighted to find that Harriet was not with her. I have hardly seen Emma without her friend these last few months. We took the boys through the woods and watched them play.

'You will never marry, will you, Mr Knightley?' she asked me.

I thought she seemed anxious, and I was gratified by her concern.

'No, never,' I said. My spirits rose. Did she feel she would not like me to marry anyone else, because she would like me for herself? 'You seem pleased,' I said.

'I am,' she replied.

Will you . . . I tried to say the words, but I was suddenly nervous and they would not come out.

I cleared my throat and was about to try again when she continued by saying: 'I would not like little Henry to lose his inheritance.'

Foolish, foolish fantasy! She was not in love with me after all, she was simply concerned for Henry.

'Oh, so that is the reason,' I said, subdued.

'You would not like him to lose it either, would you?' she asked anxiously.

'If I had a son of my own, I must reasonably assume I would rather see the Abbey go to him than my nephew,' I replied. 'But since I have no plans to marry, I see no reason for you to worry about Henry.'

No plans, as yet, I thought, as she smiled at me. But I fully intend to marry if I can persuade Emma to marry me. I do not despair of it. She does not seem set on Churchill and she likes me, I know. In time, I hope she will come to see me as a husband.

She put her hand through my arm as we walked back through the gardens, and as we reached the Abbey the sun came out.

Friday 23 April

Frank Churchill was in Highbury today, but he spent very little time at Hartfield. He paid a call in the morning, and then went on to the Bateses, and had lunch with Mr and Mrs Weston before going back to London.

Monday 26 April

I joined Emma and her father at Hartfield this morning, and I found the Westons there. They had called to say that Mrs Churchill felt no better in London, and that she had taken a house at Richmond for May and June.

I looked at Emma, wondering how she would take the news, for Richmond is very near.

'He will be with us all the time,' said Weston, delighted. 'It is only a short distance, no more than nine miles, and what is nine miles?'

'And now the ball can go ahead,' said Mrs Weston to Emma.

Emma was delighted, and I was downcast. I did not begrudge her her happiness, but I was left to trust in her good judgement and hope she sees through him in the end.

Mr Woodhouse was not happy with the idea of the ball, either, though he likes it better in May than he did in February, as the chance of draughts are fewer. But he was still worried that the boys might be taken ill whilst Emma was away.

'You will have Mrs Bates to sit with you,' said Emma, 'and if either of the boys is unwell you can send a message to me at the Crown and I will come home directly.'

Thus soothed, he subsided into vague hopes that no disasters would mar the evening. I hoped so, too, though the disasters I envisaged were of a different kind.

MAY

I did not enjoy this evening. Emma spent most of it with Frank Churchill. He was already talking to her when I arrived, and though he seemed restless, he scarcely moved from her side. He claimed her hand for the first dance, and though I tried not to look at them, I found it hard to keep my eyes away, for Emma was looking very beautiful.

'They look well together, do they not?' said Otway, who was standing at the side of the room, next to me.

'Yes. Mrs Elton is very pleased to be opening the dance, and Weston is happy to be partnering her,' I said, deliberately misunderstanding.

'I was not talking about Mrs Elton and Mr Weston, but Mr Churchill and Miss Woodhouse. I think we will see a match there before long. It would please everyone in Highbury, I am sure. Mr and Mrs Weston would be delighted, and all Miss Woodhouse's friends must be glad to see her so well married. Mr Churchill is to inherit Enscombe, and a very fine fortune besides.'

'I see nothing in it, beyond an inclination to dance together,' I said. 'I cannot believe Miss Woodhouse will ever leave Highbury. She could not leave her father.'

'Very true, it would be difficult, but might she not take him to Enscombe with her?'

'Mr Woodhouse, to leave Hartfield? That is something he would never do.'

As I spoke, I realized I was trying to reassure myself.

'Perhaps not. But Miss Woodhouse and Mr Churchill would have a house in town, and London is only sixteen miles away. They could visit Hartfield often from there.'

'I am sure Miss Woodhouse has no more idea of marrying him than she has of marrying Longridge,' I said, surprising myself as much as Otway.

He looked startled, and then begged my pardon, but it was I who should have been begging his pardon. I had spoken to him roughly, and should not have done so.

Emma caught my eye and her happiness forced me to smile, but I could not be easy. Otway's thoughts echoed my own. They made a good pair – except that I knew they would not be suited; Frank Churchill with his fly-about ways, his unreliable nature and his inconsistencies, and Emma, with her love of family and delight in her friends.

Whereas Emma and I would be a perfect match.

I could bear to watch them no longer. I retired to the card-room and played until it was almost time for supper, then returned to the ballroom. Emma was still dancing. She danced very well, and it gave me a great deal of pleasure to see her.

After a while, I noticed that her little friend was not dancing. I felt sorry to see her sitting out by herself.

To my surprise, I saw Elton walking towards her. I had thought he was too small-minded to overlook the wound Emma had inflicted on his pride, but it seemed I was wrong. It was clear he was going to rescue Harriet from her place at the side of the room and lead her on to the floor.

And why not? Now that he had married, no mistake could be made, no attention read into his action. It was a kind thought. It would set the lady at her ease, and make future intercourse between the two of them easy and pleasant. We all live in a small neighbourhood, after all.

He stood in front of her. She looked down, embarrassed, but glad that she was to be rescued from her ignominious position. But then, without saying a word to her, he moved on.

I could not believe it! To treat a young lady so! And at a private dance!

I had never thought so ill of a man in my life. To withdraw to the card-room would have been sensible; to have avoided her would have been unkind but permissible; yet to stand directly in front of her, and then to move away – that was abominable.

Things grew worse. Mrs Weston asked him if he danced, and he offered to partner her, or Mrs Gilbert; but when she mentioned Harriet, he had the effrontery to say that he was an old married man and his dancing days were over.

I was so incensed that I walked over to Harriet and asked her to dance myself. She looked up at me with such an expression of humble gratitude that my heart swelled.

I had not thought Elton could be so small-minded. Marriage had not made him better; it had made him many times worse. He had never been petty-minded before. Vain, yes; proud, yes; thinking well of himself, yes; but cruel towards others – no. And what another! A young girl with no family to offer her protection. I was disgusted with him, and did not trouble to conceal it.

I led Harriet on to the floor with all the deference I would have given to an heiress with £50,000, and I was gratified to see Elton's black look, as well as Harriet's radiant smile.

Emma might have chosen unwisely for Elton, but not as unwisely as he had chosen for himself. Harriet was shy at first, and said little, but she soon gained confidence and answered me freely, with an openness that was very attractive. She danced joyfully, bounding down the room like a lamb in spring, and I am sure the sight of her lifted the spirits of all reasonable men and women in the room.

During supper, I wondered again at Elton's slight, for it was not only Harriet whom he had ill-treated. He had slighted Mrs Weston, his hostess, when he had refused to dance with a partner she offered him, and he had sent a message to Emma, that he would not do anything to oblige her; more, that he was happy to disoblige her. And, by the glances that passed between Elton and his wife, it was clear she encouraged him.

When supper was over, Emma beckoned me over to her with her eyes. She thanked me for my kindness to her friend and we joined in censuring Elton and his abominable behaviour.

'The Eltons aimed at wounding more than Harriet,' I said. 'Emma, why is it that they are your enemies?' She said nothing, so I continued.

'*She* ought not to be angry with you, I suspect, whatever he may be. To that surmise, you say nothing, of course; but confess, Emma, that you did want him to marry Harriet.'

'I did,' she confessed at last, 'and they cannot forgive me.'

Poor Emma!

'I shall not scold you,' I said kindly. 'I leave you to your own reflections.'

'Can you trust me with such flatterers? Does my vain spirit ever tell me I am wrong?' she asked ruefully.

'Not your vain spirit, but your serious spirit. If one leads you wrong, I am sure the other tells you of it,' I said, loving her more than ever.

'I do own myself to have been completely mistaken in Mr Elton,' she confessed. 'There is a littleness about him which you discovered, and which I did not: and I was fully convinced of his being in love with Harriet. It was through a series of strange blunders!'

I was touched by her confidence.

'And, in return for your acknowledging so much, I will do you the justice to say, that you would have chosen for him better than he has chosen for himself. Harriet Smith has some first-rate qualities, which Mrs Elton is totally without. An unpretending, single-minded, artless girl – infinitely to be preferred by any man of sense and taste to such a woman as Mrs Elton. I found Harriet more conversable than I expected.'

She was gratified. There was time for no more. The dancing was about to begin again.

My heart was warmed when, on asking her whom she meant to dance with, Emma said: 'With you, if you will ask me.'

My spirits surged.

'Will you?' I said, looking down into her eyes as I offered her my hand.

'Indeed I will,' she replied, taking it. She was back to her old self. 'You have shown that you can dance, and you know we are not really so much brother and sister as to make it at all improper.'

'Brother and sister! – no, indeed.'

As I led her on to the floor, I wondered if she saw me as a brother. I knew I had an opportunity, in the dance, to make her see me as something more. She was not in love with me, perhaps, but I felt confident I could make her love me. And then . . . a happy future opened out before me. Emma and I at the Abbey, with our own children.

Little Henry will have to make his own way in the world, I fear!

Wednesday 5 May

There was a most unfortunate incident today. I was just about to set out for Kingston when I was greeted by a messenger from Hartfield. He gave me a note, and I was alarmed to see that Harriet had been attacked by a group of gypsies on the Richmond Road. She and a friend had been walking along when they had seen the gypsies and, taking fright, had run away. Harriet had not been able to run very far as she had suffered from cramp, and it was only the timely intervention of Frank Churchill, who just happened to be passing, that saved her from bodily harm.

I set out at once to see that the road was made safe again, but by the time I arrived the gypsies had hurried off. They had no mind to face a magistrate, and I am persuaded they will not trouble us again. But I am still concerned that this should have happened in my parish.

I went to see Weston straight away and told him what had happened. He had not heard of it, as his son had been on his way to Richmond when the attack and rescue occurred, and had therefore continued with his journey, but he was as concerned as I was. We decided we would speak to the other gentlemen of the parish at our whist club tonight. We must be vigilant if this is not to happen again.

I went from Randalls to Hartfield to satisfy myself that Harriet was all right. I found my nephews full of the story, and relishing it as little boys should. The story of Harriet and the gypsies will, I feel, inspire their games for weeks to come.

Harriet had been shaken by the incident, but she was much recovered. She had had Churchill to rescue her, and Emma and Mr Woodhouse to make much of her, and this had quickly restored her spirits.

Mr Woodhouse, however, was in a quake, and would hardly be satisfied until Emma promised him she would never leave the grounds again.

However, he will accustom himself to it by and by, and I have no doubt she will be walking to Randalls as usual tomorrow.

Tuesday 11 May

The boys were still talking of Harriet and the gypsies when I went to Hartfield today. They were in a boisterous mood, and Emma and I took them outside to fly a kite. The wind was high, and we had no difficulty in getting the kites to soar aloft. I handed the strings to Henry and helped him manage them, whilst Emma helped John.

The children were delighted with the game, though Mr Woodhouse, when we returned to the house, was unhappy.

'I do not think you should have played with a kite in such a wind,' he said to Henry. 'It is particularly strong today, and it might have carried you away.'

'But we were holding the strings, too, Papa,' said Emma. 'Did you not see? Mr Knightley held on to Henry's kite, and I held on to John's. The wind looked strong, perhaps, but once outside it was not so very bad. It tugged now and again at the kites, but we were never in any danger, and if it had tugged too hard, we could always have let the strings go, you know.'

'You mean well, my dear, I know, but I cannot like it. You should not play with kites when the wind is so high.'

'We have to play with them in the wind, Grandpapa,' said Henry, 'otherwise they will not fly.'

Mr Woodhouse told the boys that kites were for grown-ups, not little boys, and this so upset the children, who thought they would have to wait another twenty years before being allowed to fly a kite again, that Emma had three sets of nerves to soothe before tea.

I cannot believe we will be sending the boys on their way again in a few days. It hardly seems like any time since they arrived.

I almost spoke to Emma this evening; almost gave her an intimation of my feelings; but I felt the time had not yet come – that she did not yet see me as more than a friend – and so I held my peace.

Saturday 15 May

John arrived to collect the boys and we all took luncheon together.

'Will you not stay?' asked Emma.

'No, I must get home,' he said.

Emma was resigned, knowing that nothing can keep John away from his hearth and home, unless it is unavoidable.

Emma had made a new cap for the baby, a shirt for little George, a handkerchief for Isabella, and a doll for Bella. John thanked her for the presents and promised to deliver them. Then it was time for him to go.

Mr Woodhouse mourned their absence, though I think the boys were here long enough. He had been getting more and more worried about them as they had grown more and more confident. It is as well they were going home, where they could play to their heart's content without worrying Grandpapa.

JUNE

Tuesday 1 June

I was dining at the vicarage this evening when I saw something disturbing. Frank Churchill kept catching Jane Fairfax's eye, and I am sure some secret intelligence passed between them. I thought at first that Churchill had switched his affections, but this was not the case, as he went on making love to Emma. I was at a loss as to what it could mean.

Had he said something compromising to Jane Fairfax? Paid her some extravagant compliment? Given her to understand he liked her? That would explain the look of intelligence, but if that was the case, why did he continue to pay attention to Emma? It did not make sense. Nor did it make sense that Jane Fairfax, a young woman of good sense and good principles would be interested in the attentions of a man like Frank Churchill.

Unless women are all fools when it comes to handsome young men?

Nay, I will not believe it. I know it cannot be so. Yet Emma and Jane Fairfax both seem attracted to Mr Weston's son – and he to them.

Saturday 5 June

The weather being warm, I decided to walk up to Hartfield this evening and as I found Emma and Harriet setting out for a walk, I decided to accompany them. We fell in with Mr and Mrs Weston, Mr Churchill, Miss Bates and Miss Fairfax, and as we returned to Hartfield, Emma pressed the whole party to go in to see her father, and to take tea.

We were just turning into the grounds when Perry passed on horseback, and we spoke of his horse.

'By the by,' said Frank Churchill to Mrs Weston, 'what became of Mr Perry's plan of setting up his carriage?'

Mrs Weston disclaimed any knowledge of such a plan, but he insisted she had told him of it.

'Never!' exclaimed Churchill. 'Bless me! how could it be? Then I must have dreamt it.'

Again, I surprised a look between him and Jane Fairfax, and the thought came to me that she had told him of it. But why not say so? Why make a mystery of it?

My conviction that Frank Churchill was guilty of double-dealing became more certain as the evening progressed. He called for some alphabet bricks the boys had left behind, and he and Emma amused themselves by making up words.

'Ah! the poor little boys, how sad they were to leave us,' said Mr Woodhouse in a melancholy voice, seeing the bricks. 'I do wish Isabella would come and live here with us. Poor Isabella!' he sighed.

Under cover of his lamentations, Churchill pushed a collection of letters towards Miss Fairfax. I was watching her at the time, and it seemed to me that she had worked out the conundrum, but that it troubled her, because she blushed slightly and then mixed the bricks in with the others. But she did not mix them well enough. Harriet pounced on them, and reading the word Miss Fairfax had made, cried out: 'Blunder!'

Miss Fairfax flushed a deeper red.

So! Churchill had made a blunder with his comment about Perry's carriage, and the source of the information was indeed Miss Fairfax. Then why not be open about it? The whole thing smacked of duplicity, and worse, it was clear that Miss Fairfax was not an innocent party, but was involved in something she was ashamed of.

Churchill continued unabashed. He made a word for Emma. She smiled, but looked alarmed when he pushed it towards Miss Fairfax, who flushed again. I looked over the letters and was able to make out Dixon.

Dixon! The name of her friend's husband?

What did it mean?

One thing was certain. Churchill was not only behaving in an ungentlemanlike fashion, but he was involving others in his misdeeds, and dragging both Emma and Miss Fairfax down to his own level, involving the former in giving pain and the latter in receiving it.

Miss Fairfax could stand no more. She pushed the letters away angrily, and looked at her aunt, who read her expression and said they must be going.

The Westons and Weston's son, Miss Bates and her niece all departed. When the candles were lit to dispel the gathering gloom, I felt I must say something to Emma, for I feared that Churchill was playing a double game, and transferring his affections to Miss Fairfax. Moreover, that he was using Emma as an unwitting pawn in his game.

I began by speaking of the word he had made out of bricks, asking her how it could be so very entertaining to her, whilst so very distressing to Jane.

She was confused, and told me it was nothing but a joke.

'The joke seemed confined to you and Mr Churchill,' I remarked.

I did not know how much to say, for I did not know whether I was helping her. I had no authority to speak to her, save the authority of an affectionate friend, but I felt I must take the risk of her thinking I was interfering, rather than take the risk of seeing her hurt when a word or two of mine could prevent it.

'My dear Emma,' I asked softly, 'do you think you perfectly understand the degree of acquaintance between the gentleman and lady we have been speaking of?'

'Between Mr Frank Churchill and Miss Fairfax! Oh! yes, perfectly,' she said with assurance.

'Have you never at any time had reason to think that he admired her, or that she admired him?'

'Never, never!' she cried.

I wondered if I should stop there, but having started, thought I should continue: 'I have lately imagined that I saw symptoms of attachment between them; certain expressive looks, which I did not believe were meant to be public.'

Instead of the confusion I had expected, she was amused, assuring me there was no admiration between them: 'That is, I *presume* it to be so on her side, and I can *answer* for its being so on his. I will answer for the gentleman's indifference.'

This was plain speaking. It could not have been plainer. For her to know it so certainly meant her affections were engaged and that there was that perfect confidence between them that can only come between lovers. He must have declared himself, and been met with warmth.

How could I have been such a fool? How could I have been so slow to recognize my feelings for her, and then been so slow to speak? My hesitation had cost me dear. It had cost me Emma. I felt a wave of anguish and said no more.

I returned to the Abbey, but I could not settle to anything. I took up a book but I could not see the words. I looked over my accounts, but my mind was so distracted that I was afraid of touching anything lest I make a mistake.

Is this to be the end of Emma? I asked myself. To be married to a man like that? To spend her time tormenting others – for that is what she was doing this evening – encouraged by her lover? I cannot bear it!

And yet what can I do, except watch her, and love her, and be ready to help her if she needs me?

Wednesday 9 June

I dined with the Coles this evening, and I found the Eltons there. Mrs Elton was lamenting the fact that her sister and her brother-in-law, Mr Suckling, would not be able to visit after all. She had been living in expectation of a visit from them for some time, but it had had to be put off until the autumn.

Mrs Elton was very disappointed. No pleasure trips in the barouche-landau, no dinner parties, no discussion of Maple Grove; for even Mrs Elton seemed tired of talking about a place no one else had seen.

'Why not come with us?' said Weston.

I looked at him in surprise, and his wife did likewise. We had talked of a pleasure trip ourselves, but we had not thought of inviting the Eltons.

There is so much parade in their way of doing things that Emma, the Westons and myself had thought to go alone.

But now here was Weston, in an excess of conviviality, inviting the very persons we had been anxious to avoid.

Mrs Elton looked at him enquiringly.

'Miss Woodhouse, Mr Knightley, my wife and myself were intending to go to Box Hill. Now that the Sucklings have disappointed you, you must join our party.'

'The very thing,' said Mrs Elton. 'We do not need the Sucklings in order to arrange a pleasure trip. We can go there again when they visit us in the autumn.'

The weather being fine, a pleasure trip to Box Hill has been arranged. A few days ago, it would have been a great burden to me, but set next to the devastation of knowing that Emma is in love with Frank Churchill, it troubles me very little.

Thursday 10 June

I wanted to tell Emma the news about the party to Box Hill, but when I arrived at Hartfield this morning, I found the Westons had already told her.

'I am glad you approve of what I have done,' he was saying to her as I entered the room.

From Emma's expression, I could see that she did not approve at all. However, she could not say so, without revealing her reason, which was that she did not like Mrs Elton. And as that could not be said, she gave in with a good grace.

'Never mind,' I said to her, once Weston had departed. 'It will be a large party, and you need not talk to Mrs Elton.'

'No,' she agreed. 'I would much rather talk to you instead.'

Perhaps I would have been more heartened by her preference, if I had not known of her thorough dislike of Mrs Elton.

I was encouraged by her lack of enthusiasm for the trip, however. Frank Churchill will certainly be invited, and as she does not seem to be eager for the outing, then perhaps she is not as set on Frank Churchill as I had supposed. Is there still hope for me? The next few days will show me for sure.

Saturday 12 June

A most annoying day. I met Mrs Elton on my way to Hartfield, and I could not avoid talking to her. Her follies put me out of temper, so that by the time I reached Hartfield I was in a bad mood.

'What is the matter?' asked Emma.

'Nothing. Everything.' And before I knew what I was doing, I was telling her all about it.

'I have just seen Mrs Elton. She was telling me that one of her carriage-horses has become lame, and so the trip must be postponed. "Is it not vexatious, Knightley?" she asked me.'

'At least she did not call you Mr K,' said Emma.

'Hah!' I felt my mood lighten a little. 'She bemoaned her fate so volubly that I despaired of ever getting away from her, and so, in an effort to divert her thoughts, I said, humorously, that she must come to Donwell to visit my strawberry-beds.'

'She did not agree!' said Emma.

'She did!' I began to laugh. 'She said she should like it of all things. I could not believe she wanted an outing to my strawberry beds!'

'She wanted an outing to Donwell Abbey, rather,' said Emma.

'And she has achieved her goal,' I said ruefully.

'If the carriage-horse recovers in time, she can arrive in state.'

'No, she has already decided on her mode of transport. She has decided she is going to arrive on a donkey.'

'A donkey?' asked Emma in astonishment.

'You are to say nothing,' I warned her, feeling the laughter welling up in me again. 'She wants everyone to come on a donkey: Miss Fairfax, Miss Bates. . . .'

'And Mr Elton?'

'No. Her *caro sposo* is going to walk beside her.'

'I think it an excellent plan,' she said gravely. 'We must all have donkeys. I am sure Miss Bates would enjoy the experience, and Mrs Goddard would look very well in the saddle – if, indeed, donkeys wear saddles. I mean to purchase a donkey this afternoon, and I hope I may not disgrace you by my seat when you walk next to me, Mr K.'

'Oh, Emma!' I said. 'Don't . . .' *marry Churchill, marry me*, I was going to say. The words were on the tip of my tongue, but at that moment, Harriet walked into the room.

I had never been so dismayed to see her in my life.

'I have found the silk you asked for – oh, Mr Knightley,' she said.

I believe she knew she had interrupted something important, for she blushed.

'Thank you, Harriet. Mr Knightley has come with excellent news. We are to spend a day at Donwell Abbey, picking strawberries.'

'Oh, that will be lovely,' said Harriet, her eyes shining as she looked at me.

I was even more sure that she suspected my secret, for her shining eyes indicated that she expected me to propose to Emma at the Abbey.

Before she could say anything further, Mr Woodhouse joined us, and Emma turned to him solicitously.

'Is Perry not with you?'

'No, my dear, he has had to go on his rounds. He is very busy. I am not surprised. His advice is sought everywhere.'

'What did he say to you?' she asked.

'He was very pleased. There has been some improvement since the last time he saw me. He congratulated me, and told me that my diet played a large part in my constitution. If only I could persuade you to eat more gruel, I am sure you would be better for it,' he said.

'I believe I will join you in a bowl tonight. But what do you think? We have a treat in store. Mr Knightley has invited us to the Abbey,' she said.

'All, Mr Knightley, I am a sad invalid,' he said, shaking his head as though I had invited him to his own funeral.

'But there has been some improvement, Perry said so, and it is not so very far to the Abbey,' Emma said. 'Mr Knightley will do everything he can to make you comfortable.'

I added my pleas, and at last he said he would venture out. Emma was very pleased, as he has not been to the Abbey in two years, and I was pleased to have given her pleasure.

Mr and Mrs Weston arrived shortly afterwards, and accepted an invitation to join us. Weston said he would invite Frank for me, and it was impossible for me to refuse his offer, but I consoled myself with the thought that his son might not come.

We settled on the twentieth for the visit. It cannot be sooner, for I will have things to arrange. Mr Woodhouse's comfort must be provided for, and the Abbey must be made ready for guests.

Monday 14 June

I called at Hartfield this morning, hoping to speak to Emma, but she had gone out. I walked into Highbury on business and called on Miss Bates. I was hoping to see Emma, but although she had called, she was no longer there. I listened to Miss Bates's chatter with half a mind.

Longridge has chosen a house at last, it seems. He has settled on Southdean, the house of which Miss Bates herself is particularly fond. It has a large garden, with a stream, well-proportioned rooms, and comfortable servants' quarters. I think he will be an addition to Highbury society.

Tuesday 15 June

Robert Martin came to see me on a matter of business this morning, and I was struck again with his loyalty to Harriet. He did not, like Mr Elton, rush out to find a wife as soon as his hand was refused. He is a good-enough-looking man, with a prosperous living, and there are a number of young ladies in Highbury who would be flattered by his attentions, but I am convinced he still thinks of Harriet. He has read the books she recommended, though goodness knows what pleasure or information he has received from *The Romance of the Forest*, and he has encouraged his sisters to remain friendly with her. It is just a pity that he could not have rescued her from the gypsies, because if it had fallen to him to be her champion, then I am sure his work would have been done.

But he is a sensible man. He can see that Harriet belongs with him, and I am convinced he is biding his time.

In this, I hope to do him a good turn. Abbey Mill Farm is plainly visible from the Abbey, and when Harriet comes strawberry-picking, I hope to draw her attention to it.

Further than this I will not go; but Emma has meddled in separating them, and I think I may be forgiven for meddling in some small way to bring them back together.

Tuesday 22 June

I have had no success in finding Emma alone this week. She has either been out walking, or with Harriet, or with her father. But tomorrow I must speak to her. When she comes to the Abbey I mean to offer her my arm and lead her away from the others. Once in a secluded corner I can speak to her, tentatively at first, to see if I can discover whether she has irrevocably given her heart to Churchill, and then, if she has not, I mean to ask her to marry me.

Wednesday 23 June

I was walking into Highbury when I passed Mrs Elton by chance. She and her husband were taking the air. I wondered if he knew about the plan for a donkey, and that he was expected to walk beside it.

'Look, Mr E, here is Knightley!' she said.

I could not ignore her greeting, and bade her good morning.

'What do you think, Knightley?' she asked me. 'The carriage-horse has recovered. My *caro sposo* and I are planning a trip to Box Hill on the twenty-first, the day after we come to Donwell. I hope you will join us. You and I must lead the way, Knightley. We must not let this good weather pass us by.'

I could not readily think of an excuse, so I agreed. If, for any reason, the day at the Abbey does not give me a chance to speak to Emma, then a day at Box Hill will surely do so.

Thursday 24 June

I was relieved when I awoke to a day of bright sunshine, knowing it would make the strawberry-picking so much more enjoyable. Even so, I ordered a fire lit in the sitting-room for Mr Woodhouse, for he feels the cold, even in summer.

I helped Emma settle him when he arrived, and he was happy to sit with Mrs Weston, who claimed she was tired, and that she would much rather remain indoors. I gave them a collection of medals, engravings, cameos, corals and shells to look through and then went outside with my other guests.

The strawberry-picking began. Berries were picked and eaten, their relative flavours and textures discussed, and favourite var-ieties were remarked upon. Mrs Elton gave her opinion decidedly, whilst Elton danced attendance and Weston worried about his son.

'I thought Frank would be here by now,' he said on more than one occasion, looking at his watch. 'He has had time, I am sure. I thought we would have seen him here already.'

I took my chance and walked up to Emma, but to my frustration, Mrs Elton was before me, and was soon telling Emma that, as the two leading ladies of the district, they must find a position for Jane Fairfax without delay.

I had no desire to join their conversation, and I was about to join Mr Woodhouse indoors when I noticed that Harriet appeared at something of a loss. Seeing an opportunity to help Robert Martin, I went over to her and engaged her in conversation. I asked her how she liked the weather, and what she thought of the Abbey, and as I talked to her, I led her away from the others, down the lime-walk. She went with me readily, and as we stood together at the end of the lime-walk, we looked out over Abbey Mill Farm.

With this view in sight, I brought the conversation round to the Westons, and said how happy their marriage had made them.

'Yes, indeed,' she said shyly.

'The Eltons, too, seem happy,' I said.

She blushed, for the Eltons brought back unwelcome memories, but they served my purpose, and she admitted that they seemed happy, too.

Then, having turned her attention towards matrimony, I chose my next words carefully, and without actually asking her outright, I tried to discover if her affections were engaged.

She murmured something I did not catch, but her very shyness seemed to imply that they were. I pressed on, pointing out that Abbey Mill Farm was well-run and prosperous, and drawing her attention to the fine animals, the healthy orchards and the well-tended fields. She listened to everything I said with rapt attention. She blushed and murmured in just the way a young girl in love ought to do, and I felt that Robert Martin would be made happy before very long.

I would have said more, but that Emma joined us at that moment and I could not think of Harriet any longer, except to wish she would take herself off and leave us alone. She did not do so, and, Mrs Weston coming out, I had to master my frustration at so much unwanted company and play the host.

'I hope Frank has not had an accident,' said Mrs Weston. 'I thought he would have been here by now. I am worried about his horse.'

'The black mare? As safe a horse as ever I saw,' said Weston, coming up. 'Depend on it, it is his aunt.'

I had no chance to speak to Emma alone before lunch, but afterwards she declared she would stay indoors with her father. I saw my chance, and having seen to the comfort of my guests outside, I returned to the Abbey. I had resolved to call her out of the room on some pretext so that I could see her for a few minutes alone, for I was growing weary of waiting for such an opportunity to arise. As I walked through the hall, I rehearsed my speech:

Emma, we have known each other a long time. . . .

Emma, I must speak to you. . . .

I cannot stay silent any longer. Emma, I am in love with you. . . .

I shook my head. None of those openings satisfied me, and I decided I would have to trust to the genius of the moment. I opened the door . . . and found that Churchill had arrived.

There he was, the one person in the world to whom I did not wish to offer any hospitality, sitting in my house and talking to my Emma.

I was so displeased that I excused myself as soon as I could, for fear of saying something rude. I found Harriet once more alone, and went over to her, meaning to press Robert Martin's suit, but instead I found myself talking about Churchill.

'What right has he to come so late, and then to inform no one of his arrival?' I said, finding in Harriet a willing listener.

'None,' she said, with a shake of the head.

'He did not even tell the Westons, and poor Mrs Weston has been worrying about him all morning. And then to sit with Emma! What business has he doing that, instead of making himself known to his host?'

'None at all,' she said.

'And Emma sees nothing wrong in it.' I was about to say that I feared his influence on her would not be a good one, when I recollected myself and remembered that I was talking to her friend.

'But tell me, what have you been doing? Have you been enjoying the Abbey grounds?' I asked her, all thoughts of Robert Martin having been driven out of my mind by my own concerns.

As she spoke to me about her delight in the gardens, I found my thoughts returning to Emma, and I knew that I must be careful to guard my tongue. If I said anything more about Frank Churchill, it would look like jealousy – not surprisingly, for it is jealousy. I wish he had never been born.

The party at last broke up. Miss Fairfax had left earlier in the day, in case her grandmother wanted her, and Emma and her father kindly took Miss Bates home in their carriage. Harriet went with them, the Westons soon following. The Eltons stayed as long as possible, with Mrs Elton congratulating me on the fish-ponds, the strawberry-beds, the lime-walk, indeed anything that would allow her to remain a minute longer. At last she had exhausted every possible topic of conversation and was obliged to leave, saying she was looking forward to the morrow.

The morrow! I do not know whether I am looking forward to it or not. It might give me a chance to speak to Emma, but my hopes are dwindling. She seemed very thick with Churchill today. I wish I knew what her feelings were.

I have no wish to see Churchill paying court to her tomorrow, but it will hurt me more if I should stay away, for then I will not see her at all.

But I will not lose heart. The black mare might go lame, or Mrs Churchill might detain him, and then Frank Churchill will not join us at all.

Friday 25 June

I was up at daybreak, and oversaw the start of the clover-cutting before getting ready to go to Box Hill. The day was fine, and we had a good journey. Whether we were tired from yesterday's enjoyments, or languid because of the heat I do not know, but there was a lack of spirits in the party.

I myself was in despair. Churchill spent most of the day with Emma, and I had no chance to speak to her alone. I spent my time with Miss Bates and Miss Fairfax. I was, at least, able to be of assistance in helping Miss Fairfax repel Mrs Elton's overtures.

We strolled about until it was time for our picnic. Then, indeed, there was more liveliness in the party, though I liked it less than I had liked the insipidity of the morning, for Churchill made Emma the object of his attentions. His double-dealing continued when he directed sly glances at Miss Fairfax, however, and I could not think what he was about. Whatever it was, he did not behave like a gentleman.

Emma did not seem to notice anything amiss, and flirted with him in the most painful way; painful to me, as I am in love with her more every day. For, despite her follies and freaks, from which no one of us is immune, she is the only woman for me.

Her flirting grew worse. It was beyond anything I had seen, and I dreaded where Frank Churchill's influence would take her.

He became more and more extravagant in his speech, and if I had not spent the morning with him, and known he had not touched any wine, I should have suspected that he was drunk.

'Ladies and gentlemen,' he said, 'I am ordered by Miss Woodhouse (who, wherever she is, presides) to say, that she desires to know what you are all thinking of.'

Emma smiled at this mixture of flattery and silliness, instead of looking disgusted, as she should have done, and I replied curtly: 'Is Miss Woodhouse sure that she would like to hear what we are all thinking of?'

I looked at her intently, knowing she would not like my thoughts.

'Oh! no, no,' she cried, laughing carelessly. 'Upon no account in the world. It is the very last thing I would stand the brunt of just now. Let me hear anything rather than what you are all thinking of. I will not say quite all. There are one or two, perhaps,' – glancing at Mr Weston and Harriet – 'whose thoughts I might not be afraid of knowing.'

Well might she say so. They never find fault with anything she does, but to have such uncritical friends is not good for anyone.

'It is a sort of thing which *I* should not have thought myself privileged to enquire into,' cried Mrs Elton, not at all pleased with the turn the conversation had taken, though her anger was mostly caused by the fact that she was not the centre of attention.

There was whispering from Frank Churchill, and Emma showed no disgust at his behaviour, as she would have done had anyone else whispered in company. Instead she went on smiling. He then said that Emma – making her the source for all his proclamations – demanded a clever saying from everyone.

'Or two things moderately clever – or three things very dull indeed,' he said extravagantly, 'and she engages to laugh heartily at them all.'

'Oh! very well,' exclaimed good Miss Bates, 'then I need not be uneasy. "Three things very dull indeed." That will just do for me, you know. I shall be sure to say three dull things as soon as ever I open my mouth, shan't I?'

I was just about to say, 'Not at all,' and I saw Mrs Weston about to do the same, when Emma said: 'Ah! ma'am, but there may be a difficulty. Pardon me, but you will be limited as to number – only three at once.'

I could not believe it. Instead of reassuring Miss Bates that her contributions to the conversation were always valued, she insulted her in front of all her friends; worse still, in front of her niece. I felt sick with it. She would never have said such a thing before meeting Frank Churchill!

Miss Bates did not realize what Emma had said, and I was about to divert her attention by offering her another slice of pie when I saw her face change and knew I was too late.

'Ah! well – to be sure. Yes, I see what she means,' she said, turning to me. 'I will try to hold my tongue. I must make myself very disagreeable, or she would not have said such a thing to an old friend.'

I was mortified, yet Emma continued to smile and Weston went on with the conversation as though nothing was wrong. Weston! Who should have shown her what he thought of such conduct by a frown. He then made things worse by offering a conundrum, and one which could not have been more badly chosen.

'What two letters of the alphabet are there, that express perfection?' he asked.

And the answer?

'M and A: Emma!' Weston said. 'Do you understand?'

Emma understood, and was gratified, whilst I was annoyed. Emma, perfect? Emma, who had insulted her oldest friend? Emma, who had flirted shamelessly in front of all her friends?

Emma basked in the praise, though it was ill-deserved, whilst her flatterer, Frank Churchill, laughed and enjoyed it.

'This explains the sort of clever thing that is wanted,' I said without humour, 'but *perfection* should not have come quite so soon.'

It made no difference. Emma was pleased, and so was her court. Mrs Elton, it is true, was not pleased, though if she could have changed her name to Emma, she would have thought it the best conundrum in the world.

She and her husband declared their intention of taking a walk, and Churchill passed a disparaging remark about couples who met at a watering-place. I was astounded at his bad manners. Though I do not believe there is much genuine affection between Elton and his wife, it should not have been remarked on, and in such a way.

Miss Fairfax could stand no more, and said she would take a walk. I did not blame her. I declared my intention of taking a walk as well, and gave her one arm, whilst offering Miss Bates the other.

'Oh, Mr Knightley, how kind of you to walk with us,' said Miss Bates. 'I am not surprised Miss Woodhouse did not enjoy my company – so kind of her to be so forbearing – I rattle on sadly, it must be a trial to her – so good of her to trouble herself to visit me, for I am sure I am always receiving attention from her and her father,' she said, as we set out.

And for the rest of the walk, I had to listen to her apologizing for her tongue, when it should have been Emma who was apologizing for hers.

I did what I could to soothe her, and she grew easier. I was just beginning to regain my composure when Mrs Elton joined us and tried to force Miss Fairfax to take up an appointment with friends of hers. I pity any poor woman who would have to go as a governess to Mrs Smallwood, no matter how near Maple Grove she might be! This objectionable episode put the seal on a most disagreeable day.

My anger had not cooled when I stood next to Emma as we waited for the carriage to take us home again. I told myself I must not reprimand her or criticize her, but I could not help myself. I could not see her being dragged down, when a word from me might stop it.

'Emma, I must once more speak to you as I have been used to do,' I said, in some agitation. Even then, I tried to hold back, but I could not. 'I cannot see you acting wrong, without a remonstrance. How could you be so unfeeling to Miss Bates? How could you be so insolent in your wit to a woman of her character, age, and situation? Emma, I had not thought it possible.'

She blushed, but only laughed.

'Nay, how could I help saying what I did? Nobody could have helped it. It was not so very bad. I dare say she did not understand me.'

'I assure you she did. She felt your full meaning. She has talked of it since. I wish you could have heard how she talked of it – with what candour and generosity. I wish you could have heard her honouring your forbearance, in being able to pay her such attentions, as she was for ever receiving from yourself and your father, when her society must be so irksome.'

'Oh!' she said airily, 'I know there is not a better creature in the world:

but you must allow, that what is good and what is ridiculous are most unfortunately blended in her.'

'They are blended,' I said, 'and were she a woman of fortune, I would leave every harmless absurdity to take its chance – but, Emma, consider how far this is from being the case. She is poor; she has sunk from the comforts she was born to; and, if she live to old age, must probably sink more. Her situation should secure your compassion. It was badly done, indeed!'

She was not interested. She looked away, impatient with me for speaking to her thus. But I had started, and I could not have done until I had finished.

'To laugh at her, humble her – and before her niece, too. This is not pleasant to you, Emma – and it is very far from pleasant to me; but I must, I will, tell you truths while I can, satisfied with proving myself your friend by very faithful counsel, and trusting that you will some time or other do me greater justice than you can do now.'

I handed her into the carriage. She did not even bid me goodbye. She was sullen. Who could blame her? But it could not be helped. I had said what I had to say, and I returned to the Abbey in low spirits.

By and by, the sight of my fields began to restore my sense of calm. The air was sweet with the scent of clover, and the birds were singing. If Emma had been with me, I would have known complete happiness. But she was not, and as I came inside I had to acknowledge that such a thing would never come to pass.

I retired to my room, picked up my quill and gave vent to my feelings. But I cannot forget about Emma. Where is she now? Is she at Hartfield, thinking of Frank Churchill and his easy flattery? She must be. And soon she will be living at Enscombe.

I must go away, at once. I cannot bear to see her with him, to watch her permitting, even encouraging, his attentions. It hurts me too much. She is lost to me. My Emma.

Saturday 26 June

I awoke, firm in my resolve to go away, and settled on London, as it would give me an opportunity to see to some business, and to see John and Isabella.

I could not go without seeing Emma one last time, however, and I walked over to Hartfield. I was out of luck, for Emma was not at home. I meant to be on my way at once, but I sat with Mr Woodhouse, asking him if he had any message to send to Isabella, then telling him I did not know how long I would be away. I still could not bear to go, not without seeing her for one last time.

Harriet arrived, which provided a diversion, and gave me an excuse to remain a while longer.

'I hope I find you well?' I said to her, standing up as she entered the room.

She blushed prettily.

'Very well, I thank you,' she said.

'I have called to see Miss Woodhouse, to tell her I am going to London, but she is out. I would like to speak to her before I go. I cannot stay above five minutes, however,' I said firmly, but my body seemed to move of its own accord and I sat down beside Harriet.

'I should like to go to London,' said Harriet. 'It must be a wonderful place.'

'It is not somewhere I wish to go,' I said. 'I would much rather stay at home.'

She blushed, and I thought again that she must have guessed my secret, and that she knew I did not want to go because I did not want to leave Emma. I was glad of her silent sympathy.

'I hope you will not be away for very long,' she said.

It was kind of her to speak to me as though there was hope for me, but I know I have lost Emma. I will never call her mine. Never take her to the Abbey. Never see her sitting opposite me in the evening. Never go with her to London to visit Isabella and John. Never see her playing with our children, as she plays with her sister's children.

But I had to face it like a man.

I meant to leave, but I could not bring myself to do so. Not without one last glimpse of Emma, and so I continued to talk to Miss Smith.

'Did you enjoy our trip to Box Hill?' I asked her.

'Oh, yes, very much,' she said.

'I am glad,' I said warmly, and so I was: I was glad that at least one person had enjoyed it.

'I was sorry you ate out of doors,' said Mr Woodhouse anxiously. 'Perry did not think it at all wise. I hope you may not take cold.'

She assured him she was quite well.

'You were very ill over the winter,' he said to her.

'You were indeed,' I said kindly, remembering that she had had other ills, besides a cold, to bear.

'It was nothing,' she whispered.

I began to think there was more to her colourings than goodwill towards me and my suit, and I wondered if she might have caught another cold after all, for not only did she seem to colour a great deal, but also to whisper.

'I hope your throat is not sore?' I asked her.

'No, thank you,' she said, and blushed again.

The time passed slowly, but pass it did, and at last Emma returned. I rose as soon as she came in, saying I was going to London, and asking if she had any message to send to her sister. She looked surprised, but I said I had been planning the expedition for some time.

I waited for a word from her, something to give me hope to remain, but there was nothing.

I was a fool to expect it. To think that Emma, with all her advantages of birth and beauty, with a good heart and superior understanding, would sacrifice the attentions of a man who flatters her for the hand of a man who scolds her! If I had ever had a chance of winning her away from Churchill, I had lost it on Box Hill.

She said she had no particular message, and I was about to leave when her father began asking her about her morning call. To my surprise, I learnt that she had been calling on the Bateses, which is why she had been from home.

I am sure she did not go to apologize – it would have been beyond the desire of either party, for Miss Bates would have been as embarrassed as Emma – but this attention would be recognized as an apology, and I felt my heart expand. So Emma had not lost her better nature!

My face must have showed my thoughts, for she smiled at me, a little shyly, and on an impulse I took her hand. I wanted to do more. I wanted to kiss it. I lifted it, scarcely knowing what I was doing, and I was about to press it to my lips when I recollected that I had no right to do such a thing, no matter how much I might want to.

I dropped her hand, then making her a bow, I bade her and her father farewell. I said goodbye to Harriet, and set out for London.

It was a long and dismal journey, filled with gloomy thoughts, but once I reached Brunswick Square, I endeavoured to put my troubles out of my mind.

John and Isabella were surprised to see me, but I gave some pretext relating to business and they accepted it, welcoming me into their home.

I soon saw that the boys had grown since they were with us in the spring. Henry was turning into a fine boy, and John was not far behind. Bella had grown a very little, except in mischief, and George was still content to toddle behind her. The baby was showing an interest in everything, and I sat down with her on my knee.

Henry asked me about *Harriet and the gypsies*, a tale which made Isabella shudder, and John asked me what had been done to make sure the roads were safe. This led to parish business, and we talked of Highbury and Hartfield until it was time to go to bed.

I went upstairs but I could not sleep. I took up my newspaper, but I could not pay attention to it. I was not interested in the world outside, I was interested in my own world, and at the heart of that world was Emma. Emma with her good heart, Emma with her dear face. Emma. My Emma.

Monday 28 June

For the last two days I have been in torment. I have not been like myself. I have been short-tempered and out of spirits. I think I was wrong to come here. Isabella has always reminded me too much of Emma.

And then there are the children. I thought: *If I had known my own feelings last year, and spoken to Emma before she had met Frank Churchill, then she would already be my wife. I could, this very morning, be playing with my son, just as John is playing with his.*

Tuesday 29 June

I determined to rouse myself and I attended to business, but this evening, a restless spirit was on me.

As I sat in the drawing-room, with John reading his newspaper, Isabella sewing, and the children playing around us, I was given a picture of domestic felicity which set my heart aching. I wanted this for myself. I wanted it with Emma. If I had spoken – if I had not scolded her – if I had learnt my feelings sooner – if I had flattered her – if I had behaved as a lover and not a friend – if I had done all of the things I did not do, and none of the.things I did, then perhaps I could have looked forward to the same kind of happiness.

JULY

Thursday 1 July

A letter from Highbury arrived this morning.

'It is from Miss Bates,' said Isabella, recognizing the hand.

I picked up my newspaper and hid my face behind it. I did not want her to see my expression when she read the letter, for I was sure it would contain news of Emma's betrothal.

As she began to read, I could scarcely breathe.

'*Mother well – Jane still in low spirits – new gloves for Mrs Cole – Mrs Churchill dead.*' Isabella stopped short. '*Mrs Churchill dead!*'

I did not know what the information would mean for Emma. Would it delay her marriage, whilst the period of mourning was observed, or speed it, as Mrs Churchill could not put any obstacles in the way?

Isabella was so shocked by the news that, fortunately, she did not notice my silence. She began to read Miss Bates's letter more slowly: '*We were all very shocked to hear it. Poor lady! It seems she was very ill after all. Mr Churchill is better than can be expected – the funeral is to be in Yorkshire. Mother is so shocked! And poor Jane can hardly speak. She has been very ill, I fear. Perry is worried about her. She has a terrible headache—* Poor Jane,' said Isabella, breaking off from reading the letter. 'She is worried about her future, no doubt.'

'No doubt,' I managed to say.

I had recovered myself sufficiently to join in with the conversation, and the subject occupied us for the rest of the day.

Friday 2 July

I could not settle to anything. Emma is to marry Frank Churchill. It is as certain as the sun rising. I live in dread of the letter bearing the news, but a letter has not arrived. Emma will write to Isabella as soon as it is arranged, I am sure. Until then I am in torment. And afterwards. . . ? I dare not think of it.

Saturday 3 July

I had luncheon at my club, with Routledge. As we finished our meal, I found him watching me curiously.

'Well?' he said.

'Well?' I asked.

'Out with it.'

'Out with what?'

'Whatever it is that is bothering you,' he said. 'It must be something important, for you have not listened to a word I have said. You have answered me in an abstracted manner, and nothing you have said has made sense.'

'Nothing is bothering me,' I answered testily.

'You might as well make up your mind to tell me, because I will hound you until you do. I am tired of looking at your long face and hearing your sighs! It is not like you.'

'I do not sigh!' I protested.

'I distinctly heard you as you ate your beef. You sighed.'

I gave a deep sigh – then was angry with myself.

'Hah!' said Routledge. 'There you are! It is as I said! You sighed. Well?'

I could not hide it from him any longer, nor did I wish to, for I needed to unburden myself

'You were right.' I said.

'About?'

'About Emma. Everything you said was true. I am in love with her. I cannot think why I did not see it sooner. I have been blind. She is the very woman for me.'

'At last! I have been waiting for you to see it for months. Well, when are you going to marry her?'

'Never. I have missed my chance. She is going to many Frank Churchill.'

'Is she indeed?' he asked in surprise. 'What busy lives you lead in Surrey! It is only a few months ago that you told me she was going to many Elton. Elton, on the other hand, was going to marry Harriet – in Emma's mind – but instead he went to Bath and came home with Augusta. It is as bad as *A Midsummer Night's Dream*. Are you sure there are no fairies in Highbury, who are making you their sport? It seems very like it. I expect to hear next that Jane Fairfax is about to marry Mr Longridge, or that Miss Bates is engaged to Mr Woodhouse.'

I smiled despite myself.

'That is better,' said Routledge. 'A long face never helped anyone. Come now, tell me, what makes you think Emma is going to marry Churchill?'

'There is an understanding between them. From things she has said – things she has done – I asked her if she knew his mind on a certain subject, and she said she was convinced of it. In short, I thought he seemed to be casting glances at Jane Fairfax, some time ago, but Emma said she was sure of him. It was an intimate matter, one that would not have been spoken of if there had not been an engagement.'

'And so they have announced their betrothal.'

'I am expecting it any day, although it may be delayed as Mrs Churchill has just died.'

'Then, if it is as certain as you say, you had better marry Jane Fairfax instead.'

'I have already thought about it, but I cannot do it.'

'Why not? She is an attractive young woman, well-bred, agreeable and in need of a home.'

'I cannot marry her for those reasons. Befriend her, help her – yes. But marry her? No.'

'Then you had best see to your repairs at the Abbey, for it seems your nephew will inherit it, after all.'

'It seems so.' I remembered that Routledge sometimes saw John, and said: 'You will say nothing of this to John? He does not know that I am in love with Emma. I can stand your rough concern, but if my brother knew, he would tell Isabella, and I cannot stand Isabella's sympathy.'

'I understand. I will say nothing to anyone. You may place your trust in me.'

'Thank you.'

'What do you intend to do now?' he asked me.

'Do? I will do what I have always done. Tend my estate, dine with my friends, play whist, look after the parish, and visit my brother.'

'At least you will not have to see Emma, once she is married,' said Routledge. 'She will remove to Yorkshire, and not be reminding you of what you have lost.'

'Small comfort,' I said. 'I do not know which is harder to bear, the thought of seeing Emma as the wife of another man, or the thought of never seeing her at all. I cannot imagine a life without her. What will it be like to go to Hartfield and find that she is not there? To dine with the Westons and see that her chair is empty? To go to church and see that she is not in her pew? To walk round Highbury with never a chance of meeting her?'

'You will adjust,' he said.

'I suppose so,' I said, but I did not believe it.

I was in low spirits when I returned to Brunswick Square. The boys wanted to play, but I put them off, saying: 'Not now. I am tired.'

I returned to my room and took up my quill. And now here I am, dreading another sleepless night and another empty day.

Monday 5 July

No letter again today. Perhaps, out of respect to Mrs Churchill, they do not feel they can announce their engagement at once. But surely Emma would tell her sister?

Tuesday 6 July

The letter came, but what a letter! It was not from Emma, nor Miss Bates, but from Weston. My spirits sank when I saw it. It seemed that Emma's letter must have been lost, and Weston was now writing of the news. How he had always longed for Emma as a daughter, and now he would have her!

But when I began to read the letter, I discovered it contained nothing but parish business – until I reached the end. I was so astonished that I cried out, and Isabella and John looked at me in surprise.

'Frank Churchill is engaged – to Jane Fairfax!' I said.

I thought at once of Emma. What would she be feeling? She must be desolate. She had been led on by him and deceived by him. I had suspected – I do not know quite what I had suspected, except that his behaviour had not rung true to me. And now the reason was revealed, because whilst he had been flirting with Emma, he had been paying court to Jane Fairfax.

I could scarcely believe it. I read on, and was more and more astounded. There had been a secret engagement between them, entered into in the autumn, at Weymouth, and hidden from everyone all the long months since.

And so he had been engaged when he had first come to Highbury! He had been engaged when he had danced with Emma. Engaged when he had flirted outrageously with her. Engaged when he had led everyone to believe he was on the point of making a proposal to her. Engaged . . . to Jane Fairfax!

'I cannot believe it,' I said. 'A secret betrothal . . . Jane Fairfax . . . I cannot believe she would be a party to such a thing.'

'No wonder she has been ill,' said Isabella.

'No wonder, indeed. To have to keep such a thing secret!' said John.

And to have to stand by and watch her betrothed pay attention to another woman, I thought. *He is even worse than I painted him.*

Whilst John and Isabella talked over the news, my thoughts returned to Emma. She must be heartbroken. She could not even turn to her usual confidante, Mrs Weston, because Mrs Weston was too closely involved.

'I must go to her!' I said with decision, correcting myself as I saw Isabella's startled expression. '—to Highbury.'

John looked at me curiously.

'But we thought you were to stay for another week,' said Isabella.

'There is business for me to attend to – parish business,' I said, folding my letter. 'Weston writes to me of it.'

I told them how much I had enjoyed my visit, and resisted Isabella's entreaties to stay. I took my leave of the children, thanked John and Isabella, and was on my way.

I rode out of London thinking of nothing but Emma, my poor, heart-broken Emma. I scarcely noticed the rain. My horse was fresh, and I made good time. As I approached Highbury, the wind dropped to a gentle breeze, the clouds cleared and the sun came out.

I arrived at Hartfield. Emma was not in the house, but Mr Woodhouse was there with Perry. I gave him greetings from Isabella, then asked him: 'Where is Emma?'

'She is walking in the garden.'

I went outside to look for her, and I saw her walking along the path. Her shoulders were drooping and her head was down. My heart cried out in sympathy. For her to be so deceived! And by such a useless young man! He had come among us, simpering and smiling and flirting, whilst all the time his affections and his hand were engaged. The monstrosity of it! I had thought him a worthless fribble, but I had not thought badly enough of him. There could be no mistake; no misunderstanding. He had used her; deceived her.

She arranged her face as she looked up and saw me. Brave girl! She would not let me see how unhappy she was.

'Mr Knightley! I did not think to see you here. I thought you were still in London.'

'I finished my business early, and I decided to return to the Abbey,' I said, looking down into her eyes with compassion.

'You must have had a wet ride.'

'Yes,' I said.

'And how is everyone in London?' she asked, without any of her usual animation.

'They are all well, and send you their best wishes. Your sister begs me to tell you that baby Emma is starting to look just like you. She has your features, and the same shape of face.'

'And will lose them, no doubt, before she is very much older!' she said.

'Perhaps.'

'And how are the boys, and little Bella?'

'They are well, all well. The boys are continuing their riding-lessons, and Bella is begging to be allowed to learn, but her mother thinks she is too young. George is growing into a fine boy. I believe we might see them here soon before long.'

And that will help to soothe you, I thought, in your suffering.

I watched her as we walked through the shrubbery, and I thought how sad she looked. I said nothing, not knowing what to say. I did not want to raise the subject of Frank Churchill in case she did not feel equal to talking about him, but I wanted her to know that she could talk to me if she needed to unburden herself of her cares. And so I said nothing, hoping my silent company would be comforting for her.

She seemed about to speak, then checked. She began again. With a small, sad smile, she said: 'You have some news to hear, now you are come back, that will rather surprise you.'

'Have I?' I asked, looking at her. 'Of what nature?'

'Oh! the best nature in the world – a wedding,' she said brightly.

I waited for her to say more, but she could not speak. Her heart was full, and it was made worse by the fact that Frank Churchill was the son of her good friends the Westons.

'If you mean Miss Fairfax and Frank Churchill, I have heard that already,' I said, wanting to spare her the pain of giving me the details.

'How is it possible?' she cried in surprise.

'I had a few lines on parish business from Weston this morning, and at the end of them he gave me a brief account of what had happened.'

She appeared relieved, as though she had expected my correspondent to be someone different. But who, and why it should trouble her, I did not know. But what did it matter who my correspondent had been? I had no time to puzzle over it. She was out of spirits, and she needed my friendship.

After a time she said, in a calmer manner: '*You* probably have been less surprised than any of us, for you have had your suspicions. I have not forgotten that you once tried to give me a caution. I wish I had attended to it, but I seem to have been doomed to blindness.'

Her voice fell so much it cut me to the quick. I said nothing, but I took her arm and drew it through mine to comfort her.

'Time, my dearest Emma, time will heal the wound. Your own excellent sense; your exertions for your father's sake; I know you will not allow yourself—' *to sink beneath this burden*, I wanted to say, but I could not finish my sentence. I found my voice becoming choked and I could not trust myself to speak. When I had recovered I went on firmly, assuring her of my warmest friendship, and telling her of the indignation I felt on her behalf, because of the behaviour of that abominable scoundrel.

'He will soon be gone,' I continued. 'They will soon be in Yorkshire.'

'You are very kind, but you are mistaken,' said Emma. She stopped walking. 'I must set you right. I am not in want of that sort of compassion. My blindness to what was going on, led me to act by them in a way that I must always be ashamed of, and I was very foolishly tempted to say and do many things which may well lay me open to unpleasant conjectures, but I have no other reason to regret that I was not in the secret earlier.'

'Emma!' I cried, looking eagerly at her, as my hopes began to soar. She was not in love with Frank Churchill! She had not been wounded by him! Then there was hope for me yet!

A moment's reflection showed me the truth. She was being brave; pretending it did not signify; when it must have hurt her cruelly.

But I was pleased that she could say so much. It showed she had not felt it as deeply as I feared, and in time, with her friends around her to lift her spirits, I was persuaded she would recover.

'I understand you – forgive me – I am pleased that you can say even so much. He is no object of regret, indeed! and it will not be very long, I hope, before that becomes the acknowledgement of more than your reason. He is a disgrace to the name of man.'

I was astonished, then, a moment later, when she said: 'Mr Knightley, I am in a very extraordinary situation. I cannot let you continue in your error; and yet, perhaps, since my manners gave such an impression, I have as much reason to be ashamed of confessing that I never have been at all attached to the person we are speaking of, as it might be natural for a woman to feel in confessing exactly the reverse. But I never have.'

I did not know what to think. Was she serious? Or just bearing up under her misfortune? Had she ever been in love with him, or not? I thought of everything I had seen between them. I had never been sure. Her spirits had always been lively, and what I had taken for romantic flirtation might have been nothing but high spirits. I did not know what to think, much less what to say. But I did not need to speak. She went on, telling me that she had been pleased by his attentions because he was the son of Mr Weston; because he was continually in Highbury; because she found him very pleasant; and, she admitted, in a way no other woman would have admitted it, because her vanity was flattered.

'He has imposed on me, but he has not injured me,' she said.

I felt a rush of relief. Emma, my Emma was not hurt; not wounded, not injured. She was cheerful still.

I felt my own cheerfulness return. In fact, I was so much in charity with the world that I could even find it in my heart to be charitable to Frank Churchill.

'Perhaps he may yet turn out well,' I said. 'With such a woman he has a chance. I have no motive for wishing him ill – and for her sake, whose happiness will be involved in his good character and conduct, I shall certainly wish him well.'

'I have no doubt of their being happy together,' said Emma, as we walked on. 'I believe them to be very mutually and very sincerely attached.'

Lucky, lucky man to have the love of the woman he loved!

'He is a most fortunate man!' I burst out. 'Every thing turns out for his good. He meets with a young woman at a watering-place, gains her affection, cannot even weary her by negligent treatment – and had he and all his family sought round the world for a perfect wife for him, they could not have found her superior. His aunt is in the way. His aunt dies. He has only to speak. His friends are eager to promote his happiness. He has used everybody ill – and they are all delighted to forgive him. He is a fortunate man indeed!'

Emma said: 'You speak as if you envied him.'

'And I do envy him, Emma,' I said. 'In one respect he is the object of my envy.'

Because he had won the woman he loved.

She said nothing. I was afraid I had gone too far. If I spoke of my feelings for her, would I lose her friendship? We could never go back to the comfortable ease we had had before. Could I really bear to lose that?

She seemed about to speak, but I had to say something before I lost my courage; before I decided I had too much to lose and could not take the risk.

'You will not ask me what is the point of envy,' I said. 'You are determined, I see, to have no curiosity. You are wise – but *I* cannot be wise. Emma, I must tell what you will not ask, though I may wish it unsaid the next moment.'

'Oh! then, do not speak it, do not speak it,' she eagerly cried. 'Take a little time, consider, do not commit yourself.'

'Thank you,' I said, mortified that my attentions were so unwelcome to her. But how could they not be? I was so much older than she, and I had never flattered her as a lover ought. I had scolded her and berated her. I was the last man in the world she would wish to marry. And so, generous girl that she was, she sought to spare me the pain of being refused.

We walked on in silence. We reached the house.

'You are going in, I suppose,' I said.

And so it ended. My hope of marrying her.

She hesitated, and then she surprised me by saying: 'No. I should like to take another turn. Mr Perry is not gone.'

We walked on. I felt her preparing herself to say something she found difficult.

She is going to tell me she knows of my feelings, and she is going to put paid to them once and for all, I thought.

'Mr Knightley, I stopped you just now, and I am afraid, gave you pain,' she said. 'But if you have any wish to speak openly to me as a friend, or to ask my opinion of any thing that you may have in contemplation – as a friend, indeed, you may command me. I will hear whatever you like. I will tell you exactly what I think.'

'As a *friend!*' I said, and my heart quailed. But I could not say nothing now that I had a chance to speak to her. Perhaps I could convince her that I could change; that I could stop scolding her; that I could become a man she would be proud to marry. 'Emma, *that* I fear is a word—' I began, but stopped. I could not say I was not her friend, because I was. But I wanted to be so much more. I resolved to be silent; not to jeopardize what I had. But I could not. 'I have gone too far already for concealment. Emma, I accept your offer, extraordinary as it may seem, I accept it, and refer myself to you as a friend. Tell me, then, have I no chance of ever succeeding?'

I turned to look at her, and my love for her was in my eyes.

'My dearest Emma,' I went on, for I could no longer conceal my thoughts, 'for dearest you will always be, whatever the event of this hour's conversation, my dearest, most beloved Emma – tell me at once. Say "No", if it is to be said.' She said nothing. It was not as bad as I feared. She had not irrevocably decided against me. She was uncertain. There was room for hope. 'You are silent, absolutely silent! at present I ask no more.'

Still she said nothing. I dare not hope. I dare not fear. I dare do nothing. I dare not move, for fear of breaking the spell. And yet I had to go on.

'I cannot make speeches, Emma,' I said at last. 'If I loved you less, I might be able to talk about it more. But you know what I am. You hear nothing but truth from me. I have blamed you, and lectured you, and you have borne it as no other woman in England would have borne it. Bear with the truths I would tell you now, dearest Emma, as well as you have borne with them. The manner, perhaps, may have as little to recommend them. God knows, I have been a very indifferent lover. But you understand me. Yes, you see, you understand my feelings – and will return them if you can. At present, I ask only to hear, once to hear your voice.'

'Mr Knightley, I am flattered – honoured by your proposal,' she said, looking up at me with such eyes that with a surge of feeling I knew I had her heart. I could not speak; I could do nothing but look at her, as she could do nothing but look at me. 'I never knew, never expected . . .' she said.

'That I loved you? I scarcely knew it myself. It has crept up on me so slowly, so gradually, that I was in love with you before I knew it. Then I could not speak. You seemed so enamoured of Frank Churchill. My motives for disliking him were not wholly for his rash behaviour. They were also because you seemed to favour him. I could perhaps have borne it if I had lost you to a worthy man – but no, I do not believe I could. I could not have borne to lose you to anyone, dearest Emma, so tell me, put me out of my misery, have I your heart?'

'Yes, you have,' she said.

'And will you be my wife?'

'Yes, I will.'

I could think of nothing to say. No words could express my emotion. And so I kissed her.

At last, unwillingly, I let her go.

She had a flush on her cheeks and looked more beautiful than I had ever seen her.

'And did you come here, then, to propose to me?' she asked at last.

'No, indeed. I came to be of service to you, to lift your spirits. I thought no further than that. But when I learnt that you did not love Churchill, that you had never loved him, then I hoped – but you would not let me speak. You bade me be silent. I thought it was because you were afraid I would declare myself. I did not know it was from modesty. I almost said nothing. I could not bear to lose your friendship, and I thought I might. I thought that, if I told you how I felt, and you could not return my feelings, then our ease and companionship would be over for ever, that there would be a constraint with which it would not be possible to do away.'

'But you spoke, none the less.'

'I did.' I stopped and faced her. 'I had lost you once by saying nothing, or so I thought. I could not bear to lose you through my own reticence again.'

'That must have taken courage,' she said.

'Not courage. Love.'

She squeezed my arm, and we walked on companionably together until we reached the house. We went in, and sat down to tea. I could not take my eyes from Emma. She was radiant, and I had never been so happy.

But seeing Mr Woodhouse, I was brought up against the problems we would face when she wished to marry. He was such an enemy of the state in general, because it brought upheaval in its wake, that he had still not recovered from Miss Taylor's marriage; indeed he had still not stopped calling her 'poor Miss Taylor'.

I knew that Emma's marriage must strike him a harder blow, because it was closer to him. But I knew that, whatever problems we faced, we would overcome them.

He was ignorant of our plans, however, and therefore undisturbed. He told us of Perry's visit, saying that Perry agreed with him on the matter of diet, and that he would take a little less meat from now on. He told us of Mrs Bates's cold, which news had been brought by Perry, and of Mrs Elton's headache. He told us of Churchill's latest letter to Mrs Weston, at which Emma and I exchanged glances, and of Miss Fairfax's miraculous recovery.

'For it was not a cold at all, but worry, brought on by concealment,' said Mr Woodhouse. 'It is a very bad business. Marriage is always a very sad business. I said as much to Perry, and he agreed with me. It is forever making people ill.'

Emma and I said nothing, but drank our tea.

At last I had to leave. It was too soon for me, but to stay any longer, even for an old friend such as I, would have seemed strange, and Mr Woodhouse would have noticed it. And so I bade them goodnight, and returned to the Abbey.

I wandered round the rooms, too happy for sleep. Here I would bring Emma. Here we would live together. Here she would be my wife.

At last I went upstairs, and retired to my room. It seemed familiar and yet different. The last time I slept here, I had no notions of such a happy conclusion to all my worries! I thought Emma was about to marry else-where. And now she is to marry me!

As I thought of everything that had happened, I knew myself to be the happiest of men.

Wednesday 7 July

I returned to Hartfield first thing this morning and Emma and I took a walk in the grounds.

'I hope it is not too damp underfoot,' said Mr Woodhouse anxiously, as we set out.

'Not at all,' I said. 'It is particularly dry.'

'Do not forget your shawl,' he said to Emma.

She took it, though the morning was fine and she did not need it.

At last we were alone.

'I never thought, when I set out for my walk yesterday, that so much would happen,' she said.

'Nor I. I thought you were hopelessly in love with Frank Churchill.'

'When I had just discovered I was hopelessly in love with you.'

'What brought it on? What made you realize it? Was it when you heard me speak?'

'I—' She hesitated, then said: 'I scarcely know.'

There was something, I felt sure, some incident that had told her her heart. But I was too happy to press her, and my feelings overflowed.

'I was luckier,' I said. 'I had had time to come to understand my feelings, even if I did not dare hope they would be returned.'

We went indoors, and I took my leave. I returned to the Abbey to attend to my business. But I could not stay away long, and when I visited Hartfield again this afternoon, I found that Emma had had a letter, written to Mrs Weston but passed on for her perusal, from Frank Churchill.

She wanted me to read it, but as it was long I said I would take it with me when I left. This would not do for Emma. She expected Mrs Weston this evening, and wanted my opinion before then.

I read it; it was a trifling letter, as I expected. It was very bad, but it could have been worse. Once I knew Emma was out of danger from him, however, I cared little for his behaviour, except for a charitable wish that Miss Fairfax could have found a better man.

All was explained. When he had gone to London for a day, earlier in the year, it had not been for a haircut, it had been so that he could purchase a pianoforte for Miss Fairfax. His attentions to Emma had been an effort to disguise his feelings for Miss Fairfax. He admitted that he had behaved shamefully; that he had resented Mrs Elton, and her officious desire to find Miss Fairfax a position as a governess. He explained that he had had an argument with Miss Fairfax on the day of the strawberry-picking, and that he had been grief-stricken when she had broken off the engagement because of his behaviour towards Emma. And he wrote of his decision to throw himself on the mercy of his uncle after the death of his aunt, and that his uncle had approved the union, and that he was now reconciled to Miss Fairfax.

'You do not appear so well satisfied with his letter as I am,' she said, when I had finished it; and, indeed, my comments had not been, for the most part, favourable. 'But still you must, at least I hope you must, think the better of him for it. I hope it does him some service with you.'

'Yes, certainly it does. He has had great faults, faults of inconsideration and thoughtlessness; and I am very much of his opinion in thinking him likely to be happier than he deserves: but still as he is, beyond a doubt, really attached to Miss Fairfax, and will soon, it may be hoped, have the advantage of being constantly with her, I am very ready to believe his character will improve, and acquire from hers, the steadiness and delicacy of principle that it wants. And now, let me talk to you of something else,' I said, having wasted enough time on Frank Churchill. 'I have another person's interest at present so much at heart, that I cannot think any longer about Frank Churchill. Ever since I left you this morning, Emma, my mind has been hard at work on one subject: how I am to marry you, without attacking the happiness of your father.'

'I have thought of little else,' Emma confessed. 'I can never leave him; on that I am resolved.'

'He could come and live with us at the Abbey,' I suggested.

'I have considered this, too,' said Emma, 'but he will never consent to leaving Hartfield. And even if he did, his constitution is not strong. The shock would very probably make him ill, or worse.'

'Now that I have won you, I cannot give you up,' I said. 'I have another suggestion to make, which is that I should come to live at Hartfield.'

'What! Give up the Abbey?' she asked.

'No. I would not give it up. I would go there every day to attend to business, but I would not live there.'

I saw her smile. 'You would do this for me?' she asked.

'I venture to say I would do anything within my power for you,' I replied.

'And you would not mind living with my father? His foibles are sometimes a trial to you.'

'They are nothing, compared to the happiness I would receive from being with you,' I replied.

'You must have time to think of it more fully,' she said, but I could tell she spoke only in deference to my feelings, and not to hers: the idea appealed to her as it much as it appealed to me.

'I have thought of it as much as I need to. I have spent the morning walking away from William Larkins, in order to have my thoughts to myself.'

'Ah! There is some difficulty unprovided for,' said Emma. 'William Larkins will not like it. You must get his consent before you ask mine.'

I laughed. 'I am sure William Larkins will be overjoyed. He will have his old master back, instead of a man who is distracted.'

'Then I will think about it,' she promised me, and I am confident she will agree.

Thursday 8 July

When I returned to Hartfield this morning, I found that Emma wanted me to move to Hartfield as much as I want it myself. It is the best solution to our present difficulties. Emma and I can be together, and Mr Woodhouse will not be alone.

Whilst I was there, Mrs Goddard called, and as we all took tea together, she broached the subject of Harriet.

'Such a toothache, poor girl!' said Mrs Goddard.

Mr Woodhouse was all solicitousness.

'She must see Perry at once.'

'Would it not be better for her to see a dentist, Papa?' asked Emma.

'You are quite right, my dear, as you always are, but there is no one I would trust near by,' he said anxiously.

'We must send her to London, to see Isabella's dentist. I am sure Isabella will be glad to have her for a few days. Harriet was so good with the children when they were with us,' said Emma.

'Indeed she was,' he said much struck.

I caught Emma's eye, and she coloured slightly: she was feeling guilty for encouraging her friend to think of Elton, and wished to give her some fun to make amends, I could tell, for once the trip to the dentist was over there would be trips to the London amusements. The delights of the shops and the entertainments would be there for Harriet to enjoy.

It was arranged that Emma would write to Isabella, and that Mrs Goddard would arrange the affair with Harriet. Mrs Goddard went away full of the news, and if her own excitement was anything to judge by, I thought Harriet would be very well pleased.

After tea, Emma and I took a walk around the gardens.

'I will go to your father this evening and ask him for your hand,' I said.

'No! I must be the one to tell him,' she said. 'It will be easier for him if it comes from me.'

'Very well, if you are sure.'

'I am.'

'Perhaps you are right. If you speak to him whilst I am still here, then I can add my reassurances to yours when the news has been broken.'

'No,' she said, 'I cannot tell him just yet. He is very nervous about Mrs Weston. It is only a fortnight now until her time, and I will not add any more anxieties to his present store. He does not need to know about our engagement yet. It will only cause him needless worry.'

I was impatient to reveal my happiness to the world, but at last I agreed.

Thursday 22 July

Mrs Weston has had a daughter! I could not be happier for her! She and her little girl are doing well, and Weston is beside himself with joy.

'She is the most beautiful baby in the world,' said Emma, when she had seen the infant. 'She looks just like Mrs Weston.'

I remarked that, with such parents, the baby would be indulged, and Emma cried mischievously: 'At that rate, what will become of her?'

'Nothing very bad,' I said with a smile. 'She will be disagreeable in infancy, and correct herself as she grows older. I am losing all my bitterness against spoilt children, my dearest Emma. I, who am owing all my happiness to *you*, would it not be horrible ingratitude in me to be severe on them?'

She laughed, and said that she had had me to correct her. But I could not let this pass.

'My interference was quite as likely to do harm as good. How often, when you were a girl, have you said to me, with one of your saucy looks – "Mr Knightley, I am going to do so and so; Papa says I may" – something of which, you knew, I did not approve.'

'What an amiable creature I was! No wonder you should hold my speeches in such affectionate remembrance.'

' "Mr Knightley". You always called me "Mr Knightley", and, from habit, it has not so very formal a sound. And yet it is formal. I want you to call me something else, but I do not know what.'

'I remember once calling you "George", in one of my amiable fits, about ten years ago. I did it because I thought it would offend you; but, as you made no objection, I never did it again.'

'And cannot you call me "George" now?'

'Impossible! I never can call you any thing but "Mr Knightley". I will not promise even to equal the elegant terseness of Mrs Elton, by calling you Mr K. But I will promise,' she added presently, laughing and blushing, 'I will promise to call you once by your Christian name. I do not say when, but perhaps you may guess where – in the building in which N. takes M. for better, for worse.'

I am looking forward to that day. I can think of no greater happiness than having Emma as my wife.

Friday 23 July

Isabella has invited Harriet to stay on for another two weeks, so that she and John can bring her back to Highbury in their carriage when they visit us in August. I am glad. It means I will have Emma to myself, without her friend always being by.

Monday 26 July

I wrote to John of our engagement today. It will be a loss to his boys, there is no doubt about it. Little Henry will soon be replaced in his position of heir to Donwell Abbey, God willing. But John has always urged me to marry, and I do not think he will be displeased.

Tuesday 27 July

I have had a letter from John, congratulating me on my engagement. I showed it to Emma. It was brief, and wished me well.

Emma and I spoke again about when to tell her father the news. 'I have resolved to do it this afternoon,' she said.

'Do you want me with you?'

'No, I will do it better alone. Then, upon your arrival, you can add your assurances that it will be for the good of all.'

'Very well. What time do you want me to call?'

'At four o'clock. I will have tea with Papa first, then tell him the news, and then I rely on you to add your cheer.'

And so we agreed.

I arrived punctually at four o'clock, and found Mr Woodhouse in a state of misery.

'Ah, Mr Knightley, this is a sorry affair,' he said, on greeting me.

Not many men can have been met with these words when they announced their engagement!

'What! A sorry affair! To have Mr Knightley always with us!' said Emma rousingly. 'Someone to write your letters, and attend to business, and give us diversion when we are low in spirits!'

'That is very true,' he admitted.

'I count myself a lucky man to have won the hand of such a sweet, beautiful woman, for you know there is no one better than Emma in all the world,' I said.

'Yes, that is so,' he remarked, much struck. 'No man ever had a better daughter, unless it was Isabella, who was so happy, here at Hartfield before she married. Poor Isabella!' he said, shaking his head. 'Marriage is a dreadful thing.'

'But not this one, Papa. This one will not be taking me anywhere,' said Emma. 'I will still live at Hartfield. And I will have Mr Knightley here as well, as you will, Papa. It is quite a different matter from Isabella's marriage.'

He was at last brought round. He reminisced about Emma, and praised her many perfections.

I was not exasperated, as I used to be, when he spoke of them. Instead, I agreed with every one.

And so, slowly, he became accustomed to the idea.

To the idea, but not the fact. *That* will take some time to accomplish. But at least we have made a start.

Wednesday 28 July

Weston called on me at the Abbey this morning, to offer his congratulations.

'Mrs Weston and I could not be more delighted!' he said. 'It is a wonder it did not occur to us before. It is the most suitable thing. Who else would have agreed to move to Hartfield? Who else would have been so understanding of Mr Woodhouse? It is one of the things that concerned Anne and me, when we hoped Emma would marry Frank. Emma would have had to go to live in Yorkshire, and that would have been a sad thing indeed. But everything has turned out for the best, as I knew it would. We are not to lose Emma, and Anne and I are still to gain a beautiful daughter-in-law in Jane Fairfax. Two daughters in one year! I am truly blessed.'

'And how is Anna?' I asked.

'Thriving. The joy of having a baby daughter! I hope you will soon know the same joy, Knightley. Anna is someone to brighten our lives, and to keep us lively as we grow old. I could not have wished for anything better. To think, I have a son and a daughter! And at my time of life! I am the most fortunate of men.'

'I think you will have to fight me for that honour!' I said.

'Will you join us for dinner tomorrow night?' he asked. 'Emma and her father are invited. Mrs Weston feels she may be of some assistance in reconciling Mr Woodhouse to the marriage.'

'Thank you, yes,' I said. 'I will be there.'

Thursday 29 July

We dined at Randalls this evening, and Mrs Weston was as great a help as she had meant to be.

'This is very good news,' she said cheerfully to Mr Woodhouse. 'Mr Knightley is just the person to take care of Emma, and of you. He is always so kind and considerate, and we all love him so dearly. It could not be a better arrangement.'

'Ah, poor Miss Taylor, it would be so much better if you had never married. You always liked living at Hartfield with us,' he said.

This was not encouraging, but she persevered.

'But if I had never married Mr Weston, I would never have had Anna,' she said, smiling at the baby on her knee. 'You know you love her. See, she loves you too, for she is smiling at you.'

I could not see the smile, but Mrs Weston and Emma were certain it was there. Mr Woodhouse was very happy to believe it, and his cries of 'Poor Miss Taylor!' and 'Poor Emma!' soon subsided, to be replaced by cries of: 'She is a pretty little thing.'

'And she will have soon outgrown her first set of caps,' Mrs Weston said.

'I will have to make her some more,' said Emma.

And so the evening passed, and by the end of it, I felt we had worn away the worst of Mr Woodhouse's resistance.

AUGUST

Monday 2 August

Robert Martin called to say he was going to town on business, and he asked if there was anything he could do for me whilst there. I asked him to take charge of some papers for John, which he took very readily.

Thursday 5 August

I was surprised to find Robert Martin at my door as soon as I had breakfasted this morning, but when I saw his face, I guessed what he would say.

He had delivered the papers to John, and had then been invited to join John's party to Astley's in the evening. He had accepted the invitation, and had gone with John, Isabella, Henry, little John – and Harriet.

'There was quite a crush, and on quitting our box at Astley's, Mr John Knightley took charge of his wife and younger boy, whilst I followed with Harriet and Henry. Harriet was uneasy. I gave her my arm, and steered her safely through the crowd,' he told me.

By his recital of this small incident, I could guess what was coming, but I did not interrupt him. I was only too pleased to see him happy.

'Your brother asked me to dine with them the next day,' he went on. 'Very kind of him it was, and I accepted his invitation. In the course of the visit I had a chance of speaking to Harriet. I asked her to be my wife, Mr Knightley,' he told me, with a smile spreading across his face, 'and she said yes.'

I was delighted, and told him so, but I was pensive as I walked to Hartfield, not knowing how Emma would react to the news. I greeted her warmly, and then said: 'I have something to tell you, Emma; some news.'

'Good or bad?' she asked.

'I do not know which it ought to be called.'

For myself, I knew; and for Harriet and Mr Martin; but for Emma? I did not know how she would regard it. I said as much, and then said: 'It concerns Harriet Smith.'

She flushed, but said nothing.

'Harriet Smith prepares to marry Robert Martin. I have it from Robert Martin himself. He told me not half an hour ago.'

I thought she did not like it, and I said as much, but she replied: 'You mistake me. I never was more surprised – but it does not make me unhappy, I assure you. How – how has it been possible?'

I told her everything, and she made no reply.

'Emma, my love, I know you think of his situation as an evil; but you must consider it as what satisfies your friend; and I will answer for your thinking better and better of him as you know him more. His good sense and good principles would delight you. As far as the man is concerned, you could not wish your friend in better hands.'

I was relieved to learn that she had been silent only from surprise.

'You need not be at any pains to reconcile me to the match. I think Harriet is doing extremely well. *Her* connections may be worse than *his*. I have been silent from surprise merely, excessive surprise. You cannot imagine how suddenly it has come on me! how peculiarly unprepared I was! for I had reason to believe her very lately more determined against him, much more, than she was before.'

'You ought to know your friend best,' I said, 'but I should say she was a good-tempered, soft-hearted girl, not likely to be very, very determined against any young man who told her he loved her.'

It is a happy conclusion to the affair, and Emma sees it quite as well as I do.

As Emma and I walked in the garden at Hartfield this morning we were talking of Harriet again, and Emma laughed, saying: 'Only Harriet could be in love thrice in one year.'

'Thrice?' I asked. 'Mr Elton and Mr Martin are but two men.'

She coloured, but then said saucily: 'I see I must tell you all. I am very much afraid that, until recently, Harriet was in love with you.'

'*Me?*' I asked, astonished.

'You need not be so surprised. You are a very easy man to fall in love with. I have managed it myself without any difficulty.'

I smiled and pulled her hand through my arm.

'But Harriet . . . I cannot believe it. I gave her no encouragement. I barely spoke to her!' I said.

'You saved her from humiliation when you asked her to dance, and you singled her out at the Abbey, asking her if her affections were engaged.'

'The first was an act of charity, the second – she did not think I was asking if she was attached to me?'

'Yes, she did.'

'But I was thinking of Robert Martin! I wanted to know if she was still in love with him.'

'So I hoped, but she was adamant that nothing had been further from your mind – or hers. And then you sat with her at Hartfield just before you went to London, the day after Box Hill. She distinctly remembered you saying you could not stay for five minutes, but then you stayed with her for half an hour.'

'That is because I was waiting for you.'

'So I hoped—'

'You hoped?'

'When Harriet told me she was in love with you, and she was sure her feelings were returned – that is when I knew I loved you. I told her she must be mistaken, but she gave so many proofs of your affection, I thought it must be true. I was thinking of it as I walked in the garden when you returned from London, and it was at the forefront of my mind as you said you had something to tell me.'

'You thought . . .' I began in surprise. 'You cannot mean to say that you thought I was about to talk of Harriet?'

'Yes. I thought you were about to tell me that you were in love with her.'

'So that is why you looked so sad.'

'I thought I had lost you. I had spent so long meddling with other people's hearts, I had neglected my own.'

'So when I spoke, and you tried to silence me. . . .'

'. . . it was because I could not bear to hear you say that you intended to marry Harriet. But I realized that, as a friend, I could not refuse to listen, and so I said you might speak. And then you said that you loved *me*.'

'Oh, Emma,' I said.

Words failed me, and so I abandoned them, and kissed her. It felt so right that I kissed her again. And then again.

Tuesday 10 August

John has arrived from London with his family, and Harriet has returned with them. When I called on Emma this afternoon, she had spoken to her friend, and after a little awkwardness on each side, they had congratulated each other with a warm and sincere affection.

Emma has invited Robert Martin to call on her, and I am sure he will be happy to accept the invitation.

Thursday 12 August

Robert Martin called at Hartfield today, and Emma was delighted to meet him. Harriet was as happy as it is possible for a woman to be, and Robert's happiness, I do believe, approached my own.

Harriet's father has been discovered at last. Mrs Goddard revealed his name to Mr Martin, and Harriet now knows she is the natural daughter of a tradesman. Robert Martin has applied to him, and he has given his consent to the marriage.

Autumn will be a season of weddings!

SEPTEMBER

Friday 10 September

Emma and I have decided to marry whilst Isabella and John are still here. It will allow Emma and me to go to the seaside for a fortnight after the wedding, and we will not have to worry about leaving Mr Woodhouse alone. As Harriet is marrying in a few weeks' time, and Churchill is marrying in November, we have settled on October. John and Isabella approve the plan; so do the Westons. But we still have to get Mr Woodhouse's consent.

Emma said, this evening: 'Papa, Mr Knightley and I have decided to marry in October. Then you can have a quiet fortnight with Isabella and John and all the dear little children whilst we are away.'

'October!' said he, looking stricken. 'But that is next month.'

'That is a good thing, Papa,' said Isabella, 'as it means you will have Mr Knightley's company all the sooner.'

'But we already have his company. He walks over from the Abbey to see us every day. You had much better not get married, Emma. It will be better if we stay as we are.'

He was so troubled that I despaired of ever seeing my wedding-day.

'I cannot marry if it will cause him so much pain,' said Emma, when he had retired for the night.

'He will accept it as soon as it is a settled thing,' said John. 'It is only this indecision that makes him anxious. Tell him the date; go ahead with your plan; and he will accustom himself to it. That is how Isabella and I managed.'

But Emma is unhappy, and I hate to see her so.

Monday 13 September

Isabella again tried to reconcile her father to our marriage.

'I will be very pleased to see Emma so well settled,' she said.

'Poor Emma!' said her father, with a heavy sigh.

Isabella did not give up, but her father was not any more sanguine as she continued to talk of the marriage. He did not oppose it; indeed he talked about it as though it was a settled thing; but in such a drooping tone of voice that Emma said to me, after dinner, that she thought we should abandon the plan, at least for the moment.

I rallied her spirits, but she could not proceed. She took no interest in the arrangements, and said at last that, if it was going to make her father so unhappy, she could not do it.

I talked to John and Isabella. John felt we should go ahead, and that when it was done, we would hear no more sighs; and Isabella said she wanted her sister to know the happiness she herself had known. But Emma was firm. She felt that her father had had to suffer one marriage already, that of Mrs Weston, and that he had been made anxious by the news of two more, so that to force him to confront a third, and one so near to home, was a cruelty she could not bring herself to inflict on him.

We parted unhappily, and I can see no way forward. But we must find one, for I am determined to make her my wife.

Monday 20 September

Today Robert Martin was married. What a splendid outcome to all the tribulations of the year! He has proved steadfast in his love, and Harriet could not have looked happier when she became Mrs Martin. It is not to be wondered at. She is moving into a family who sincerely love her, and who will make her happy. And she will have the added blessing of knowing she is bestowing happiness by being there.

Mr Elton performed the service, and he did it very well. No recollections were allowed to interfere with his duty, and he behaved as a gentleman and clergyman should. It was something of a relief, as I wondered whether some trace of hostility would be evident, but all the misunderstandings are so long ago, or he is so aware of his duties, that nothing of that nature was allowed to intrude.

Harriet looked very pretty in white, and Robert's sisters, who attended her, were equally pretty in blue. I will venture to say it was a wedding enjoyed by all, though Mr Woodhouse sighed over it, and added 'Poor Harriet!' to his collection of young ladies to pity.

But Robert's wedding has made me even more impatient for my own.

Saturday 25 September

There must be something in the air, for when I visited Longridge at Southdean this afternoon on parish business, I found him in the drawing-room, hand in hand with Miss Bates!

Miss Bates, saying: 'Oh, Mr Knightley, whatever will you think!' blushed a deep crimson.

'I beg your pardon,' I said retreating, but his words stopped me.

'No, Mr Knightley, do not go. I will explain everything,' said Longridge. He turned to Miss Bates. 'You will not object to Mr Knightley's knowing?'

'No indeed, I am sure – so good, so kind to Jane – so good to mother.'

'Wonderful woman,' said Longridge, wiping his eyes. 'And she has made me the happiest of men.'

I was struck dumb. I had never suspected! I had seen Longridge paying attention to Miss Bates for months, and I had attributed it to kindness, and nothing more. But as soon as he had told me the news, I thought she was the very woman to make him happy, and he the very man for her.

Miss Bates began to murmur with embarrassment: 'Too kind – past the first flush of youth – hope my friends will not find it too ridiculous—'

'Your friends will be as delighted as I am!' I said, congratulating her heartily. 'It is a wonderful piece of news.'

She smiled, and blushed, and said: 'So kind, but then you have always been so kind, Mr Knightley. I am sure I do not know what I have done to deserve this.'

'There is no one who deserves such happiness more,' I told her.

'There, Hetty, you see, my dear, I told you how it would be. All our friends are pleased for us. I never thought, when I lost my dear wife, that I would meet another such woman,' said Longridge. 'One who was interested in all the details of life, and who took such pleasure in them. One who never thought of herself, but always of others. One who could bring such happiness to an old man.'

'Come! You are not old,' I said.

'I'm past my prime, but even so, I can give my dear Hetty a good life,' he said, pressing her hand. 'It's a comfort to me, Mr Knightley, to be able to do that for her, and it's a small recompense for the joy she brings to me.'

'And Mrs Bates?' I asked.

'She'll live here with us. We've plenty of room. There's a room for Frank and Jane, too, whenever they choose to come, and a spare or two for when they bring their children with them! I'm a lucky man, Mr Knightley. In marrying my dear Hetty, I'll have not only a cheerful wife, but I'll have a mother and a niece as well. And in the future, God willing, the house will have children playing in it. I little thought, when I came to Highbury a year ago, that this would be the result.'

'I am very happy for you,' I said, shaking his hand heartily.

Miss Bates stood by, and if I needed proof that her feelings were genuinely touched, I had this; that she spoke not once during his recital.

'We're saying nothing yet. My dear Hetty wishes it that way,' he said. 'We don't want to take anything away from the young people. Let them have their glory. Then, when it's all done, Hetty and I will marry quietly. I hope we can prevail upon you to come to the wedding?'

'Yes, indeed you can.'

It is a very happy outcome. I have often worried about Miss Bates and her mother. Their fortune, small to begin with, has been ever declining, and they had little to look forward to. Miss Fairfax would have helped them, I am sure, but she will be living in Yorkshire, which is a long way off. Miss Bates's Highbury friends would, of course, have made sure she had food and fuel enough, and have varied her life by inviting her to dinner, but it is not the same as suddenly finding herself married to a good and respectable man, with a home of her own. And what a home!

Southdean is a fine residence, such as any woman might be proud of, and, moreover, a house she has had a fancy to live in since she was a child.

As I thought this, I saw that I had indeed been blind. Longridge had asked her to help him choose a house so he would know which one she liked!

I decided that this was not the time to discuss parish business, as I had intended, but I could not resist asking a household question: 'Will you need a maid, by any chance?'

'A maid?' Longridge asked in surprise.

'Why, the very thing,' said Miss Bates, recovering her power of speech and understanding me at once. 'James has another daughter, just the right age – if she were to work here then Mr Woodhouse would visit us, I am sure. How fortunate to be able to return my friends' hospitality, for it was never easy to hold a dinner party in the apartment, though it was very snug, and mother and I were lucky to have it. But now we will be able to invite our friends to dine with us, only Mr Woodhouse will not come – he does not like to bother James, you know, though I am sure James never thinks it any bother – but if he feels that James can see his daughter he will not mind giving the instruction for the carriage to be brought round.'

I left them to their plans, and the words Bath . . . Brighton . . . Weymouth . . . followed me out of the room.

Saturday 25 September

We dined at Randalls tonight, and when we had admired the baby, and all sat down to dinner, Mrs Weston said: 'Have you had any trouble with your poultry recently?'

'No, what kind of trouble do you mean?' asked Emma.

'Our poultry house was robbed last night. We lost all our turkeys.'

'What?' exclaimed Mr Woodhouse in alarm.

'Was it a fox?' Emma asked.

'No, nothing of the sort. There were no feathers. The turkeys simply vanished. They were taken by thieves.'

'Thieves!' said Mr Woodhouse, in great consternation.

'There is nothing to worry about, Papa. It was an isolated incident, I am sure of it,' said Emma.

But Mr Woodhouse was very anxious, and suggested going home at once, lest the thieves should be at Hartfield.

'If there are thieves at home, you had better remain here,' said Weston.

Mr Woodhouse did not know what to do: whether to go home at once, or never to leave the safety of Randalls again.

At last, I soothed his fears by offering to return to Hartfield with him, to make sure there were no miscreants on the premises.

Wednesday 29 September

Everywhere we go, we hear of poultry-yards being raided. Hens, chickens and turkeys are no longer safe. It is a problem for those of us who seek to uphold the law. William Larkins was very upset.

'We need to find the culprit, Mr Knightley,' he said.

'I have had a watch set around Highbury,' I assured him. 'We will catch the villains.'

I did not want to catch them too soon, however, as the incident had had an unexpected, but very welcome, consequence. When I went to Hartfield this evening, Mr Woodhouse was so perturbed by the thought of the robberies that he could talk of nothing else.

'Mrs Cole has had a dozen hens taken,' he said. 'And there have been turkeys taken from Abbey Mill Farm. Mrs Goddard was telling me about it only this morning. She had it from poor Miss Smith' – he has still not learnt to call her Mrs Martin – 'who visited her to say she was sorry she could not take her a turkey, as they had been stolen. I am afraid the thieves will come here next, and once they have taken our chickens, what will they do?'

'There is nothing to worry about, Papa. The poultry yard is a long way from the house.'

'You do not know these people, Emma. They will break the windows and steal the silver, I am sure of it,' he said.

'We have John to protect us,' said Emma soothingly.

'But he cannot stay for ever,' said Mr Woodhouse. 'He has to be in London in November.'

We could not have wished for a better opening.

'If Mr Knightley were in the house, Papa, we would be safe. It was what we arranged, you know, that Mr Knightley would come and live here once we are married.'

'Oh, yes, so it was,' he said in relief. 'A very good plan. The wedding is to be in October, I think you said, Emma, my dear?'

'Yes, Papa,' said Emma, with a smile at me.

'October the eighth was the date decided on,' I said decisively, so that there would be no more arguments.

'Well, my dear, I am sure it cannot come soon enough for me,' said Mr Woodhouse. 'I will not sleep easy in my bed until Mr Knightley is here with us at Hartfield.'

Thursday 30 September

Now that a date has been set for our marriage, it is the main topic of conversation in Highbury. I admired Emma's fortitude this evening when we dined with the Westons, and the Eltons, too, were there.

I wondered how they would take the news. Elton said little, but Mrs Elton quickly made up for his deficiencies.

'My dear Emma, what is this I hear? You are to be married, and to Mr Knightley? You sad girl, how could you not tell me of it? I am quite put out. Selina will stare when she knows how sly you have been.'

Emma was too happy to pay much attention, but Mrs Elton went on: 'Selina is to pay us a visit. We will tell you how to go on. Two married ladies, you know!'

'I cannot put you to the trouble—'

'My dear Emma, it is no trouble, no trouble at all,' said Mrs Elton gaily. 'I flatter myself I am an old hand.'

'I need very little—'

'My dear Emma, you need say no more. Simplicity shall be our watchword. Satin there must be, and lace veils; we will make you the most beautiful bride. But hush, here comes Knightley,' she said as I approached, though she had whispered so loud I had heard every word. 'The menfolk know nothing of dresses. My *caro sposo* declared himself mystified by all the talk of satin and lace.'

I rescued Emma, and Mrs Weston kindly distracted Mrs Elton, who, apart from occasional references to *pomp and feast and revelry* and *Hymen's saffron robes*, was persuaded to talk of other things, until she discovered we are to marry next week.

'But Selina will not be here! She does not come to us until November. How she will stare when I tell her. There is not time to arrange everything in a week.'

'Simplicity is our watchword,' Emma reminded her, but Mrs Elton was still exclaiming over it when she and Elton set out for home.

OCTOBER

Today, Emma and I were married. I had the satisfaction of knowing I was marrying the best woman in the world, because she is the only woman for me. I have seen few sights better than the sight of Emma walking into the church on her father's arm. Elton performed the ceremony and, if he remembered that he had once hoped to marry Emma himself, he gave no sign of it.

As we made our vows, I had the pleasure of hearing Emma call me George. She seemed to like it, too, for she called me George again at our wedding-breakfast, and I do not despair of her calling me George as a general thing.

Isabella and Mrs Weston argued over whether Emma's first child would be a boy or a girl, Isabella pressing the merits of a boy as firstborn, and Mrs Weston pressing the merits of a girl.

'Whatever the case, Emma will be a very happy woman,' said John. 'Will she not?' he asked Mr Woodhouse.

Mr Woodhouse looked up from his gruel and sighed.

'Poor Emma!' he said.